MURDER WAS MY NEIGHBOUR

What would you do if, during your first night in a rented house on the sea's edge, you happened to observe a neighbour behaving in a mysterious way? For John Chadwick, one-time policeman and Private Inquiry Agent, there was only one thing to do. He investigated . . . with astonishing results.

The trail takes him back to London, where he attends the oddly convened meeting of a blackmailer's victims. George Swinton, hard, self-assured business man, has a cut-and-dried plan for dealing with the blackmailer if he can get the co-operation of his fellow victims. But is Swinton quite the man he claims to be? Chadwick is suspicious but lends his aid to the plan.

How the plan misfires, and threatens the secrets of the glamorous Kate Malone, Doctor Gribble, and other victims makes an absorbing, swiftly moving tale. Chadwick gets many a shock as he probes deeper into the mystery but none as great as the final one when he learns the real reason for the house by the sea wall, and tough as he is, has to fight and overpower a killer, maddened by the threat of exposure.

MURDER
WAS MY
NEIGHBOUR

GUY COBDEN

THE MYSTERY BOOK GUILD
178–202 GT. PORTLAND STREET
LONDON, W.1

This Edition November 1956

Printed in Great Britain
by The Anchor Press, Ltd.
Tiptree, Essex

CHAPTER I

IT WAS the lobster that started it. I'm rather fond of lobster. When Freda told me that she had accepted the offer of a friend's house for a month at Selsey Bill, and we discovered on arrival at supper time that the housekeeper had laid on a lobster, caught locally that morning, I staked an immediate claim on the claws, and waded in. Very nice too, but I can never be certain of my reaction to lobster. Maybe it is the time of the year, or maybe what the damned thing has been feeding on, but sometimes I can eat a plateful with no ill-effects whatsoever, at others I get the gyp. This was one of the other times.

I went to bed, fell asleep, had a hideous nightmare, the details of which are mercifully forgotten, and finally woke up bathed in perspiration with some playful demon poking me in the tummy, its claws as powerful as the lobster's but red hot.

I got out of bed, found my dressing-gown without any bother—the room was flooded in moonlight—and padded round to the bathroom to see what I could find in the medicine cabinet. I remembered that it had looked pretty well stocked when I had seen it earlier. I was in luck, for I found a tin labelled "Stomach Powder". It was of no known brand, but with my tummy in knots I wasn't fussy. I helped myself to a stiff dose. It was probably nine-tenths chalk, but it did the trick. The demon grumbled a bit at the treatment, then retired.

By that time I had lost all desire for immediate sleep. I wandered back into the bedroom. Our travelling clock propped on the table between out beds said three o'clock. Freda, whose sylph-like form conceals a constitution as robust as the average lumberjack's, was sleeping peacefully, unaffected by lobster. In the dim milky light she looked astonishingly beautiful. I could see the sweep of her long dark lashes against her cheek. With her short hair tousled by sleep she appeared gamin-like and very young. For the thousandth

5

time I wondered why she, who had everything from looks to wealth, had married a roughneck like me, who had neither, and for the thousandth time gave up seeking an answer.

I moved across to the window, wide open to the midsummer air. The house was on the sea's edge. Indeed, if they had not built some expensive and belated defence in the shape of a huge wall the previous winter, it would probably have been in the sea by then. A quarter of its long garden had gone and the bottom of what remained was still scarred and lumped where the dumpers had filled in behind the new sea-wall.

The night was absolutely still, undisturbed by any noise except the faint shirr of the sea lapping on the sand below the wall. The tide was nearly full. A three-quarter moon had moved far round to westward, and a long, faintly shimmering path of silver led up to it across the black and oily-looking sea. The air by the open window was cold and the sill was moist from a heavy dew.

I stayed there for a minute or two absorbing the bizarre black and silver beauty of the scene. I was contemplating returning to bed, or staying out of it a little longer in order to smoke a cigarette, when a movement at the bottom of the garden next to ours caught my eye. A shape, dark and amorphous in the moonlight, but a man's for all that, moved out of the shadow of the cypress hedge growing between the two gardens, stood for a moment in the recess cut by the top of steps in the sea-wall, then moved slowly downwards out of sight and onto the beach. I had been able to make out in the instant he had been motionless that he was carrying an object in each hand. These had been hanging at his sides, and had looked as though they might have held buckets.

I used to be a policeman before setting up on my own as a private dick, a profession I had neglected sadly after marrying Freda. At any rate I've always maintained that the training made me inquisitive, though Freda says that I must be a Nosey Parker by instinct or I would never have become a policeman, and certainly not a private one later. Nosey or not, our old hound dog in one of his brighter moments could not have come to the attention quicker than I did when I saw that figure slip over the wall. There had been something undeniably furtive about it. Perhaps it had been its utter silence. But why had he taken the trouble to go down the length of the garden in the shadow of the cypress hedge instead of straight down the lawn in the full light of the moon? And buckets or pails, unless you are particularly careful, usually rattle a bit when they are carried, especially so when empty. Maybe the ones I had seen him carrying had been full though he'd not looked strained, merely furtive. Maybe they'd not been buckets at all.

The conjecture only prompted me to find out. I found my slippers, tied my dressing-gown tighter, and tiptoed downstairs. It was in my mind to go through the lounge and out by the french windows, but I remembered that Montmorency, the hound, was sleeping in his travelling basket beneath the kitchen table, and since he was in a strange house he might be restless and set up the hideous noise that serves him for a bark if he heard me without seeing me. It was unlikely, for if there is one natural function that dog performs without any prompting it is sleeping. The other is eating. He is not really old, but there is something in his wrinkled and ugly expression that invariably makes him appear so. He was supposed to have been a bloodhound, and at one time gave promise of becoming a true member of that noble breed. However, the shape of his ears betrayed him early on, and later he went on growing, getting bigger and bigger, finishing up somewhere between a Boxer and a Great Dane, both of which breeds may have been in his ancestry. As a pup he was given to Freda for a birthday present by a friend with a warped sense of humour because she had learnt that, bored with doing nothing, I was setting up office as a Private Inquiry Agent again. Whatever he is, Montmorency, whose name we lifted shamelessly from the pages of *Three Men in a Boat*, is no bloodhound.

I moved into the kitchen. He condescended to get out of his laundry basket, stepped into a patch of moonlight, yawned and stared at me with reproachful eyes.

"You stay where you are!" I hissed at him in a fierce whisper.

He slunk back into his gargantuan basket—a monstrous thing which has to travel on the top of the car like a boat—and gave a muffled grunt of satisfaction.

I opened the back door very quietly. It was cold outside with that extra nip the air acquires about an hour or so before the dawn. My slippers left dark tracks in the dew-laden grass behind me as I moved quietly and quickly towards the cypress hedge.

Macrocarpa grows thickly and well at Selsey. I'd hoped to find a gap in the hedge through which I would be able to observe our mysterious neighbour from close quarters without walking the length of the garden, but in fact I reached the end of the hedge down by the sea-wall before I was able to see anything of next door's plot.

I waited, while the chill of the early hours crept up on me via my bare ankles and pyjama legs. The chink of metal on stone as he came over the sea-wall gave me warning of his approach. As before he contrived to look strangely furtive, and as he had done on his outward journey, he chose the shadow of the cypress hedge as soon as he had gained the sanctuary of his garden. But this brought him diagonally across the grass towards the spot where I was lurking, and I was able to get a glimpse of him in the full light of the moon.

I noticed first that the objects he was carrying were indeed buckets, one in each hand. This time they were full; brimming with what could have been only sea-water. I saw it slopping over the sides of the buckets in spite of the rigid care with which he appeared to be carrying them. He was a big bull-necked individual with a strong fleshy face. His hair had been clipped close at the sides and left brushy on top. There were beads of sweat on his forehead, which was creased in concentration as though he was carrying a couple of grenades that might explode if he was unable to get them to the house within a stipulated time. He made absolutely no noise, and had it not been for my slippers wet from the dew and my cold ankles I could have been dreaming the whole thing.

I saw him for barely a second, and then he had slipped away on the other side of the thick hedge. I gave him a minute, then crept back into the house. I waited at the bedroom window for some time to see whether or not he would make another journey but he failed to appear. Finally I climbed back into bed wondering what the hell a man could want with a couple of buckets of sea-water at three o'clock in the morning. I was asleep before I could make even a reasonable guess at it.

In the morning Freda was up bright and early. She was wearing jodhpurs by the time I had my eyes open. She has done her best to persuade me to take up riding, but golf is my idea of exercise. I've contrived to look silly enough at that game before now, but nothing like as silly as I would look trying to sit on a moving horse. It meant that breakfast would be latish, which didn't worry me since I'd had a disturbed night, and it gave me a chance to have a word with Mrs. Mulraney, the daily housekeeper, who came clattering down the front garden path just as Freda was getting the car out.

Mrs. Mulraney was neither Irish as her name suggests nor Sussex as might be supposed. She was pure Cockney, a prodigious worker and a heavenly cook. Her only failing was her general noisiness in which her voice played a major part, for it was remarkably strident and must have been trained at a stall in the New Cut. I heard her bawl out to Freda:

"Caw! You're early, mum!"

Then Montmorency, grouchy probably at being denied right of entry to the car by Freda, decided to take it out on Mrs. Mulraney, and set up his hideous baying. She soon put him in his place, however, with what sounded uncommonly like "Shut yer bleedin' row!"

There was peace for a moment or two during which I contemplated another half-hour's sleep, but by that time Mrs. Mulraney had reached the kitchen where she set to work upon the pots and pans. She could not have made more noise had she arrived in a suit of armour and tripped over the kitchen step. Freda and I were to learn later that no matter how late we went to bed no sleep was possible in the house after the arrival of Mrs. Mulraney.

I made a leisurely toilet, and went down to the kitchen. Here Mrs. Mulraney had knocked off clattering for a minute or two, and was sitting drinking a cup of tea. In repose her appearance completely belied her character, for she looked a motherly little old lady who would never raise her voice except to sing in chapel. She was watched by Montmorency, who was squatting on his haunches with his tongue lolling out of the side of his mouth and hope in his limpid eyes. It had evidently penetrated his dim brain that this strange woman would be responsible for his food from that day on, and that greeting her in hostile fashion had been a gross error. Every now and again the end of his tail would give an apologetic knock on the floor, which is as much as he can achieve by way of a tail-wag whilst sitting.

"Morning, Mr. Chadwick!" she greeted me. " 'Ow did the lobster treat yer?"

"Roughly," I said. "How did you know?"

"My old man was up 'alf the night. 'E must 'ave 'ad its twin. Like a cupper tea?"

I accepted a cup and whilst drinking it chatted about this and that. I led the conversation round to our immediate neighbours, and in particular the one on our eastern side.

"I don't know the tenant," Mrs. Mulraney told me. "It's let furnished like this one. 'Ouse belongs to one of them women novelists . . . Ethel Primrose. She give me one of 'er books to read once. Talk about mush! Fair give me the willies. Sooner 'ave television any day."

"How long has the present tenant been in occupation?"

" 'Im? 'Bout a week. Maybe more. I've never set eyes on 'im. Place is about as lively as a perishin' graveyard during the day. 'E's out all the time. Mrs. Croxted—she does for Ethel when she's in residence—went up there the day 'e arrived to see if 'e needed 'er services, and 'e said 'e could look arter 'imself. Crank, I expect." Mrs. Mulraney added, by way of explanation, "Selsey's full of 'em."

I didn't press the subject for I suspected that Mrs. Mulraney, when she got amongst her cronies, was as big a gossip as any of them and I had no wish for the man next door to learn by some devious means that I was nosey about him.

Two buckets of sea-water at three o'clock in the morning, and collected even at that hour with an obvious care to avoid being seen, certainly had me guessing, however. I was as curious as an alley cat. The more I thought about it the more I wanted to know all about it; not perhaps so much why the man had wanted the stuff but why he had left it till the early hours before he had collected it, and acted so furtively. After all, he had not been stealing it.

Later in the day it occurred to me that the time of high tide must have had a good deal to do with it, and I took care to be on hand that afternoon when high-water time came round. But our mysterious neighbour failed to show himself at all, which merely added to my interest in the reason for the secrecy of his action. He may have gone down to the beach to pick up something else which he had placed in the buckets along with the sea-water. If so it had been a remarkably easy process. I judged that he had been gone long enough to scoop up two buckets of water and not a minute more. If he was involved in some smuggling operation and stuff had been planted on the beach for him to pick up, why take the buckets at all? And if they had been taken to act the role of containers, why fill them with sea-water?

When it became obvious that the afternoon tide and the resulting proximity of the sea had no interest to our neighbour I whistled for Montmorency, and strolled up to the village.

The first of the House and Estate Agents I visited regretted that he had not the name of Miss Ethel Primrose on his books, but the second one on the opposite side of the road was actually handling her business. I explained that I had just taken up the tenancy of the house next to hers, which appeared to be empty, and what were the chances of obtaining a let to some friends of mine?

The House Agent, who was a sandy-haired man, wearing a hacking jacket of outlandish tweed, regretted that Kohinoor, which was the name of Miss Primrose's house, was already let.

"I don't think there would be any objection to a sub-let," he added, "not on the part of my client, but of course it will depend primarily on the present tenant, who has taken the house furnished for three months."

"I'll ask him if I run across him," I said. "What's his name?"

He had to consult his books, and then gave it me.

"A Mr. George Swinton," he said.

I thanked him, and we parted the best of friends. At least

I feel certain that we would have done, but the door to the street had been propped open to relieve the heat of the day, and at that precise moment Montmorency came snuffling into the place. I had left him down the High Street endeavouring to make the acquaintance of the local butcher. There was a big ginger tom-cat asleep on one end of the House Agent's small counter. I'd barely noticed the animal for it was so much in repose that it might have been stuffed. Normally Montmorency adopts a very tolerant attitude towards cats. It's probably more prudence than goodwill for he once took a pasting from one whilst still a pup. On this occasion, however, he let go immediately. I dare say the butcher had kicked him out, which would not have improved his temper, and the cat, being asleep, offered an unsuspecting target which he could not resist.

The cat came to instinctive and immediate life by leaping a yard in the air, and disappeared behind the counter. Montmorency, excitement turning his normal hideous bark into an even more horrible sound akin to a strangled screech, lunged across the counter after it. I hauled him back by his tail, but not before he had knocked over a couple of inkwells which splashed their contents over the startled House Agent.

We left in disgrace, but I had the name of our mysterious neighbour, which I hoped might prove to be worth the cost of a cleaner's bill for the House Agent's jacket.

I have always had the knack of being able to wake at roughly any time I wish after going to sleep provided I think about it hard enough beforehand, and provided I am not too physically tired. That night I put the trick into practice. As usual I awoke too soon, but thereafter I cat-napped for about an hour, crept softly out of bed and took post in an easy chair by the window. It was another perfectly still and moonlit night with long streaks of very high and thin cloud straddling the sky like vapour trails. It was nowhere near as cold as the previous night had been, and this may have accounted for the presence of an early cricket below the bedroom window, who was putting in some steady work, every now and again buzzing like a band saw. Apart from the cricket and the persistent shirr, shirr of the sea against the beach, there was no other sound to break the stillness. The tide was then, I judged, about half an hour from its full.

It had occurred to me earlier that my time would be put to better account if I could so arrange things that I was able to observe what it was in fact that Mr. Swinton collected from the beach, if indeed it was anything in addition to sea-water. With this object in view I had reconnoitred the beach before going to bed but there had been absolutely nowhere I could see what he was doing without being plainly in view myself. No large rocks. No bathing huts. At that stage, too, my curiosity extended only as far as learning whether his trip with the buckets was a nightly occurrence or a single isolated incident. I waited while the minutes dragged, the cricket buzzed, and Freda slept peacefully, unaware that I was playing truant from my bed. Sure enough he came.

He was a trifle careless this time. I heard him close the back door of his house. It was a mere click but the night was so still I could have heard a key turn in its lock. As before he chose the shadow of the hedge and it was a good minute before he slipped over the wall and down to the beach. He was back in no time at all. It could have been only sea-water he collected. There was absolutely nothing else there but sand. The moon was higher in the sky than last night. I saw it splash silver from the tops of his buckets as he darted back to the shadow of the hedge. But he made two trips. For all I knew he had made two trips the previous night and it had been the second one I had chanced to witness.

I waited for a long time but he didn't venture out again. Four buckets of sea-water, collected with the utmost care against being seen, for there had been no doubt that he had waited a long time within the shadow of the hedge to make certain that there had been no chance prowler along the sea-wall or on the beach before he had moved out into the moonlight. Why? What on earth was he doing with the stuff?

I told Freda about it the next morning. There have never been any secrets between her and me, and she was going to notice my extreme curiosity concerning Mr. Swinton before very long. She has a sixth sense for it.

"But, John," she exclaimed, "what an extraordinary thing! Do you think he needs it for his feet or something, and is too shy to paddle?"

"I don't know," I said. "I just don't know, darling. But the fellow looked so damned furtive about it. You know how I've got a nose for trouble? Mr. Swinton reacts that way on me. He had guilt written all over him last night when I saw him close to. I don't like it, Freda. I'm going to learn a bit more about him."

"Well . . . be careful, darling. After all, this is Monica's house. Not that it matters as far as we are concerned, but she lives here for the greater part of the year."

"I'll watch it," I said. "I wonder what Miss Ethel Primrose would make of her tenant sneaking out in the small hours to collect sea-water. She'd probably invent some tender romance for him with a beautiful mermaid he keeps in his bath. Now where's that damned dog going in such a hurry? Never seen him move so purposefully."

Montmorency, nose down and looking something like Walt Disney's Pluto, had scuttled the length of the garden and disappeared over the sea-wall.

Freda gurgled with laughter.

"He's found a new line. Yesterday afternoon, after you'd got back from the village, he discovered the beach. You know how the kids love him? He cadges sweets off them. He adores ice-cream and chocolate."

"And probably liquorice and toffee as well. There's something porcine in that animal's ancestry. What's our programme for today, Freda?"

"I simply must go into Chichester and make an appointment with a hairdresser. This salt air makes my head positively sticky. You coming?"

"Thought I'd try a swim this morning. This weather is too good to miss."

"Well . . . wait for me, John. I shall be back by eleven. Once I've fixed a hairdresser I shan't mind if my cap comes off."

When Freda had gone I lounged in a deck chair and read the paper for a while till a gnarled old gentleman, pushing a

wheelbarrow in which were arraigned various gardening imple-
ments, came unexpectedly round the side of the house. I
remembered Monica Field mentioning the jobbing gardener,
who came twice a week, when she had told us of Mrs. Mulraney.
Unlike the housekeeper this member of the staff was pure
Sussex.

"Marning, sir," he intoned.

He didn't bother to introduce himself but trundled his way
to the extreme end of the lawn where, after setting down his
barrow and sitting on its edge whilst he lit his pipe, he began
attacking the mess left behind by the builders of the wall.
I waited till he took a breather then strolled down the lawn
for a chat. He was ready enough to talk for it meant that he
could lean on his rake instead of work with it. I can't say that
I blamed him. To have to slave away in the hot sun with a
beach full of idlers in full view must be galling at times even
when you've done it all your life.

I led the conversation round to the house next door.

"I'm told the place is let," I said, "to a Mr. George Swinton.
Haven't seen anything of him yet."

"Ah. Don't suppose you will, either. Proper queer 'un 'e
is. Never at 'ome. Goes off in the early marning in that motor
of 'is, and don't come back till night. I'm supposed to do that
garden twice a week same as this 'un, but 'e won't 'ave me
near the place. 'But Miss Primrose is payin' me twelve hours a
week whiles you're 'ere,' I says. 'Then what you got to grumble
about?' 'e says, 'I'll cut the grass and keep it tidy like. I don't
want you in the place.' Makes it proper arkward, sir. I collects
me money last week from the Agent but I ain't done no work
for it. The missus says, 'You write and tell Miss Primrose.'
Well . . . I done that . . . but she's abroad somewhere. I don't
suppose she'll get the letter anyways."

He rambled on for a bit. I was glad when Montmorency,
evidently out of luck so early in the day, came galloping into
the garden and gave me the excuse of taking him for a walk.

That afternoon, whilst Freda browsed in a deck chair
wearing a sun suit that guaranteed an absolute maximum
area of tanning without being improper, I made a detailed
study of Kohinoor. It was roughly the size of the house we

were occupying, which meant that it was detached, had four bedrooms and everything else that goes with a house in the post-war four or five thousand class. More than enough for the odd, lone-living Mr. George Swinton.

The back door out of which he emerged for his nightly forage was set in a tiny porch attached to an extension to the house on its south-western corner. Not very clever designing since it faced the prevailing wind, which in winter must come tearing in at gale force straight from the South Atlantic via the Channel and the Isle of Wight. However, it suited me. His back porch was about the nearest point of Kohinoor to its neighbour. The macrocarpa hedge ran the whole length of the land between the two houses, but it had been clipped to reasonable proportions in the front, and after a careful examination I found a hole in its base. This would need improvement before I could use it for the plan I had in mind, and the work could not be put in hand till the old jobbing gardener had finished his ineffectual raking at the bottom of the lawn.

I filled in the time by walking up to the village. Montmorency came with me. The ironmonger's shop where I bought a hefty pair of secateurs was refreshingly free from cats, and apart from a brief encounter with a big black Alsatian, who curled his lips at Montmorency and generally frightened him to a point just short of death, the journey was without incident.

As soon as old Pipe-and-Whiskers had trundled away with his barrow I set to work on the hole in the base of the hedge, which at that point was about four feet thick. I soon clipped myself a nice little hidey-hole from which I could observe the back door of Kohinoor, and later, I hoped, Mr. George Swinton as he went over the sea-wall with his buckets. His side of the hedge remained undisturbed and all I had to do to gain his domain was to brush aside a thin screen of lacy twigs.

Montmorency had been an interested spectator of my activities, and as soon as I had finished testing, he dived into the hole himself, twirled round once or twice, then flopped down in it with a grunt of satisfaction. Evidently he regarded the hole as having been constructed for his special benefit and refused to come out when called. I lugged him out by the scruff of his neck, at the same time making a mental note to see him well locked up for the night. To come down in the small hours and find that clown of a dog snoring in the hole would wreck my plan from its start.

I told Freda what I proposed to do. She was too loyal to criticize and knew me too well to make an attempt at dissuading me, but she didn't like it.

"It's not all plain noseyness, darling," I told her, trying to justify myself. "I'm following a hunch that the man's a wrong 'un. My hunches usually play out. Besides, he's acting altogether too carefully and too furtively. The dead of night. A full minute inspecting the beach and sea-wall before he moves out of his garden. No servant allowed in the house or even in the garden. That he's up to no good is practically a deduction, not a hunch. You see."

"Well . . . perhaps you're right, John. But don't get caught.

"I won't," I said.

Later in the evening I saw Swinton arrive home. He was driving a big black Austin. The car looked reasonably clean and free from dust as though it had not travelled very far, and I made a note of its number. He was wearing a business suit and a black Homburg hat. I got the idea that his early morning departure was probably to catch an electric train from Chichester either to London or Portsmouth. If he did he probably parked the car in the station yard all day. I could check that easily. He didn't see me at all. He put the car in its garage, locked up and walked straight to the front door of the house without a glance to either side. In his town suit and in daylight he looked a hard bargaining customer; a man who knew what he wanted, ruthless, self-sufficient and hard. I realized that if he caught me snooping I should be for the police court and no mistake. But it failed to damp my enthusiasm for my plan. I still thought he was a wrong 'un.

B

CHAPTER II

THAT night, as such things will, my automatic waking mechanism failed me and I awoke almost too late. Maybe I had willed myself so hard to wake up before I went to sleep that I had tired myself out. Fortunately I had laid on everything beforehand. Flannels, sports shirt, rubber shoes and a torch. I dressed in a panic almost, fearing I was too late. Freda slept on, and I had time to grin to myself because I'd been reasonably certain that she had intended to wake up and watch points from the bedroom window.

Downstairs in the kitchen Montmorency greeted me joyously, eager anticipation in his eyes, tail going round in circles. He would feel frisky tonight of all nights. I ought never to have let him see me make that hole in the hedge. I cursed him luridly and fairly pushed him under the table, where he stayed I think out of sheer surprise.

The night was again fine and warm but with rather more cloud. The moonlight was not so hard, but soft and shimmery through its veil of high white cirrus. There was no dew. This was just as well. I had some grass to cross before I could reach Mr. Swinton's back door, and I had no wish to leave any tracks to set him wondering if he chanced to see them.

I reached the hole in the hedge without incident, and settled down to wait, my only fear that he had already come and gone. High tide was getting progressively nearer to dawn but he still had an hour or two to play with either side of high water when he could get to the sea's edge without making himself conspicuous. It seemed obvious to me that his whole method of fetching the water was designed to avoid being seen. If he went when the tide was out any distance at all even at night there was still a chance of him being spotted by somebody from an upstairs window in one of the neighbouring houses. But if he went only when the tide was near to lapping the wall then he was shielded completely by the wall itself from the houses at his back. The only possible moments when he could be spotted was coming or going over the wall. That I

had chosen those moments to be gazing idly across the bottom
of his garden was just too bad for him.

Crouched in the hole with my eye glued to a gap in the
tracery of shielding twigs I waited with as much patience as
I could muster for him to emerge. The house was in complete
darkness, but it had been that way as far as I had been able to
observe on the previous nights, and to my suspicious mind it
was just another indication of his wrong intent.

From the point of view of comfort, or rather lack of discomfort, I could not have timed things better. I waited barely
five minutes, and out he came. He was so damned quiet and
quick I could have missed him. The door opened. He closed it
behind him, then slipped across the strip of lawn to the shadow
of the hedge, the two buckets held carefully away from him to
avoid rattling. He was just a black and white moving picture
without sound.

I waited till he had slipped over the wall, and then I moved
as quickly and as silently as he had done. Through the tracery
of hedge, over the grass. Door open. Door shut, and I was
wiping my feet on the mat.

I was in a scullery. The door to the kitchen was standing
wide open, and so was the door beyond that into a hall. At the
bottom of the staircase a low-wattage bulb was burning in a
pedestal lamp mounted at the foot of the banister rail. I
ignored the stairs and chose the door to a room on the right.
The door was standing ajar and I was careful to close it just
that much behind me.

I had time to spare the room a glance with a flash from my
torch; not that I was particularly interested in it for it was
Ethel Primrose's not Swinton's. As a matter of fact it was
rather sombrely furnished for a lady's dining-room, a great
deal of dark oak and an immensely wide sideboard that could
have done duty in a club. On the bare table-top in front of me
were Swinton's black Homburg and his yellow string gloves.
Beside them was a pile of sealed envelopes, addressed but not
stamped. I glanced idly at the top one and drew in my breath
with a jerk of surprise. The address on it was not written,
nor typed, but printed in crude capitals like the first efforts of
a child. Yet, unlike a child's, the capitals, though they sloped

this way and that, and some were big and some were small, were not entirely ill formed. The idea behind the disjointed symbols was obvious. The writer had intended to take all character out of his hand and disguise it utterly.

I snapped out my torch and stood with my back against the wall, my right ear almost in the slight gap left by the partially opened door. I'd seen notes written that way before during my brief career as a policeman. Blackmail notes!

A moment later I said to myself, "Come off it, Chadwick. You're getting altogether too suspicious." But the idea persisted. I pushed it away. I'd sneaked into his house for another purpose entirely. What did he do with the sea-water?

I was soon to know. Once inside the house he threw away all pretence to silence. I heard him come padding into the hall. The place was so silent I could hear his hard breathing, and the creak of a floor board under his weight. He came nearer. Whatever he did with the stuff I felt tolerably certain that he was not storing it in the dining-room, but my mouth went dry with suspense as he came nearer. His shadow flashed across the gap left by the open door, and then the stairs went creak, creak, creak as he climbed them.

He must have prepared his way upstairs, leaving the room doors open as he had downstairs. I listened intently and heard two long rumbles as he emptied the buckets, and then he was on his way down, the pails jangling merrily. His shadow passed the door again, and his footfalls died away down the hall. The slightest of draughts could be felt as he opened the back door and closed it again.

I went quickly up the stairs. There was one door standing wide open and I scarcely needed the torchlight to tell me it was the bathroom. Quite a luxury job, expensively tiled and fitted. There was the sea-water in the porcelain bath. He must have made a number of journeys before I had spotted him, for it was a big bath and nearly half full. Away from its natural setting the water looked green and rather dirty, cloudy with sand, and with one or two morsels of weed drifting through it. There was nothing else there—just half a bath full of sea-water. I could smell the salt of it above the faint odour of Ethel's bath soap that still haunted the room.

I hadn't much time. If he made only two journeys he would probably lock up after the second. I had no wish to lurk in a downstairs room while he prepared himself for bed. Quite apart from the obvious fact that I could not bolt a door behind me, and would thus be compelled to leave evidence of my visit, it was more than possible that Swinton would not go to bed. A man who was crazy enough to collect sea-water by the bucketful at that hour of the morning was quite capable of sitting down and dealing himself a hand of patience as soon as he had finished.

I moved swiftly downstairs to the dining-room where I flashed my torch on the pile of letters on the table. I would dearly loved to have examined them all at my leisure but I dared not disturb them. The name and address on the top envelope burned itself on my mind.

Mr. Nigel Pendleton,
32 Plutox Gardens,
S.W.1.

I wouldn't forget the name or its address.

By this time Swinton must be scooping up his second load. I ran through the house. I opened and closed the back door as quietly as he had done, and then I dived for the hedge. Like a fool I'd forgotten that from this side the hole I had made to give me access was completely concealed. I had a moment's panic, then reason returned. I must have made some faint track across the grass. I found it and lost it in the shadow of the hedge, but it was near enough. I found the hole and stayed there till Swinton returned. I was not going to chance him hearing me move around the house. I gave him time to emerge for a third trip, but he never came. Two journeys a night. Did he consider that to make more, to fill the bath in one spell of duty, was tempting Providence? I was getting the glimmering of an idea about that bath. If he intended it for what I was thinking then the man had the patience of a fiend.

Freda was awake when I got in. She sat up on one elbow.
"Well, John?"
"The bath," I said. "He keeps it in the bath."

"But, darling, wasn't that rather obvious? Where else could he keep it—I mean, if he intended keeping it?"

"I am more concerned now with why he keeps it," I said.

"Did he see you?"

"No."

"Thank heavens for that. I haven't slept a wink thinking that he might have done."

"That," I said, crossing to her bed and kissing her, "is a typically wifely statement that bears no relation to the truth. You were snoring your head off when I went out. Good night, darling."

Although Swinton left presumably at his customary hour the next morning he was back early. It was about eleven o'clock when I heard the sound of the Austin being driven into Kohinoor's garage. I kept out of sight for I had no wish for him to know that I was interested in his movements. Then later he had a visitor. It was a woman and she came on horseback. This was unfortunate for she led the animal into the front garden of Kohinoor and used the macrocarpa as a hitching rack, choosing a branch of it not very far from the spot where I had cut the hole. Montmorency was asleep in the hole. He waited till the horse had backed itself around till its hindquarters were practically overhead, and then with diabolical timing let go a frenzied yelping. The horse shied violently, and whinnied loudly with fear.

I happened to be in the bedroom at the time changing into swimming trunks. From there the noise sounded like jungle warfare at its most savage. By the time I had whipped into a pair of trunks and got down there Freda had already reached the scene. She had Montmorency by his tail but he was too strong for her, and I had to give him a cuff before he would stop his racket. He backed out of the hole as soon as he felt my hand on him, licked his chops and grinned foolishly. From the other side of the hedge a female voice could be heard making soothing noises to the horse. This was the first intimation I had of a visitor to Kohinoor, and I was immediately curious about her. By the time I had got it into Montmorency's thick skull that he was banned from the garden for the rest of the morning, and manœuvred myself up to the front of the house to get a better view, she had taken the nag to the other side of the garden and hitched him to a shrub, and was just going back into the house through the front door. I caught a fleeting glimpse of the back of a dark head, of a figure a little too dumpy to look well in jodhpurs, and that was all.

Freda, of course, had been watching for some time.

"I do believe it's Pansy," she said.

"Pansy who?" I asked.

"Idiot—I mean the mare. She comes from Stanton's stables. I took her out myself our first morning. She's tubed."

"Too bad," I said. "Silly name for a horse, though. All right for a cow. The horse is a noble animal. Do you think you can find out the name of its rider?"

"I'll try," Freda laughed. "Darling, you really are impossible—the world's biggest snoop. Don't you think all the mystery you are building round a few buckets of sea-water to be a little far-fetched?"

"I don't know," I demurred. "Notice one significant feature about the rumpus we've just experienced? No Mr. Swinton. Not even the Goddamned awful row Montmorency makes when roused, not to mention it being mingled with the scream of a frightened horse, can bring Swinton out of that house. And he's in there all right. I saw him come back about half an hour ago. Makes you think."

"Probably enjoying a salt-water bath," Freda said. She was as good as her word concerning the identity of Swinton's visitor. She either had, or made, occasion to call in at the stables that afternoon and came back with the information that Swinton's lady friend had been a Miss Helen Arnett who was staying at the Marine Hotel.

I had intended to get a good look at the woman when she rode away from Kohinoor, but in spite of my almost burning curiosity concerning next door I was not going to make myself a martyr to it. I had my swim, and Swinton's visitor left while I was splashing around in the surf.

If he collected more sea-water that night he fetched it unwatched by me. I kept to my bed.

Next day after lunch Freda drove me into Chichester where I caught a train for Victoria.

"I'll stay at the flat tonight in any case," I told her, while we waited for the train to move. "If I find that I've got to stay longer I'll give you a ring."

"All right, darling." Freda lugged angrily on Montmorency's lead. "Keep still—blast you!"

The dog was showing every indication that he wanted to come with me. His perverse mongrel mind can never accept the fact that he belongs to Freda. She pets him on every occasion and I do nothing but cuff him and curse him, yet every time I leave on a journey of some duration he knows it instinctively. He shakes like an aspen, and big tears roll down his ugly face. The astonishing thing is that when I'm away he behaves less like a clown and more like a responsible hound.

The train slid away at last, and I sat down feeling foolishly sentimental about leaving my lovely wife and her big plug-ugly dog. Was my suspicion of Swinton, a complete stranger, worth it? What the devil business was it of mine? The fact that I had nothing better to do was only half an excuse. The other half was that I cannot leave a mystery alone. At any rate the evening should at least prove whether I was on to something or merely wasting my time. But I needed some luck, and at first I thought I was not going to get it.

I filled in time round at the flat, had some dinner at an expensive restaurant—the meal was nowhere near as good as the one Mrs. Mulraney would have prepared for Freda—and took a cab to Plutox Gardens, S.W.1.

After the nectar of the seaside air and its accompanying sunshine London seemed sweaty and stifling that evening, and most of its inhabitants looked like tired and pallid ghosts. The weather was indeed changing. The sky was overcast. It was hot and humid. There was no relief from the reek of exhaust fumes in the traffic-packed streets.

I had failed deliberately to give the cabby the number I wanted and he dropped me at the end of Plutox Gardens. It was just a street like millions of others. There were no Gardens, not even in front of its crowding houses. The sight of it did nothing to relieve the depression that had been creeping on me ever since I had arrived in town. A long row of terrace-built houses, homely as a gaol, and not so well preserved. It probably had legitimate claim to wealth and gentility at one time but now the disease of commerce had crept upon it, and the private dweller had departed, leaving it for offices and agencies, with here and there a lodging house calling itself a hotel.

No. 32, when at last I drew level with its peeling stucco front, had nothing save its number painted on the fanlight to prove its identity. It was just a house. The basement windows, protected from the perils of the pavement by thick iron railings, were ablaze with light and the clatter of dishes being washed came through their opened tops.

I rang the door bell. A light clicked on in the hall, and the door was plucked open to reveal a short middle-aged woman with wispy untidy hair and harassed eyes. She was dressed in black and her thin face, sour at the mouth, expressed plainly her displeasure at the interruption. She looked a mean type to me.

"Mr. Nigel Pendleton?" I asked, raising my hat.

"What of 'im?" she snapped.

"He lives here. I'd like to see him if I may."

" 'Es out. Went out 'alf an hour ago."

As far as she was concerned that was the end of the conversation and she began closing the door.

"Have you any idea where I can find him?" I asked desperately. "It's vitally important for me to see him."

"I dunno," she said dully. " 'E just went out." She advanced her scraggy head as far as the door post and looked carefully up and down the street as though she expected to see Mr. Pendleton come striding along it. "Boozin'—I shouldn't be surprised," she said venomously. "Why don't you try the Fevvers or the George and Duck? They're 'is favourite 'aunts."

I wanted to ask her where exactly I could find these establishments, but she slammed the door in my face leaving me no choice.

I backed down the two hearthstoned steps to the pavement. "Hell!" I thought. "Is it worth it?"

My mind dwelt longingly on Selsey, the house against the sea-wall, on Freda and our evening stroll through the Sussex lanes with Montmorency snuffling in the fragrant hedges, and I called myself the mug of all mugs.

Maybe if I had been teetotal I would have chucked the whole thing in then and there, but I needed a drink at that moment. I thought that I may as well have it at the Feathers or the George and Duck as anywhere else.

I couldn't remember seeing a pub at the bottom of the street where the cab had dropped me so I went hopefully along the length of Plutox Gardens, and sure enough, when I reached the top where it debouched into a wider and busier thoroughfare there were two pubs, one on each corner. One was the Feathers and the other was the George and Duck.

I chose the Feathers simply because it happened to be on the same side of the street, and force of habit took me into the saloon bar.

I ordered a double, and not until I had a good half of it inside of me and doing its warming work did I bother to look around me.

The pub was one of those relics of prosperous Edwardian days. The saloon bar was spacious and high-ceilinged, with a prodigious amount of mahogany and glass amongst its more permanent fittings. The only modern note was formed by the leather-topped chromium-legged stools ranged along the bar. I perched myself on one of these and studied the clientele.

Nothing outstanding about any of them. Three old ladies in one corner with tall glasses of stout on the table in front of them. A group of four gentlemen flashily dressed at another table engaged in a great deal of argument. A boy and his girl at another. The inevitable type making eyes at the barmaid from a stool farther along. Beyond him two more lonely ones just sitting and drinking. Was one of them Pendleton? I didn't know, and it came to me that unless I started asking questions I never would know. Pendleton might be any shape or any age. Guesswork was useless.

I waited till I had finished my drink and ordered another.

The barmaid handed me my change—wet as usual—and then I popped the question.

"Do you happen to know a Mr. Nigel Pendleton? I'm

"Why my hotels are open all the year round"

BY BILLY BUTLIN

Many people have been good enough to tell me that my kind of holiday, which they enjoy so much in the summer, is just as perfect for spring, autumn and winter, when the choice of outside amusement and entertainment is generally very much restricted.

I am therefore keeping my Holiday Hotels open throughout the year, and whether you come in June or January, April or October, you can be sure of a full programme of entertainment on the well-known Butlin lines, and all included in my All-in Tariff.

The famous Butlin 'Redcoats' will be there to welcome you and, if you wish, help you make new friends and enjoy to the full the amenities provided. You will find too, plenty of opportunity for quiet rest and relaxation.

Whenever you come, you can be sure of a real happy holiday.

W. E. Butlin

BRIGHTON: Ocean Hotel, Saltdean
BLACKPOOL: Metropole Hotel
MARGATE: 4 Butlin Hotels, Cliftonville

FULL DETAILS of all the Butlin Hotels will be sent on receipt of the coupon below. Tear off and post to

BUTLIN'S LTD., HOTELS DEPT., 439 OXFORD STREET, LONDON, W.1.

- -

PLEASE SEND ME FULL PARTICULARS OF BUTLIN'S HOLIDAY HOTELS

Name ....

Address ....

....

ALSO MY FRIEND

Name ....

Address ....

....

(BLOCK LETTERS PLEASE)

A happy welcome awaits you

all year round at

Butlin's HOLIDAY HOTELS

OPEN ALL FOUR SEASONS—FOR EVER

BRIGHTON : Butlin's Ocean Hotel, Saltdean, an ultra modern holiday hotel with acres of glass-screened sun-decks.

BLACKPOOL : Butlin's Metropole Hotel, in the heart of Blackpool's wonderful entertainment centre.

MARGATE : Butlin's Hotels, Cliftonville, with all the amenities of 4 big hotels for the price of one !

ALL-IN TARIFF includes many of the famous Butlin Holiday entertainments and novelties. *The popular Butlin 'Redcoats' are always there !*

FREE BROCHURE—see overleaf.

anxious to meet him and I'm told he's a regular at the Feathers."

"Why—sure! He's here now." She raised her voice. "Hi—Nigel! There's a gent here wants to meet you."

I could have done without the publicity. Her call had the momentary stupefying effect on the customers that a gun shot might have done. Dead silence. A craning of heads, and then the buzz of conversation got going again.

Pendleton was one of the lonely types at the far end. He stood up from the stool when his name was called and I walked along towards him carrying my fresh drink with me.

I saw a long and lean man of about my own age—which is thirty-two. He had a mop of rusty hair and the freckles that sometimes accompany it. Not a strong face at all—weak round the mouth and an insignificant nose. Blue rather prominent eyes somewhat bloodshot. Just at the moment they were completely blank as though he couldn't see the joke, then, when he realized that I meant it, suspicion and fear chased themselves across his face. He was not badly dressed but his squarish-cut suit was worn and frayed at the cuffs. He had tiny neatly darned holes in his shirt where the points of his collar had rubbed.

"What's the idea?" he demanded. "I don't know you from Adam." His voice, though it rasped, was not uncultured.

"I'm trying to remedy that," I replied, putting as much friendliness into it as I could muster. A couple of whiskies and the relief at finding him helped a lot. "My name's Chadwick. John Chadwick. I'm well aware that it still means nothing to you. But there is a little business I'd like to talk over with you if I may. It would be better discussed—at a table say rather than here at the bar."

For a moment I thought he would refuse. His face took on a mulish look and he stuck out his lower lip. Then he shrugged his shoulders.

"If it's money you're after, you'll be damned unlucky," he said, feelingly.

"Nothing like that," I said. "I think maybe you'd better let me buy you a drink first."

He didn't say "No" so I gestured at the barmaid, who had

been standing within range, her ears waggling, and she whipped him up a double scotch as though she was a mind-reader.

I led the way to a table which was conveniently far away from the others to ensure our not being overheard. He sat down opposite me in a challenging sort of way. He was puzzled but there was just a trace of concern in his eyes as well that encouraged me into thinking that I was not wasting my time.

"All right, Mr. Pendleton," I said, "I'll come to the point quickly. Here's my card. Take a look at it. You'll see that I'm a Private Inquiry Agent." He started to say something but I cut him off. "Now wait a bit. Hear me out. This pub is not the place nor is this the time to discuss matters freely. I think you're being blackmailed. I know that this morning or late yesterday you received a letter sent you in an envelope addressed in a deliberately disguised hand. I know the man who sent it to you. Here's what I want you to do. Call on me at my office tomorrow morning—the address is on my card. I'm out to help you if I can. It won't cost you a penny. What do you say?"

He didn't say anything. He sat there with my card twisting in the fingers of one hand, and his whisky glass gripped in the other. I finished my own drink.

"Think it over," I told him. "I'll be there from ten o'clock onwards."

Still he said nothing whilst he stared at the blank table-top seeing God knows what.

I got up and left him there and pushed my way through the swing doors of the pub without looking back.

CHAPTER III

I FELT pretty sure that Pendleton would turn up the next morning. Given the rest of the previous night to chew over my offer, he would come all right, if it was only curiosity that brought him. The almost stunned silence, after his first attempted question which my next words had obviously answered, proved that he had something on his mind and if it was not blackmail then it was a matter of equal concern to him.

I wondered what it was I had stumbled on when I became curious about Mr. George Swinton. Well—I would know soon. All I hoped was that Pendleton would be early. But he wasn't.

I had given Connie, my office girl, secretary, and general factotum, a holiday while Freda and I were away at Selsey and the office was depressingly empty when I arrived there at ten. There was a little heap of letters in the mail box— circulars mostly—and the inevitable bills. I sorted these over, put through a call to Freda telling her I'd be down that afternoon with any luck, then sniffed around the building a bit thinking that Pendleton might be sitting and twiddling his thumbs in the wrong waiting-room. The building houses all types from dentists to bookmakers. I didn't see him.

At eleven I began to worry about it. Had I misjudged him? Was my guess that it was blackmail right off the mark? If I'd not sworn off the stuff till the evenings I would have had a drink. Why the hell had he not come? Where had I gone wrong?

Later I began asking myself why I was so certain that I had guessed right about him. I couldn't answer the question. It was instinct. I knew it—could feel it in my bones. Swinton was a wrong 'un.

At twelve I was prowling round the office like a wild man. At five past I had chucked in my hand and was looking up the trains to Chichester in the A.B.C. At six minutes past I heard the office door open, looked up, and there he was. Pendleton. Just the same as I had seen him the previous evening. Same suit. Same shirt. He had a green felt hat this time, which he took off as he came in.

I kicked a chair towards him.

"Jiminy!" I grinned. "I'd almost given you up."

"Sorry," he said, "but strange as it may sound I have to work for a living. This is my lunch hour. Ten o'clock was impossible."

He sat down. I reached for the deep bottom drawer and lifted out the bottle but he shook his head. I put it back.

"You're quite right," he began, "I am being blackmailed I'd like to know how you come into it?"

He was watching me intently, still not liking the idea of taking me on trust.

"I get to know things," I answered. "I'm a Nosey Parker by instinct as well as by trade. By the way, if you want a reference on me ring up Chief Inspector Mackintosh at Scotland Yard. If he's there he will tell you I'm all right."

I waited, even indicated the telephone, but he made no move. I was glad of that. The Chief Inspector knew me well enough but he would have been livid to know that I was giving his name as a reference.

"How long has the screw been on?" I asked Pendleton.

"Two years—roughly."

"Cost you much?"

"More than I can afford. He's clever with it. He takes care not to kill the goose laying the golden egg."

"Professional touch, eh? Well—don't worry. I can put my finger on him any time. . . ."

"Can you? I wonder." Pendleton made himself more comfortable by crossing his legs. "If you mean the writer of the letter I received yesterday morning you're in for a shock. That was something entirely different. Care to see it?"

He took my assent for granted, put a hand in his pocket, pulled out an envelope and gave it to me. I took it, wonderingly. It was Swinton's letter all right; the top one of the pile I had seen on his dining-room table. If it was not a blackmail note . . .

"I don't get this," I said. "Do you mean to tell me that this is not a customary demand note?"

"I do. I don't get it myself. That is why I am more than willing to seek the advice of a professional—particularly when he has offered his services for nothing."

"Yeah?" I drawled. "I thought I was on the tail of a blackmailer when I made that offer. I'll even pay to put one of that kidney behind bars. This may be different."

Pendleton smiled lopsidedly. I decided that I didn't like him very much. He was smooth, and in the light of day conceit oozed out of him.

I pushed a box of cigarettes towards him and while he was helping himself and lighting up I read the letter. The paper matched the envelope in texture and the writing was the same hotchpotch of assorted capitals. It read as follows:

You are being blackmailed by a man named Bilter. So is the writer. If you are interested in ridding yourself of this pest come to the George Public House, Gracey Lane, Chelsea, next Friday evening the 22nd. Ask for the room reserved by Swinton. Be there at eight o'clock.

The cigarette was slack in Pendleton's lips when I glanced up. Without bothering to remove it he said almost with a sneer:

"Well, Mr. Chadwick?"

"Definitely not what I expected. Far from it. Illuminating in its own odd way." I paused. "To a certain extent it explains how I came into the picture. Swinton and I are temporary neighbours. He has been behaving in such a furtive fashion that I felt impelled to investigate him. That is how I came to see your name and address on this envelope. I've seen blackmail notes written in the same childish way. So—I followed it up. Obviously Swinton has something up his sleeve, and if this Bilter is a professional blackmailer, Swinton is taking care to keep himself more or less hidden for fear of retaliation. There were six or seven of these envelopes all ready for posting, presumably to others who are also victims of Mr. Bilter. Interesting. I wonder how Swinton learnt of his fellow victims, and their names and addresses?"

"Ah!" said Pendleton. "I wondered when you would come to that. It's the part that worries me."

"Could be an attempt to hi-jack the business. It has been done. Tell me about Bilter."

"There's precious little I can tell you about him. I don't know him. I've never set eyes on him. The whole thing has been done through the post. The first demand came in the form of a letter accompanied by photostatic proof of the . . . er——"

"Crime?" I suggested.

He didn't like that. I saw his mouth set in the mulish way I had observed the previous evening. His protuberant eyes, as smeary in the daylight as they'd been at night, were suddenly hostile. Then he recovered himself.

"Possibly," he said, coolly. He went on: "The first demand was not exorbitant. Five pounds in old one-pound notes to be sent to Mr. Bilter, unregistered, at a *poste restante* address. And so it has been ever since. The demands are not at strictly regular intervals—sometimes I don't hear from him for three months. He'll demand more then. I can pay because he never asks for anything exorbitant. I prefer to find the money rather than face the alternative—which might be distinctly unpleasant. I'm practically enured to it by now. After all, if you do—foolish things, then you can expect to pay, but sometimes I wonder when it will end."

"Never. While you're mug enough to go on paying," I said, brutally. "And you don't know the man? Have never set eyes on him?"

"No."

"But you must have done. How the hell did he get the low-down on you?"

"I don't know."

"You don't . . . For God's sake!" I swore at him. "Talk sense, man. Listen. This man Bilter carries the hall mark of the professional. Obviously he has a nice little coterie of victims from whom he enjoys a comfortable tax-free income. These birds are often in partnership. Very often it's a woman who takes a post as a domestic servant or a private secretary. She sets out deliberately to search for the family skeleton. She looks for letters, photographs, things like that. She snoops. She listens at keyholes. She's usually an adept at the task. When she finds something she passes it on to her accomplice, who will find out what he can about the proposed victim, and if he's not likely to cause them trouble, down they come on him with a demand note." I grinned at Pendleton. "Simple, isn't it? When you know how."

He stirred in his seat uncomfortably, not liking the homily.

"Now you come to mention it," he said sullenly, "I was living at home at the time. I recall that my mother sacked a maidservant whom she caught nosing into her desk. I wondered afterwards . . . As a matter of fact I could have sworn that I destroyed . . ." He stopped awkwardly.

"Letters?" I asked lightly. "Never mind. I don't want to

know what hold he has on you. For all I know you deserve it. Trouble with blackmailers is that they rope all sorts into their nets—many of them quite innocent and respectable folk who suffer because of one isolated very human lapse. What was the girl's name?"

"I don't remember it now," he answered petulantly. "I think she was Ella something-or-other."

"Think you can find out? I mean that. It may be important."

"I suppose I could. But what's all this leading up to? Do you think you can nail this—er—Bilter?"

"I can try," I said. "These gentry are not so anonymous as they sound. Their fellow rats know how they make a living, and like rats they sometimes squeal. I've got a man on tap who keeps a gazeteer on crime. The police themselves will sometimes oblige with records. I don't suppose Bilter is the fellow's real name any more than he is likely to have left his finger-prints on the demand notes he's sent you. I'll tell you what though, Pendleton. If you had come to me, or indeed to any competent dick, or to the police if you could have borne the thought, two years ago when this first happened, we'd have had the pants off this blackmailer within a fortnight. As it is the trail is as cold as the man's own heart."

"Maybe," Pendleton complained. "Of course I'd like the swine scuppered. Who wouldn't? But if you go turning him up to the light of day other things may be revealed as well, for which I, and probably other victims too, won't thank you."

I shrugged my shoulders.

"It's a risk," I replied lightly. "The police are usually co-operative. Of course if Bilter is blackmailing you because he knows that you have committed a serious crime the authorities won't let you go unpunished because you've been a blackmailer's victim."

"I'm not a criminal," he declared hotly.

"I never said you were. What about Swinton? He seems to be in fair way towards 'turning Bilter up to the light of day'. Surely the same risk of other things being revealed in the process applies. You going to this meeting?"

He stirred restlessly and dragged fiercely on the remains of his cigarette.

"I'm damned if I know what to do. I've been thinking—a great deal more so since I met you in the Feathers last night. I don't like the idea of other people knowing I'm a victim of a blackmailer, let alone them learning why. Seems to me the time has come for the affair to be placed in the hands of a competent investigator. . . ."

"That may well be precisely what Swinton will propose at the meeting."

"Perhaps. . . ."

"Or he may have a plan of his own. From the little I've seen of him he doesn't look the type to knuckle under to a blackmailer without fighting back. Suppose you let me handle this, Pendleton? Swinton doesn't know me. Let me go to this meeting in your place."

"Why?" he demanded. "I can't pay you a fee." He laughed mirthlessly. "Bilter keeps me on a subsistence level. I left home to live in that dump of a boarding house because it was becoming obvious to my parents that my money was not being spent or even banked."

"I don't want a fee. I want to attend this meeting because —well frankly this letter from Swinton considered as a development in a case of blackmail is about the craziest thing I ever saw. It's a little too pat to be true. I think Swinton has a plan all cut and dried. It'll need vetting by someone who understands these things."

"And are you the man for the job?" he asked in his half sneering way.

"I'd like to be."

He said nothing for a full minute, just sucked on his cigarette and stared dully at the floor. Then he got to his feet.

"All right," he said. "Go ahead. But for God's sake try and keep my name out of any *dénouement* that may arise. I'm not particularly worried on my own account although I should probably lose my job. My employer is a sanctimonious old bible puncher in everything except business, in which he's something akin to an undetected rogue. It's my parents who would suffer. I'm an only son, and, quite mistakenly of course, they idolize me. Anything else you want to know?"

"Your telephone number."

He gave me two, one for the office. I jotted them down.

"Anyone else know about this?"

"Not a soul."

"No girl friend?"

"Not now," he said, bitterly.

"Sounds like a moral lapse," I suggested. "Not with that Ella something-or-other?"

"Good God—no!"

"Well—don't forget that I would like her name as soon as possible."

He repeated his earlier promise to do what he could and left after noting my telephone number.

I sat still for a little while marshalling my thoughts. Friday night at the George, Gracey Lane, in Chelsea, and this was Wednesday. Not much time. I picked up the telephone and dialled TOL to give them the Selsey number. Freda was still at home and I explained the situation, pointing out that I might have to stay in town for a day or two.

She had one little bit of news for me before she rang off.

"S. has bought a boat," she said. "I thought you'd like to know. It's a small seagoing dinghy with an outboard motor. He's fixed up a mooring below the wall at the bottom of the garden. He was out in it last night. Fishing, I think."

I could not make much of the information immediately and stored it away for future reference.

My next contact was Delaney Slater. He was the man to whom I had referred when telling Pendleton of the gazeteer on crime. A useful fellow, Del Slater. Apart from an uncanny knowledge of the seamy side of life I had used him as an operative on many an occasion. He was adept at trailing a man without being spotted himself. A rough-spoken and out-spoken little fellow, cocky at times, but a gem at his job.

I dialled his number and he answered it himself.

"Thought you was away, guv'nor. Left your missus all on 'er own? Ain't you lucky!"

"Blackmailers, Del," I returned, coming to the point. "Got any professional ones on your list?"

I heard him suck his breath through his teeth.

"Not a very popular line, guv. Penalties too severe—they

come down heavy on blackmailers. Sort of trade you don't
'ear anything of till the bloke's in the dock and wondering 'ow
the 'ell he's going to survive seven years on the Moor . . . if
you know what I mean."

"I know what you mean," I said. "You never learn of one
till his career is over, and I want one in practice. I was afraid
of that. This one calls himself Bilter and it is more than likely
that he has a female accomplice."

"Ah!" he exclaimed. "Now there used to be a couple 'oo
was generally supposed to be working the black—last I 'eard
of them was six or seven years ago. But you know how it is
with me, guv. I only learn of the little ones. These birds
prosper and grow big or else they get nabbed and sent down.
Either way I crosses 'em off me list. But Bilter! I've never 'eard
of that one. I'll look up some names and give you a ring."

I thanked him and rang off.

Whenever I get my teeth into a case I invariably accumu-
late all the possible information I can gather on the principals
in it. An awful amount of useless data comes into the net, but
very often some odd piece, of which I would have had no
knowledge at all in the ordinary way, pays off handsomely.

I use a man named Patey, who runs what he calls a
Reference Bureau, to do all my dirty work for me in this
connection. I've helped him financially before now, and he and
I are now firm friends.

"Morning, Patey," I said, as soon as I heard his voice in
the instrument.

"Hell! It's you, Chaddy. I thought you were at the seaside
and nicely out of my hair for a month at least. What's
cooking?"

"I want to know all you can learn about a man named
George Swinton. I think he's a Londoner though at present he's
residing at Selsey in a rented house. Yes. There may be five
or six of that name in the London Telephone Directory. I
don't know. But this bloke is a man of some substance, and if
there should be more than one in your reference books, then
give me the dope on them all. O.K.?"

"Done," he said, and rang off.

I had the feeling that perhaps I ought to have told him to

collect some information on Nigel Pendleton, but then I decided that he was too small a fish to be catalogued.

Having set the ball rolling I went to lunch with an easy mind.

Slater was the first of the two with some information. He brought it in person. I was having a shameless forty winks by the side of the telephone with my feet propped comfortably on another chair when he came in.

"What it is to be the boss!" he exclaimed.

My feet vacated the chair. He sat down on it and pushed his bowler to the back of his head.

"Warm out," he remarked tentatively.

I found the bottle and a glass, pushed them towards his end of the desk. He raised his scrubby eyebrows when he saw that I was not joining him.

"Sworn off it till the evening," I said.

"Me too," he said, tipping the bottle comfortably. "He smacked his lips noisily. "As far as I'm concerned, guv, the shades of night are falling fast. Good luck!"

He had his drink, and we got down to business.

"Nothing doin' with Bilter," he said, shaking his head. "Never 'eard such a name before. It can't be real."

"It isn't," I returned. "Couldn't be more obviously false. I'm more interested in the couple you mentioned . . . the man and woman who used to practise the black."

"Ah. Now that feller's name was Spirelza . . ."

"And the woman's?"

"She was supposed to 'ave been 'is missus. Maybe she was."

"What happened to them?"

He shrugged his shoulders.

"Couldn't say, guv. I can't rightly remember, now, 'ow I come to 'ave 'em ticketed as blackmailers. Process of elimination I daresay. Spirelza used to be in the stolen-car racket, working with a man named Gunton. They fell out. Shortly afterwards Spirelza teamed up with a girl 'oo used to be missing for weeks at a time. They always seemed to be in the money but Spirelza did nothing to earn it. He wasn't working honestly. 'E wasn't smuggling or 'ousebreaking, or keeping a red-lamp house. Where the 'ell was he getting it? He was a crook and 'e was in the money. Answer, blackmail.''

"He could have won a football pool," I pointed out. "Was he ever convicted?"

"I don't reckon so, guv. He was one of those the war threw up. Refugee, I dare say."

"What did he look like, Del?"

"Cor, stone the crows, Mr. Chadwick, what d'you think I am? This must 'ave been eight—nine—years ago. I was interested in Gunton at the time—one of 'is mechanics used to talk a lot when he got the drink in 'im. I suppose I did set eyes on Spirelza. . . .'' Slater put a finger under the sweat band of his bowler and rubbed at his hair. "Mind you," he said, "we worked all this out about Spirelza after he'd gone from Gunton's. Let me think . . . Yers. I did see him once. I remember now. I used to think he was a Pole, or a Greek, or somethin', but he spoke the King's English like a gentleman. Biggish feller— be about fortyish now—swelp me, guv'nor," he said plaintively, when he saw that I was frowning, "I can't remember the colour of his eyes or anything like that. But I do remember being told that 'e'd teamed up with a woman and was working a black- mail racket. That got me interested and I started some notes on 'im. But something happened to him. He went—like that." Slater snapped his fingers.

"All right, Del," I said. "Thanks a lot. It's all very nebulous, but you know how it is with me. I don't like to disregard anything however remote. Mackintosh may know him."

"What's on your mind, Mr. Chadwick?" he asked.

For answer I dug out the letter Pendleton had left with me and flicked it across to him. He read it and looked baffled.

"That's rich!" he exclaimed. "I've never seen anything like this before and that's a fact! If the bloke that wrote it is being blackmailed himself how in tarnation did 'e learn about the others?"

"You ask me," I said. "Another thing—perhaps not so obvious. He takes care to disguise his handwriting but at the end of the note he puts his name. Incidentally I've prevailed upon Mr. Pendleton to let me attend this meeting using his identity. Should be interesting. Will you be around for a day or two? I may need your services."

He said that he would be on call, and after I had told him how I had come to notice Mr. George Swinton, he took his leave.

I grew impatient waiting for Patey to call and finally got through to himself.

"Have a heart, Chaddy!" he groaned. "I've dug out three of that name. One is a clergyman. Can I cross him out do you think?"

"Why?"

"A man of the cloth—a priest. Not exactly one of your criminal types."

"Clergymen have erred before now. Let me know all about him, Patey. If you've not finished your compiling Friday morning will do. I'll ring you then."

I sat tapping fingers on the desk for a little while wondering if I had the courage to beard the lion, Chief Inspector Mackintosh, in his den. Finally, after seeing in the time table that I had about an hour to spare before the next train to Chichester, I picked up the telephone and dialled Whitehall 1212.

I had to state my name and business. I gave my name but said that the call was personal. I waited. I could imagine the operator getting through to Mac and the Chief Inspector's reaction to a personal call from me. Outside of the profession I hardly knew him at all. The ice was thin. The whole thing depended really on whether he was busy or not.

The instrument clicked and he said, "Mackintosh here."

"Mac," I replied, "I'm sorry to bother you . . ."

"You're not a bit sorry," he said. "Speak up, Chaddy, and make it brief. I'm hellish busy."

"You sound fine," I retorted, "which suggests the opposite. Will you do me a small favour, Mac? Will you get your myrmidions to look up two names in the records? One is Bilter. The other is Spirelza."

I spelt them for him.

"They're sufficiently unusual not to demand initials," he

remarked dryly. "I don't know Bilter. Spirelza is vaguely familiar. What have you smelt out this time, Chaddy?"

"Blackmail, chief. I'm just groping at the moment, though. May I call for the answers, if any, on Friday morning?"

"You may. If I'm not here ask for Sergeant Williams."

Then Chief Inspector Mackintosh really astonished me.

"How is your wife?" he asked.

"Fine. She's fine. We've rented a furnished house at Selsey for a month. She's down there now."

"That's odd," he said, "I've got a boat in Chichester Creek. I'm down there week-ends whenever I get the chance, which is not often. I must look you up. Where is the house?"

By this time the Chief Inspector's friendliness had me in a daze. Come to think of it he had shown an interest in Freda the last time we'd had occasion to meet, but to my certain knowledge he had never set eyes on her. Mac himself was a hardened bachelor old enough to be my father, and having worked under him for a short time years previously I'd always had a job to believe him human.

"The name of the house is Tenderleas," I told him, "and it is on the West Beach. Come whenever you like."

"Splendid," he said. "I will. I've always wanted to meet Mrs. Chadwick."

With that he rang off. I put down the receiver telling myself that wonders will never cease.

An hour later, after telephoning the glad news that I would not have to stay in town after all, I was on the train for Chichester. I was feeling reasonably pleased. Inquiries were out, and in due course the information would trickle through to me. I found the outlook intriguing. I had not done so badly in twenty-four hours, with one possible exception. Swinton's buckets of sea-water had started me on this and I still had no clue as to the meaning of them. What the devil did the man want with it, storing it in his bath? At one time I'd thought I had the glimmerings of an idea, sinister though it might have been, but now that notion seemed ludicrous. Evidently Swinton had got something on the blackmailer Bilter, and for safety's sake had rented a house on the coast to get away from his normal place of abode. It explained his presence in Selsey mostly during the evenings only, and the care he had taken to keep himself to himself. But the sea-water in his bath?

I thought about it for a long time while the train flashed through the southern suburbs, but it had me guessing. That was as far as I could get with it.

CHAPTER IV

THURSDAY at Selsey was uneventful save for the weather, which was foul. Lashings of rain driven by a south-west wind with the devil behind it. I caught one glimpse of Swinton as he went over the sea-wall, this time in daylight. He was anxious about the moorings of his newly acquired boat. The glimpse was nearly an encounter. In a way it was a narrow squeak, for if I was to impersonate Pendleton at Swinton's oddly convened meeting of blackmail victims, then it was essential for me to remain unseen myself.

The same thing nearly happened again on Friday morning when Freda drove me into Chichester to catch the seven o'clock train. Swinton's big black Austin was ahead of us on the road into the city, and was parked in the station yard when we got there. He was waiting on the platform, but his nose was buried in *The Times*, and he was completely un-suspecting. Freda said a hasty good-bye, for if Swinton glanced up idly he was more likely to recognize her than see any evil intent in my presence there. I was fairly confident that he had not seen me at Selsey, but there was always the chance. It was one I could take and feel reasonably safe when the time came to present myself as Pendleton in the private room of a Chelsea pub. Under those conditions he would never identify me as the loutish husband of his pretty neighbour in Selsey; a man whom he might have glimpsed lazing about the place in bathing trunks.

Freda had not missed a thing going on in Kohinoor while I had been in town. Apart from reporting Swinton's boat she had seen him receive another visit from Miss Helen Arnett.

This time the lady had arrived over the sea-wall dressed in nothing but a scarlet-hued Bikini. Freda, being a woman, had naturally paid great attention to this unconventional approach, and in consequence had seen Miss Arnett's departure ten minutes later. The lady had been looking plainly annoyed as though she and Swinton had quarrelled violently.

I didn't see Swinton at Victoria for he was at the front of the train and I had taken care to keep in the rear.

Five minutes after I had arrived at the office Patey came through.

"Who will you have first?" he demanded. "The parson? If he's a crook, then so am I. Bet you there is not a more blameless cleric in the whole of Crockford. Are you ready?"

He was probably right about the parson, but I said:"All right. Take it easily. Connie is on holiday and I'm no shorthand queen."

I scribbled steadily for five minutes, and when Patey had rung off, sat back and studied what I had written. The cleric was out. He was the vicar of an obscure parish in outer London, married with three children and as poor as most of his parishioners. Patey had found his name in a trade gazette that published the names of people with County Court Orders against them. If he was the George Swinton who had taken on Kohinoor then I was the Lord Chamberlain.

The next, George Swinton, was a University Lecturer, who lived at Malden. He was a Doctor of Philosophy. He had been educated privately and at Oxford. He was unmarried. His hobbies were motoring and breeding cats, which led me to suppose that Patey had lifted him straight from the pages of *Who's Who*. But he was a possible.

The third and last one looked the more likely of the three to match my Selsey neighbour. He was managing director of a firm called Rabal Products Ltd., who had premises in the Goswell Road. His private address was a flat in Millbank, which I recognized as being part of a block that was practically a hotel. He too was unmarried. In addition he was a director of Radleys the toffee makers, being, according to Patey, the nephew of Mrs. Agnes Radley, widow of the founder and therefore virtual owner of the firm.

"He's my boy," I thought.

I glanced at the clock and dialled Pendleton's office number. The girl who answered obligingly quoted the name of the firm who were enjoying the doubtful honour of Mr. Pendleton's services, and I made a note of that too.

Pendleton, when at last he answered his extension, was as sour as soda and milk.

"I rang your office three times yesterday," he complained. "Why the hell can't you get a girl or someone to look after the place when you're out?"

"My wife doesn't trust me," I said. If he'd not been so curdled I would have apologized. "Did you get that girl's name?"

"I did. It is Ella Price. Look here, Chadwick, you're going to keep me informed, aren't you?"

"What leads you to suppose that I won't?"

"I don't know." He sounded irritable but a little more humble. "It's just that I have a hell of a lot at stake. I've been thinking——"

"Don't," I said. "I've already got a line on Bilter if that's any comfort to you. The thing to do is to watch that this fellow Swinton doesn't queer the pitch. I'll see to that."

"You mean you've identified him already?"

"Bilter? I think I know who he is. I told you that these professional blackmailers cannot remain entirely anonymous. Leave it to me, Pendleton. I'll keep you posted."

I put down the receiver hoping that Pendleton would judge me far more confident than I was.

Fifteen minutes later I was beefing about in an empty waiting-room in Scotland Yard wondering how long either Chief Inspector Mackintosh or his stooge, Sergeant Williams, would keep me waiting. In actual fact it was ten minutes, though it seemed more like an hour; a phenomenon peculiar to all waiting-rooms, particularly those smelling of disinfectant.

Mac was out, and I saw Sergeant Williams, whom I knew as well as I knew the Chief Inspector. Williams was a big affable man, incredibly handsome in a film-starrish sort of way with his white teeth and thin black moustache. He had the bright berry-brown eyes that so many of his profession seem to have

"Nothing on Bilter," he said. "Name's odd enough to have been invented."

"Probably was. Spirelza?"

"Ah. Now you're talking." He referred to a file he had been carrying under his arm. "Would he be S. B. Spirelza? Sergius Borodic Spirelza?"

"Sergeant," I appealed, "you tell me. I don't know any Christian names. The surname like Bilter is odd enough to merit distinction, if not invention. Del Slater had him listed some nine or ten years ago as a blackmailer."

"Blackmailer eh?" Sergeant Williams tapped the folder in a sinister sort of way. "This bird," he said, "was a murder suspect."

"When?"

"Seven years ago."

"Could be the same bloke. Slater says that something happened to him. By that he means that Spirelza vanished from his usual haunts. If he was a murder suspect he might have felt impelled to push off elsewhere."

"He did," Williams grinned. "He went to Scarborough. No doubt he felt in need of a little bracing air."

"Who was killed?"

"A girl—name of Elsie Gold. Ring a bell with you?"

"No. How was she killed?"

"Strangled with her own stocking. Not a very original method, but—sort of handy for a man in a hurry. Spirelza knew the girl. He had been a constant caller at her flat. She was undoubtedly his mistress. Unfortunately her body was not found till twenty-four hours after she had been killed, nor could we find a witness who could swear to have seen Spirelza calling on her the evening she was killed. On top of that he produced the usual alibi. Even so he was the only suspect, because he was the only man with whom she had associated in the previous two years."

"Motive?"

"None. May have been robbery. If it was we don't know what was taken. It was a clean job. The victim wasn't clutching a button like they do in the story books. There were no finger-prints that could not be satisfactorily explained. One or two places, door handles and the like, had been wiped. He knew what he was doing all right."

"Think it was Spirelza?"

"I'd bet a year's pay on it. What we had to do was to prove it—that's different."

"What was the girl? I mean what had she been doing for a living?"

"Various jobs at various times. Chambermaid in an hotel. Domestic service. Milk bar help."

"She could have been Spirelza's accomplice in his black-mailing schemes?"

"Perhaps. We never found evidence of it. If she was that useful why bump her off?"

"I don't know. It was an idea. How much have you got on Spirelza, Sergeant? Any pictures?"

"No. He was never arrested. We've got his dabs, of course."

"Description?"

Williams consulted his file.

"For what it's worth," he said. "Age 39. That was seven years ago. Height, six foot. Complexion, ruddy. Hair, brown. Eyes, ditto. Heavy build."

"Lucid," I remarked. "That could fit you."

"Or you," he retorted.

"My eyes," I replied with dignity, "are green flecked with brown. It says so on my passport. Talking of passports—what nationality is Spirelza?"

"He's of Russian origin. Possibly an Englishman by now."

"I see." I picked up my hat. "Well . . . Thanks a lot, Willy. His finger-prints might be useful."

"What are you after, Chaddy?"

"A blackmailer."

He tucked the folder under his arm again.

"Don't forget the law," he said.

"I never do—unfortunately the victims fight shy of it for obvious reasons. If I can catch him with the goods you'll have him quickly enough. My regards to the Chief Inspector. By the way—what's come over the great man? He was positively friendly on the 'phone the other day."

The sergeant's white teeth flashed in a biggest-ever grin.

"He's courting," he said.

"No!"

"It's a fact. Nice little widow. Did he tell you he had a boat on Chichester Creek?"

"Yes."

"Don't you believe it. The boat is hers. Mac's on a good thing there, and it's practically all over. Banns up soon. By—— I'll get drunk the day the old man is hitched if I never touch another drop!"

"That's a date," I said, and we shook hands, grinning like a couple of kids.

Back in the office I sat down to mull over what I had heard about Spirelza. I decided after a very short time that he might be Bilter, but I could have arrived at that conclusion without bothering Scotland Yard. The one crumb of comfort was the fact that his prints were on record. I toyed with the idea of getting some demand notes from Pendleton if they had not been destroyed with the idea of testing them for prints, but discarded the notion before it had taken root. A man systematically blackmailing a number of victims was living on the edge of a gaping pit. He would make no simple errors. He had probably built up an elaborate system of collecting his money once it had arrived at a *poste restante* or accommodation address that would take a great deal of breaking down. It would not be easy. Swinton knew something, of course, and it was a waste of grey matter to go on speculating ways and means till I had heard what he had to say.

The rest of the day passed slowly till eight o'clock. The George, in Gracey Lane, Chelsea, was just like any other pub in any other back street in the vast sprawl of inner London, when I arrived there five minutes after the hour. I pushed my way into the saloon bar. It wasn't very big, and though it contained only six customers, it seemed crowded. The landlord was one of those people who collect brass junk, and hang it polished all over the walls. These were teeming with harness badges, toasting forks, warming pans, brass plates and trays. The place looked like a pseudo antique shop in a seaside town.

Before leaving the flat I had changed into the oldest pair of flannels and put on the most ancient tweed jacket I could find, with the idea of trying to look like a man living on a much depleted income. Maybe I succeeded, for the bar-keep took one look at me and said:

"Mr. Swinton's party? Up the stairs, first door on the right."

He had to show me the stairs, which were tucked away in an alcove in the corner.

I paused for a moment outside the door. There was a mutter of voices coming from the other side but I couldn't make anything of them. I waited long enough to convince myself that Swinton had seen me at Selsey and was bound to recognize me, then took a grip on the doorknob, turned it, and went in.

The room was a plainly utilitarian one and had never been used for anything except committee meetings of local clubs and the like. A table, with a once polished top, occupied the centre of it. Some hardwood battle-scarred chairs stood around the faded walls. Facing me over the fireplace at the far end was a tattered buffalo's head, with an advertisement for tonic water dangling from one of its horns. The names of the officers in the Local Order were inscribed in gilt letters on a large board. That was all the furniture the room contained. Throughout the years vast quantities of beer had been spilt on the worn linoleum, enough to reach the floorboards below, and now the air in the room contained a permanent and sour reek of stale beer.

There were five people in the room. Swinton was one of them. Of the other four, two were ladies. That jolted me. I had not expected women to be mixed in Swinton's party. What the devil did he expect from them?

They all turned to stare at me. I saw at a glance that I was about as popular with them as they were with each other. Suspicion, speculation, fear, and even derision were in the looks they gave me. Swinton could find no welcome for a newcomer. He stepped forward, big, hard, ruthless looking, formally dressed as though for a board meeting, his dark eyes one menacing question mark.

"Pendleton," I said, tersely.

He nodded. His eyes swept over me quickly as though he

was matching me up with what he had expected. Apparently
he was satisfied. I was, at any rate, because he had given no
sign of recognition. He turned his back on me and addressed
the others.

"Ladies and gentlemen, we now number six with Mr.
Pendleton. I sent out seven invitations. The response is better
than I had hoped. For all I know the seventh victim is a
commercial traveller away from home. I suggest we make a
start. Will you pull up chairs to the table?"

By the way he said it Swinton was not expecting any
argument that evening, and by the way they all complied he
was not going to get any—yet.

The two ladies chose one side of the table, the two men the
other, and I found myself facing Swinton, who took a standing
position with his back to the fireplace and the buffalo's head
leering over one shoulder. The thing seemed faintly symbolic,
for there was something of that bulky animal to be seen in
Swinton himself.

"Pendleton," he said, "you have not yet been introduced.
On my right, Miss Piper and Mrs. Malone. On my left, Captain
Ellery and Doctor Gribble."

I nodded genially all round, which was a gross error, for
there was nothing particularly pleasant about this meeting.
I reminded myself that I was supposed to be a nerve-worn
victim of a blackmailer. There was one thing only that had
dragged these people to this obscure pub in the back streets of
Chelsea at the behest of a total stranger, and that was Fear.
They all had something on their conscience. They lived in
apprehension. Anxiety was their bedfellow. They sat around
that ring-marked table in Fear. It would not engender any
comradely spirit towards a fellow victim. The only pity they
could have would be Self-Pity.

Till then I had not paid any particular attention towards
my fellow guests. They were there. Two were men and two
were women. That was all. Now I studied each one, quickly
and covertly.

Of the four Miss Piper was the oddity because she was the
most insignificant. She was a small and thin woman, perhaps
thirty years old, dressed unrelievedly in black, and not very

stylishly. Her narrow face was pale except for a smear of red on her lips and even that had been put on half-heartedly. She sat and stared with uninteresting eyes at the table immediately under her nose, while she pulled nervously at the finger of an empty glove. What she had done to receive the attention of a blackmailer was completely beyond me. She looked as harmless as a soft drink.

By contrast Mrs. Malone, who was a year or two her senior, was as glamorous as a movie star. She was a big Junoesque type of woman immaculately dressed in a costume of pale saffron colour. There was nothing cheap about her from the rings on her finger to her neat close-fitting hat. She had nice hair, a wide inviting mouth, and large lustrous eyes as warm as an Indian girl's. Mrs. Malone had everything, and knew it. She sat with a trace of a smile on her rich red lips glancing at the men opposite her, but the smile was missing from her eyes, which held a suspicion of worry mixed with their habitual boldness of glance.

Of the two men Captain Ellery was sitting at Swinton's end of the table. In build he was not unlike Pendleton, being long and lean. He was big boned, however, and he had the type of wide shoulders that sometimes invoke jokes about coat-hangers left in the jacket. Though he was wearing a Guards tie he was too old to be on the active list, not with the rank of captain. His hair was thin and greying, and he had a long nose with a perceptible bump on its end which gave him a prying look. He was scruffy round the neck, and his hands, which he had humped on the table-top, were noticeably dirty. Seedy, he looked to me.

His neighbour, Doctor Gribble, and the man immediately on my right, though he was altogether more spruce in his dress, was at first glance no more likable. He was as hairy as an ape, with a long black bar of eyebrow, and little dark tufts high on his cheek where for some reason he neglected to shave. There was a malevolent gleam in his black, deeply set eyes, and he had a tight squarish mouth that looked ready to snarl at the slightest provocation. I could imagine him wielding a hypodermic and the thought gave me the shudders. I could be wrong. For all I knew then he was a Doctor of Music, except

D

that he had a surgeon's hands, slender and strong, but matted with dark hair.

Swinton, having rid himself of the introductions, was all set to get down to business, when there was a timid knock on the door. We all jerked round, but it was only a waiter, an old man in a not too clean white jacket, who, following his knock, came shuffling into the room. He had some affliction of the eyes. They blinked perpetually like the Morse Code.

"You folks want any drinks?" he whined. It was more of a complaint than an invitation.

Mrs. Malone gave a husky chuckle.

"Sure," she drawled. "Right now—a bottle of nerve tonic."

So she was either an American or Canadian. I never could tell the difference.

Swinton didn't care for the interruption but he covered it well, asked everybody what they would have, and passed on the order.

Miss Piper shuddered at the idea and shook her head violently. The others wanted whisky. I ordered a pint of beer. It seemed to me that to drink anything else in that particular room was to mix drinks whether you liked it or not.

Swinton said that he would wait for them to be served before he started again. When at last they came, five perfect strangers wished each other "Good Luck", each wondering what the hell the other had done to bring him or her there. Miss Piper sat with downcast eyes and punished her glove.

I thought it a good idea to strengthen my deception by breaking in on Swinton before he could start his Chairman's act again.

"I don't know what's been said already," I called down the table to him. "I was the last to arrive, but there is one question I'd like to put immediately. I'm sort of sensitive about it. How the devil did you get hold of my name and address and to know that I was being blackmailed?"

Ellery said, "Hear! Hear!" in a very pointed way.

Swinton leant forward, his hands spread out on the table-top.

"Mr. Pendleton," he said, "I'm not at all surprised to hear

you ask that question. Everybody has done the same. Believe me, it is the very first explanation that I shall give. I know what is worrying each and every one of you. Have I learnt as well *why* you are being blackmailed? I have not. I know no more about you than your names and addresses, and that is all."

He paused to let this sink in, and also to see from the expression on our faces whether or not he was believed. It was fairly obvious that without further explanations everyone was ready to call him a liar and he hurried on:

"We are all in the same boat, ladies and gentlemen. I too am a victim of Mr. Bilter's, but I don't take kindly to blackmail. Yes. I paid him because his demand was comparatively moderate, but I fought back right from the word go."

That was fair enough. Bilter had slipped somewhere when he had chosen George Swinton for a victim. His trap set to catch a lamb he could fleece had caught instead a tiger. I felt pleased with the analogy but vaguely uneasy about it. One of the necessary, almost vital, prerequisites of blackmail is for the blackmailer to know his victim. It seemed odd to me that such a slick operator as Bilter could have made such a grave error. Swinton was one of those men who hate to be beaten at anything. It was not his pocket being bled that worried him, but the blow to his not inconsiderable ego.

"Right away," Swinton was saying, "I engaged a discreet firm of Private Inquiry Agents and they tried to trap Bilter at the places where I was told to send the money. They failed every time. I daresay you have all received the same sort of instructions. If he used a *poste restante* it was always at a Central Post Office, very crowded and very busy. Without the active co-operation of the authorities, which I was reluctant for them to use for obvious reasons, it was practically impossible for my Agents to catch him. They suspected that he had already left instructions for the letter to be sent on to another *poste restante*, or that he came in with an addressed registered envelope already prepared into which he put the money and posted it away again without leaving the counter."

Swinton paused as though to invite comment but nobody said anything. The saturnine Gribble had one hand on his now empty whisky glass and was twisting and turning it as though he wanted to screw it into the table. He didn't look up when Swinton stopped. Next to him Ellery had teetered back in his chair, and cocked up his head as though he had to sight his long nose on Swinton in order to see him properly. Mrs. Malone had her shapely and crimson-nailed fingers comfortably interlocked on the table in front of her and looked surprisingly placid. She was instantly aware of my glance at her, switched her luminous eyes to mine and smiled. My natural reaction to a smile from a pretty woman is to grin back at her promptly, but keeping in mind that I was Pendleton I just looked, and she glanced away unperturbed. I didn't have to glance at Miss Piper to know her reaction to Swinton's words. She may have changed hands but she was still at her glove.

Swinton, having taken time off for a quick drink, and drawn no questions, went on.

"I got on to Bilter eventually," he told us, "by an extraordinary stroke of luck. My firm sells amongst other things large quantities of stationery. We had as a remnant some very poor stuff, hopelessly inferior, which we sold in one lot at a give-away price. Four days later I received a demand note from Bilter typed on that very same paper. It was unmistakable— made originally from straw, and in colour a dirty grey. We were not the only firm to have handled that paper, but there was a chance—a very faint chance—that Bilter had bought from the retailer who had bought from us. I got my Agents working on it. The retailer had sold two packets—one to a schoolgirl, who could be ignored, but the other to a man whom they were certain they had seen on more than one occasion in the very Post Offices they had been detailed to watch—a man with a certain physical characteristic whom they could not possibly mistake." Swinton leant back from the table, and stood to his full height. "That man, ladies and gentlemen, was Bilter."

Doctor Gribble looked up from his perpetual fiddling with the empty glass.

"How did your Agents learn that?" he inquired, quickly. His voice was not a growl as I had imagined, but firm and resonant, completely at variance with his appearance.

"Bilter is well known by sight at least in his own neighbourhood," Swinton snapped back. "He is a big heavy man. His real name is Edward Ward. The shopkeeper knew him and where he lived, though not his name. The rest, of course, was easy."

I wanted to point out that it had been gross carelessness on Bilter's part to purchase material for his blackmail notes almost on his own doorstep. It sounded unlikely. But criminals do make the most stupid mistakes, particularly so after a year or more's undetected success, and I kept my own counsel.

"O.K., Mr. Swinton," Mrs. Malone observed. "What happened next? Nobody knows this guy Bilter. I thought we'd established that before we sat down—that is, all of us except Mr. Pendleton here. I guess we're all pretty anxious to know how you learnt about us."

"From then onwards," Swinton resumed, "I was on my own. You may have noticed that on no occasion did my Agents approach the authorities or seek their assistance in any way—not even Post Office officials. From my point of view it would have been too risky. The Post Office would have wanted to know a great deal of detail before they co-operated, and from them it was but a short step to the police being called in.

"Now, I will be perfectly frank with you. I don't want the police in on this. If I did I would have gone to them when I received the first demand note. Obviously the same condition applies to each of you."

"I don't know that it's obvious." Captain Ellery stirred in his chair. "Are you trying to imply that we have all broken the law?"

"Nothing of the sort. But if you, Captain Ellery, want the police to know that you are being blackmailed, why have you not gone to them? Obviously because you don't want them to know why you are being blackmailed."

"Look," Doctor Gribble cut in, "this is hardly worth arguing about. Of course it is obvious. Can we not get on, and argue later?"

"Thank you, Doctor. I'll make it short. I studied Bilter for a long, long time. I flatter myself that I have learnt in the process a great deal about him without him knowing that I was doing so. The fact is that he possesses certain documents

involving me that I must have before I can be free of his
attentions. Much the same conditions apply to you, I daresay.
I was on my own. He was outside the law, which I argued
gave me a certain amount of protection. I don't believe in
half measures. I chose my time. I burgled his house." Swinton
smiled grimly. "Naturally I failed to get what I wanted
because he keeps it in a quite formidable safe. I'm no
cracksman. But what I did find—and I think I was excep-
tionally lucky, for I feel sure that normally it would have been
kept in the safe and not in an unlocked drawer of his desk—
was a little black book containing all your names and addresses.
Since my own heads the list I felt safe in presuming that you
were all fellow victims. Here is the book."

Swinton groped in the top pocket of his vest, brought out
a shiny covered notebook, and with a dramatic flourish, for
which he could probably be excused, flung it onto the table.

CHAPTER V

ALTHOUGH the book had been pitched to the middle of the
table it was Captain Ellery's long hand that closed over it almost
before it had come to rest. His fingers probed it open, and then
he swept it up, ducked his nose and peered into it short-
sightedly. He grunted, closed the book and passed it to Gribble.
The doctor spurned it, and pushed it along the table to me.

"My name must be in it!" he said. "If it were not I should
not be here."

He had a point there, but if he expected me to follow his
lead, presumably to save time and come quickly to the next
item on the agenda, he was mistaken, but then he didn't
know that I was not Pendleton.

The names and addresses had been neatly written, each to
a page, in tiny handwriting of an almost copybook quality.
I saw not without some satisfaction that Swinton's address
was listed as being care of Rabal Products Ltd. in the Goswell
Road. One up to Patey. Doctor Gribble had a fashionable address
and Miss Alice Piper a most unfashionable one. I had time to

notice that Mrs. Kate Malone's was listed as The Can Can Club, Priden Street, W.1, when some slim fingers curled over the top of the book and the lady herself, in a voice with no trace of offence, drawled:

"Seen enough—pal?"

I let the book go. She flicked through the names and passed it to Miss Piper, whose thin face flushed hot with self-consciousness. She took a quick peep at one page then let it go to Swinton. He picked it up and pocketed it.

"Right you are," Ellery said irritably. "You guessed correctly. We all have to kow-tow to Bilter, or Ward, or whatever his damned name is. You've got us here. Now what?"

"I should have thought that was childishly simple," Swinton retorted. "Surely we can get together and think up some way of ridding ourselves of this pest?"

Gribble laughed.

"Come now, Mr. Swinton. You've been batting all the evening. You would not have asked us here if you had no plan of your own to offer. Suppose you open the innings again?"

Swinton, suddenly growing tired of standing, pulled up a chair and sat down. But even sitting he dominated the proceedings. In spite of his formal dress and the cut of his starched collar there was something elemental about the man. With his thick hair cut close to the sides and left like a wire brush on top he reminded me vaguely of an Army R.S.M. under whom I had once suffered. That man had not had an ounce of human compassion in his make-up, and I felt certain that Swinton would prove to be the same. Had his eyes been blue they must have resembled ice. As it was their colour dispelled the illusion of coldness, but they were hard, and when emotion caught him, as it had momentarily when Ellery had riled him, they turned black and menacing. More than ever I wondered that Bilter had been such a fool as to attempt a fast one on him. But criminals never learn, or they would not be criminals.

"Yes," Swinton announced, "I have a plan, but I warn you there is nothing squeamish about it. I do not expect the ladies to take an active part in it. Nevertheless I sent them an invitation because I thought they should know what is going on. Briefly the plan is this. I suggest that we get hold of Bilter, or Edward Ward, which is what I think we should call him from now on, take him to some place where we shall be undisturbed, and persuade him that blackmailing us is no longer a profitable proposition."

"Why wrap it up?" Ellery demanded. "You mean kidnap the blighter. How the devil are we to do that?"

Swinton shrugged.

"I'll tell you, but first I would like your opinion on the idea."

Gribble cut in:

"Why consult us at all? It is your plan. You have done very well by yourself up till now."

"That's easy, Doctor," Swinton explained. "I need help. I'm no lily, but Edward Ward is a mountainous man—most of it lard. If I knocked him down I could never pick him up. The detectives I have employed would never acquiesce in a scheme that is outside the law even if the victim to be is a law breaker himself. I suppose there are dubious characters who could be hired for the job, but I don't know any, and if I did I would not employ them. I would only be offering myself as a victim in another blackmail effort."

"It's risky," the doctor said. "I don't like it. This man Ward is no fool. He must have allowed for the chance of his victims turning nasty."

"All at once?" Ellery demanded. When he turned to speak to the doctor I saw him full face and the result was not inspiring. His eyes were set too closely together for my liking. Nor were they healthy looking, being bleary and red rimmed. He went on:

"It seems to me to be a peach of an idea if it can be properly organized. The question is—can it? Are you a Doctor of Medicine, Doctor Gribble?"

"I am. What has that to do with it?"

The captain's thin lips twisted into a smile.

"If we catch him you could be useful. I'll lay a fiver you know a few tricks with a hypodermic syringe that would scare the living daylights out of him, eh?"

Ellery bleated with laughter.

"You damned idiot!" Gribble spat at him. "If you think I'll lend my professional services to——"

"Take is easy, Doc.," I put in hastily. "I don't think he means it."

"Don't let's quarrel, boys," Mrs. Malone drawled. She glanced at her watch. "Do I have to remind you, Mr. Swinton, that I work nights? I've got a business to attend to. . . ."

"Yes. Yes. What is your opinion, Mrs. Malone?"

"You go ahead, Mr. Swinton. I'm sure any plan you have will work out all right. So long as it means that I don't have to go on paying good solid money I don't care what you do to the guy." She turned to Miss Piper. "How about you, honey?"

Miss Piper, her self-consciousness accentuated by the unexpected delight of being called "honey", went redder than before and whispered something that nobody heard.

"Pendleton?" Swinton snapped.

"The doctor's right, of course," I replied casually. "It's bound to be risky however perfect the set-up may sound. On the other hand our unity gives us strength. Ward can deal with any one victim who might choose to mutiny, even if that victim should go to the police and confess his own sins in the hopes of killing Ward's racket. The man is a professional. He will have allowed for such a contingency and will conveniently vanish. Using alternative means of collecting he will in the meantime sustain himself on the money he receives from his other victims, till in due course he can replace the one he has lost. But if his victims collaborate and are able to get him in a spot from which he cannot vanish—well, then he is practically powerless. He may have allowed for such a chance, and arranged for a confederate to spill the beans on his victims, but the fact remains—he himself cannot vanish, and if his victims stay consolidated, then it will mean ultimately that Ward must be arrested and be sentenced. Since that is the very last thing he wants there's a chance of success."

A split second after I had finished speaking I realized once more that I was supposed to be Pendleton, and not John Chadwick, Private Inquiry Agent. The assembled company were staring at me rather as though I was a prophet descended in their midst. I went on quickly:

"Ward will have missed that book, Mr. Swinton. He may be expecting something of the sort you are planning."

Swinton, who had been gazing at me in a way that suggested he had hitherto neglected to give me proper attention, nodded briefly.

"I know. Do you think I lifted it from his desk only last week? It was four months ago. In the meantime his routine has gone smoothly. Demands have been met. Why should he be suspicious now?" Swinton rapped the table with his clenched fist. "I tell you I've spent a hell of a lot of time and money in perfecting this plan. Ward has been watched for weeks. I've taken no chances. He may have become aware of it unbeknown to me—I don't know. But that is a risk we must take. I'm well aware that although his identity has been carefully kept from us, it is practically certain that either he or an accomplice knows each one of us. Before calling you together in order to enlist your support—we cannot possibly employ outsiders in this—I took the precaution of moving down to the coast, of renting a furnished house there, just in case Ward had retaliated and was perhaps keeping an eye on me. Nobody knows I am there—not even my own firm."

I wondered. Who then was Miss Helen Arnett, staying at the Marine Hotel? A little local relief? A man must grow lonely even when his exile is self imposed.

"Could we not hear the details of the plan?" Ellery growled. He turned quickly to the rest of us. "I must say," he went on, raising his voice a trifle, "that I'm almost sure Mr. Swinton is going to get my wholehearted support in this. He's displayed an initiative and an energy in fighting this man Bilter for which, quite frankly, I envy him. I feel grateful to him. Obviously you are all interested or you wouldn't be here. . . ."

"Of course not," Gribble murmured.

Mrs. Malone drawled, "That goes for me too." I contented myself with a nod. Swinton was a go-getter all right, but I was not certain that his enthusiasm was not blinding him to the hazards. Unless this man Ward's undoubted success over the years had blinded him too, Swinton might strike some terrible snags.

My rumination was cut short. Swinton was on his feet and taking out some sheets of paper from an inside pocket.

"The plan," he announced. "This is where and how we will take him. These sheets are rough copies of the official One Inch Ordnance Map of the district round Stoke Mandeville Station. Take a look at them." He distributed them round the table, and when we had each flattened one on the table in front of us he continued:

"I must tell you," he said, "that Ward is a creature of habit in one respect only. Every Tuesday evening, without fail, he pays a visit to the cottage marked at the top of the map with a cross. He catches the seven o'clock train from Baker Street which gets him to Stoke Mandeville round about eight o'clock. The exact time of his arrival is not important. A motor-car from a local firm of car hirers meets him at the station and takes him a distance of approximately two miles and a furlong to a spot marked A on your maps. You will observe that this spot is directly below the cross marking the cottage which he visits, and that the distance between them is roughly two hundred yards. The line I have drawn on the maps represents a footpath through some woods to the cottage which at one time was a gamekeeper's set in the corner of a field backing onto the wood. The spot marked A is the closest that any sort of vehicle can get to the cottage."

"Who lives in it?" I asked.

"Ward's old mother."

Doctor Gribble laughed harshly.

"I suppose even blackmailers have mothers," he remarked, "though one would suppose them to have been spawned rather than born."

"Well, he has one human emotion at any rate," Ellery backed him up, "filial devotion—very touching."

I noticed that both of them sounded more cheerful and enthusiastic. Swinton's attention to detail was impressive. He waited till the chuckles had died and then went on expounding.

"The hired car returns to the spot marked A later in the evening to pick up Ward and take him back to the station in

time for the last train to Baker Street. The firm supplying the
car is situated on the Aylesbury Road and is primarily a
garage. It owns two cars. Both are Humbers, identical models,
of a type very popular with a number of car hirers. I can get
one easily—to drive myself. My plan is simply this. I propose
to drive down to Stoke Mandeville next Tuesday, if everyone
is agreeable, arriving about an hour before Ward is due to
leave the cottage. I shall telephone the garage that supplies
the hired car, and I shall say that, owing to his mother being
not very well, Mr. Ward has decided to stay the night and has
asked me to cancel the car on his behalf. There will be nothing
odd about that because the cottage is not on the telephone.

"At the appointed time I shall drive my own hired Humber
car to the spot marked A, and Ward, if he does not actually
step into it before spotting the deception, will have at least
approached it so nearly as to make persuasion an easy
matter."

Swinton paused.

"Now, gentlemen," he went on—"I exclude the ladies because this is so obviously not a job for them—I need your assistance. Ward is a mountainous man as I have told you. I cannot
handle him alone. Even if he should be completely unsuspecting
and actually step into the car I must have others to step in
after him and keep him quiet."

"What do you propose to do with him once you have him?"
Gribble demanded.

"Take him to a place where we can point out to him the
error of his ways. In particular borrow the keys to his house and
his safe. These are not to be returned to him or he himself
released till the evidence he uses in his blackmail schemes is
safely in our hands. As to the place—failing other suggestions
which I welcome—it will have to be the house I am renting on
the coast. Unfortunately it will mean a drive of about a hundred
miles from Stoke Mandeville, which might seriously incon-
venience us. On the other hand, once there, we shall not be
disturbed. I must admit I would welcome a place much nearer
London if anyone has anything to offer. I'm certain that it
will not be used for any length of time. Once Ward realizes
that we are in earnest he'll be only too pleased to play ball.

Any suggestions? Captain Ellery? Doctor? Mr. Pendleton?—
or the ladies, perhaps?"

Mrs. Malone, who during his recital had lit a cigarette,
took a long pull at it, inhaled, and let the smoke dribble slowly
from her open but still shapely mouth.

"Why not bring him to my club, Mr. Swinton? I've got a
flat over the top, with two or three empty rooms. I'll look
after the guy."

"You really mean that, Mrs. Malone? But your club is in
the heart of the West End."

"What's so wrong about that? You take this guy to your
house in the country, and what'll happen? Some busybody
will see you. Folks get nosier than a pack of hounds in the
country, but in town . . . they mind their own business. Sure
you could carry him in upside down and nobody 'ud say
anything or do anything."

This shrewd observation was greeted with exclamations of
delight, particularly from Ellery, who gave his own characteristic bleat of laughter. Even Swinton allowed his lips to twist
in a smile.

"The idea sounds attractive, Mrs. Malone. Thank you.
Do you live alone? I mean, you have a husband. And what
about servants?"

"Oh, I've no husband, Mr. Swinton. Don't get me wrong.
I'm what they call a *feme-sole*."

"Servants?"

"Sure, I've a few employees in the club but they go home
nights, all save one. He's an old man I employ about the place.
He cleans up, looks after the gents' cloaks, deputizes for the
commissionaire, that sort of thing. He sleeps in the office
downstairs."

"Can he be trusted?"

"Sure. I trust him, Mr. Swinton."

This was not quite the answer the master mind wanted, but
a glance at Mrs. Malone seemed to tell him it was the only
one he would get on that particular subject and he went on:

"You don't mind if I come in and look the place over?
Say tomorrow evening? I dare not leave anything to chance,
Mrs. Malone."

"Oh, you come along, Mr. Swinton. I'd be glad to have you. I've a kind of feeling you're going to save me an awful lot of good red money before very long." Mrs. Malone turned an admiring gaze upon Swinton, who liked it so much that he rubbed his hands together, and purred: "I trust so, Mrs. Malone. I trust so."

A short silence followed this little interchange, and then Swinton got back to business.

"That settles it then," he said. "If I find that Mrs. Malone's place is suitable—and I can't think why it should not be— then we'll take Ward there. It will be much more convenient for everybody."

"Except possibly Mrs. Malone," I pointed out.

"Oh, I'll get by, Mr. Pendleton. Don't you worry," the lady said.

"Now," Swinton demanded, "is there anybody who cannot manage this affair next Tuesday night? The sooner the better. The moon rises very late, and it will be totally dark when we pick up Ward."

"Just one moment," Gribble put in quickly. "I was not aware that I had promised to come into it at any time—never mind the day of the week."

"But, Doctor Gribble——"

"It may be all right for you, Mr. Swinton, but I'm a professional man." The doctor embraced us all in a single comprehensive glance from his deep-set eyes, and gave a mirthless sort of laugh. "Let's not disillusion ourselves," he went on harshly. "You will all have guessed that a doctor who has laid himself open to a blackmailer can have been guilty of one thing only—unprofessional conduct. Maybe. But you are asking me to indulge in a further act of unprofessional conduct."

Swinton leaned forward across the table.

"Doctor Gribble," he said, emphasizing his remarks by jabbing a finger on the beer-stained wood, "you must place your own construction on it. I would not call it that. It has nothing to do with your Hippocratic Oath. Consider the alternative. You will go on paying this man Ward for years. He must be stopped. Now is a unique opportunity."

"Absolutely!" Ellery backed him up. "You can count me

in, Swinton. Damn it, we can manage it between us!" He turned to Gribble. "He'll bleed you white, Doc. See how you like it then. What about you, Pendleton?"

I thought for a moment. Swinton's plan sounded risky to me. A flat tyre could wreck it. Quite apart from accidents, which could take a hundred different guises, I could not believe that a blackmailer like Ward, knowing himself to be an object of pure hate for a number of victims, any one of whom might, given the chance, slit his throat at the drop of a hat, would make a weekly journey to such an isolated spot as his mother's cottage in quite the unsuspecting frame of mind that Swinton expected. The man might go armed. After all he was living in a jungle.

Then I thought: "That's Chadwick's reasoning. You are supposed to be Pendleton, doomed to go on paying Ward a quarter of a hard-earned income presumably till the end of time. Pendleton would say it was a first-class plan." In addition it seemed to me that Swinton would push the job through with Ellery's support alone, and so I said aloud. "All right. I'll come along."

"Good for you!" Mrs. Malone's hand found mine and squeezed it. The doctor looked at me appraisingly, his dark eyes boring into mine.

"You look a man I could trust," he said, surprisingly. "If you're going then so will I. Where and at what time shall we meet you, Swinton?"

"At nine o'clock. I shall have the Humber waiting a few yards down the Edgware Road from the Marble Arch."

"Thank you. Now if you will excuse me . . ." The doctor pushed his chair away from the table. "I must be hurrying. I dare say I shall have the opportunity of returning your hospitality at a later date, eh?" He walked to the door, paused with his hand on the knob, as though he had remembered to say good night, but said instead: "There must be no violence, Swinton. I shall not stand for that."

"One moment, Doctor!" Swinton was on his feet, his dark eyes menacing. "If you come next Tuesday you will be under my command—is that clear? There must be no muddled decisions due to divided thinking. Nor will I allow the whole

plan to fail through last-minute squeamishness. Please say
nothing of this to any single person. It will be useless for you
to try to communicate with me between now and Tuesday for
I shall be neither at home nor at my business address. I shall
wait ten minutes on Tuesday night and not a minute longer.
If all else fails two of us only can do this job."

I thought at first that the doctor would resent Swinton's
dictatorial manner. Perhaps he did. I saw him stiffen and then
he relaxed.

"Very well," he said. "Good night to you." And then he
was gone.

A general buzz of conversation broke out as soon as the
door closed behind him. Swinton spoke to Miss Piper, who
shook her head. Mrs. Malone guessed that it was time she
looked for a taxi. Captain Ellery announced in a loud voice
that he was going to have another drink in the more congenial
atmosphere of the bar downstairs. He looked invitingly at me
as he said it, but I didn't fancy him as a drinking companion,
and said that I would have to be going. Swinton himself
picked up his Homburg and a rolled umbrella. He gave us a
final objurgation on the necessity for secrecy about the
evening's meeting, then with a gallantry that ill became him
insisted on escorting the ladies downstairs.

I followed in company with Ellery, who made another
effort to persuade me to have one for the road, but I pleaded
a fictitious business for which I was already late.

When I emerged into the street Swinton was handing
Mrs. Malone into a taxi. She saw me and waved a hand as the
taxi started off. I raised my hat. There was no sign of Miss
Piper, and Swinton strode away, purpose as usual in every
single movement.

I turned in the opposite direction which would bring me to
the nearest Tube Station. I had walked roughly fifty yards
when a hand fell on my arm from behind, and plucked at me
insistently. I swung round. It was Pendleton. By the look of
him he had been doing some steady drinking, and it didn't
require much imagination to realize that he'd been doing it
downstairs in the saloon bar of the George whilst the meeting
had been proceeding over his head. The idea riled me.

"Don't ever do that again, Pendleton!" I snarled. "Come up on me from behind. You're liable to get a poke on the snout. I suppose you were waiting downstairs?"

"And why not?" he sneered. "Had a right to, hadn't I? I've got a hell of a lot at stake, and I want to know what happened."

I got a grip on his elbow and yanked him along with me. "For God's sake!" I protested. "And I suppose you've been shooting your big mouth off in there to all and sundry, eh? If you have, Pendleton, you're finished! Understand that? As soon as we get Mr. Bilter behind bars I personally will see that the contents of your letters that he holds are communicated to the right quarters. How do you like that?"

He began to splutter, and made some attempt to break from my grip, but, though he was as tall as I, he was barely half my weight and I had no difficulty in propelling him away from the George, where for all I knew Ellery might be watching.

Within a short distance we came to another pub, and outside it I let him go.

"All right," I commanded. "Relax. We'll go in here and have another drink, and I'll tell you all about it. But did you, or did you not, mention our business to anyone in the George?"

"Of course not. What the hell d'you take me for?"

"I'm not sure, Pendleton. I wish I was. Come on in."

I got him ensconced in the corner of the dingy saloon and bought him a whisky in a tall glass. I pretty well soused it with tonic water before I gave it him and he didn't thank me. He took a pull at it, made a wry face, and plumped it down on the table.

"Cripes!" he said. "You drink gin with tonic." He paused and then quite suddenly he abandoned his truculent attitude. "I'm sorry, Chadwick," he muttered. "But this business has got me down. I was all right—getting inured to it—till you came along. It's the risk of the whole damned thing becoming public—and—the blasted memories it brings up. I guess I was a B.F. to go along there tonight. Should have left it to you. But I didn't say a word to anyone. Barman asked me if I was Swinton's party. I near as a touch said 'Yes', but I didn't. I just waited for you to show up."

E

"All right," I said. "Now listen. Here's what's happened." And I told him the story, omitting only the details of Swinton's plan, its time and date.

"We aim to trap Ward," I explained, "and although the outcome is about as predictable as the weather, the scheme may succeed. If it does you'll have nothing to worry about."

"And if it doesn't? I'll be for the high jump, eh? That's fine. That's dandy!"

"Look, Pendleton," I said, "pull yourself together. There were five people besides me at that meeting, and they were all in the same boat as you. For all I know some of them stand to lose a damned sight more than you if the scheme fails. Two of them were women, and, all things considered, they behaved admirably. At heart I feel sure they were worried sick, but they didn't sit around throwing an act or biting their nails. They listened and they offered their help if required. I don't know what to prescribe for you. Would it ease the tension if you told me all about it? You can trust me. I might as well tell you that, had you come to me instead of me approaching you, then I would have demanded to know all about your trouble before I would have stirred a finger on your behalf. Come on, man. Get it off your chest. You'll feel better for it."

"All right," he said, and ran a hand through his mop of rusty hair. His face had gone pale and the freckles on it showed strangely livid on the pallid skin.

"It's not a particularly edifying story," he continued, after a long pause. "At the time I was in the R.A.F. serving the last year of a Short Service Commission. I met a girl. More than that, I fell in love with her, and well . . . we misbehaved ourselves . . . and she found that she was due for a baby. I wanted to marry her, Chadwick. We'd planned to do so just as soon as I got my gratuity, but she was absolutely terrified of having the child. It wasn't all physical fear. Her parents were narrow-minded to say the most of them. Polly was frantic about it. She must be rid of it."

Pendleton gulped down the rest of his drink.

"These things can be arranged. I started making inquiries. I thought I was being rather clever over it, using a false name and that sort of thing. The upshot of it was that I was given the address of a woman in Rotherhithe. I got some leave and brought Polly to London. We went to the address three or four times before we found the woman. She told us to return on Saturday evening. I think she chose that time because most of the neighbours would be out in the pubs. Saturday was the last day of my leave and the squadron were due to fly on some local defence exercise early on Sunday. We went on Saturday. The hag was out, and when she turned up she was drunk. She said that Polly would be all right, but she would have to rest before she could go home. I left the girl there. I had to, Chadwick. Well . . . the hag had bungled. Polly died, there in that damned tenement, and I didn't know a thing about it till I read the papers and saw that the woman had been arrested. She did her best to incriminate me, swore that I had forced her into the job, that sort of thing."

Pendleton laughed sourly. "In a way I was lucky. Polly had told her parents months previously, when the squadron moved from her district, that she had stopped seeing me. I had used a false name in getting an introduction to the woman. To cap it all the squadron was posted to Germany about a week after it happened. So from one point of view I got away with it."

"So you did," I said, not with any enthusiasm. How any man, even with a summons from the Archangel Gabriel, could have left his girl under such circumstances, staggered me utterly. It left a nasty taste in my mouth. All I could hope was that the rest of Bilter's victims were more deserving of my sympathy than was Pendleton. At least it explained in part his behaviour. Nine tenths of his mental struggle was remorse.

"And Polly had written you letters which you kept?"

"Yes."

"Had you written to her?"

"No. I always telephoned her at her place of work. She had to write. I was never anywhere near a blower most of the day when she could telephone."

"The rest you know," I pointed out. "Bilter probably keeps a whole library of press cuttings on such subjects. He matched the letters which his accomplice filched and the set-up was complete. But I doubt if the police would prosecute you,

Pendleton. I dare say the girl's father would be after you
with a horsewhip, or a shot gun, and perhaps it's that sort of
thing you fear."

"All right. All right," he growled. "It needs no elaboration.
I know I'm a bastard. But believe me, Chadwick, if I'd known
that hag had bungled I'd never have left Polly there. Not for
all the service records in Christendom. She knew I'd been in
trouble before for overstaying leave. She wanted me to go.
She said she was all right. I believe she was at the time and
had a haemorrhage later."

"Maybe," I grunted, and got up to go. I never can hate for
long and I felt suddenly sorry for the man. He was sick to his
soul.

"Cheer up!" I said. "I'll get you out of this mess. I'll ring
you Wednesday morning."

He brightened a bit, and I left him there in a pub's saloon
as I had the first time I'd met him.

When I got home to the flat I 'phoned Freda to let her
know that I wouldn't be down that night. It was still comparatively early, however, and I wondered as I put down the
receiver how I could spend the rest of the evening. Then I had
a bright idea. I was not certain of the exact social status of the
establishment I proposed to visit, but to be on the safe side
I changed out of my nondescript flannels into a dinner-jacket.

By the Regents Park Underground I was lucky enough to
pick up a vacant taxi.

"Where to, guv?" the Jehu asked.

"Priden Street," I said. "The Can Can Club."

CHAPTER VI

THE entrance was the same as those of a score of such clubs
dotted about the back streets of London's West End. Two
swing doors giving on to a long corridor that ran the distance
between the shops on either side to gain access to the club
buildings that spread out behind them. There were barrels
containing evergreen shrubs, one at each end of the two horse-

shoe steps that led up to the doors. Overhead the inevitable neon sign flashed "Can Can Club" on and off, in a bright bilious blue, so quickly as to be faintly irritating. The usual ex-guardsman type of commissionaire opened the taxi door. He would have asked me if I was a member had I not slipped him half a crown, so that he was content to pass me inside where, if necessary, some other official could turn me away.

The corridor gave onto a *foyer*. Ahead of me across an expanse of fawn carpet was a curtained doorway leading into the club itself. Small alcoves on either side, signposted with illuminated glass directions, led the way to the cloaks. There were two doors marked Private, a handsome leather divan, and four deep armchairs in the same brown hide, and, placed at strategic points, big vases of summer flowers. I could hear a dance band playing in slow time way behind the curtains. The atmosphere was rich with the aroma of a good cigar mingled with the scent of face powder and cigarettes. All very typical, but a good deal better in quality than I had expected. Two couples, none of them in evening dress, were sprawled at each end of the huge divan. They took no notice of me. I waited a few seconds, then went into the alcove marked "Gentlemen's Cloakroom".

An old man shuffled round to the counter from behind the rows of pegs that filled the space in the tiny cubby-hole.

I guessed he must be the ancient retainer of whom Mrs. Malone had spoken earlier. He was wearing a brown uniform, its edges piped in pale blue. Two Cs of the same colour adorned the lapels of his coat. His head, bald and as wrinkled as a dried apple, was flanked by a pair of enormous ears. Their pointed tops reached the level of his pate. In addition he had a long chin, bony with age, and a pair of closely set bird-like eyes. He looked like a bat.

"Evenin'," he said casually. "You a member?"

"Do I have to be?"

The little dark eyes twinkled sardonically.

"You ain't obliged to be, mister. This 'ere's a free country. You don't 'ave to join this club any more than you 'as to join the Marines, but if you want to go in there and eat, drink, and be merry—I 'ope—a member of this club you has to be."

I had suspected as much. In spite of his mildly discouraging attitude I rather liked the old codger. He had an independence of mind refreshingly different from the usual servility one met with in such places.

One of his ancient eyelids fluttered in a wink and I caught on. I took out my wallet, extracted a couple of notes, and dropped them onto a plate that had contained, till that moment, a sprinkling of small silver.

His horny hand closed over the notes and whipped them away.

"Does that make me a member?" I asked.

He dragged a ledger-like book along the counter and produced a ball-point pen from a pocket.

"Son," he said solemnly, "you're practically a Vice-President! Sign 'ere!"

I scrawled my name in the spot indicated and he wrote another alongside it.

"Introduced by John Smith," he said. "The number o' new members introduced by that gentleman is nobody's business. Membership card coming up!" He produced another book from under the counter, tore a strip of card out of it and told me to sign it in the space provided. I did so. "You're in!" he announced.

I gave him my hat, and he put it on a peg behind him. "You won't want a ticket," he said. "I'll remember you."

Restraining an impulse to tell him that he damned well ought to, I strolled out into the *foyer*, and towards the curtains giving access to the club.

It was not very big. After the promising spaciousness of the *foyer* it was disappointingly small. Whether or not this made it more select I had yet to learn.

It followed the customary pattern. Microscopic dance floor. Band on a small stage. The rest of the space crowded with tables, so closely placed that the waiters had to be better contortionists than the girls in the floor show. A staircase to one side, its banister rail almost hidden by flowers, led up to a narrow balcony, on which was ranged a row of comfortable-looking chairs. Nice idea that, I thought. The walls were covered in brightly painted murals of Parisienne ladies in various stages of the Can Can. All legs, and garters and splits.

A very foreign-looking major-domo type with sideburns was standing just inside the curtains.

"You are a member, zair?" he asked.

"Sure." I waved the card I had between my fingers, and he bowed solemnly. Trouble with him was his accent was phoney, and he had blue eyes. I dare say his name was Higgins. "I'm waiting for a friend," I lied easily. "I'll help myself to a drink till she turns up."

The bar was on the left on a raised dais, and standing there offered a good view of the rest of the club. It was by no means full, but this was only to be expected for the hour, by night-club standards, was still early.

There were a few people round the bar, one or two couples jigging round the tiny dance floor like goldfish in a bowl, and some unattached ladies at a table nearest the bar. They didn't have to look at me speculatively for me to know that they were hostesses. The whole place hummed with human chatter against which the band achieved a pleasing and throbbing background.

I found a stool at one end of the bar, perched myself on it, and ordered a whisky. The price of it made me blink. On the other hand it was good stuff, smooth as a gun barrel. I sipped appreciatively and looked around for Kate Malone. I failed to see her. I was not particularly surprised. The fact that she owned the club was no guarantee that she was part of it.

One of the hostesses caught my eye and, reading an in-vitation in my glance that was pure invention on her part, sauntered over to the bar and took the stool next to mine. She was a nice little thing, with a friendly face under her bubble cut. Her figure made me think what a marvellous creation is the strapless evening frock.

"Hallo!" she said. "I'm a hostess. You can tell me to hoof it if you like. I shan't mind . . . much."

"You stay right there," I commanded. "Imbibing strong drink by yourself is a sordid process that becomes civilized by the addition of company. What is your name?"

"Clarissa," she said.

"Mine's John. How d'you do and what will you have?"

Clarissa chose whisky, and dealt with it expertly. Not wishing her to think that she had found a customer for the remainder of the evening, I had to tell her that I was expecting to be called away, but she didn't seem to mind. She could absorb whisky like a Canadian trapper. She asked me a number of personal questions, including details of my job, my income, my age, to all of which I gave fictitious answers. In the midst of this nonsense a voice behind me drawled:

"Well, well, well . . . if it isn't Mr. Pendleton!"

Kate Malone, in a white evening frock, its top a miracle of moulding, was a striking and breathtakingly lovely figure. Her magnificent shoulders gleamed like polished ivory. She had changed her hair style for the evening and it was so arranged to show off the smooth column of her neck. Some skilful art of make-up had been used round her big dark eyes, and these appeared more warm and lustrous than before. I goggled a bit. I couldn't help it. She made poor Clarissa, whose charms were by no means negligible, look like a painted doll.

I slipped off my stool.

"This is marvellous," I said. "I was hoping to see you, Mrs. Malone. Shall I be out of order in asking you to have a drink?"

"Not just now, thank you, Mr. Pendleton."

She was puzzled a little, and it wasn't hard for me to guess why. Apart from my presence on her doorstep so soon after our earlier meeting, Pendleton in scruffy flannels in the back room of an obscure Chelsea pub was one person, and Pendleton in a natty line of dinner-jacket was another.

"Have you really called to see me?" she wanted to know. "Or have you come for entertainment?"

"To see you, Mrs. Malone. I should like a talk with you if I may."

The bar was no place for it. Clarissa was beginning to fidget. The barman, with the boss in the offing, was ready to whip up a drink at the lift of a finger. For their benefit Kate simulated surprise, and said:

"Surely. I'd be glad to. Give me five minutes, and then come up to the balcony . . . eh?"

"Fine," I said.

She gave me a dazzling smile, and moved away, the full lacy skirt of her dress billowing gracefully.

"So I had to pick a friend of the boss," Clarissa remarked.

"Not really," I replied. "I knew she owned the place. Does she manage it as well?"

"Oh yes. She sings too. She's got a lovely contralto voice. She's pretty good is Mrs. Malone."

Clarissa went on chattering about the club. Until Mrs. Malone had acquired the place it had been nothing but a restaurant, and it was she who had made a club of it. There was not much doubt that its success as such was due entirely to her personality.

At the appointed time I left Clarissa at the bar and went up to the balcony where Kate was waiting at the top of the stairs. There was a door marked Private at the side of the balcony and as soon as I had gained the top of the stairs she turned towards it.

"I guess you'd better come up to the flat, Mr. Pendleton. We can talk without fear of interruption there."

I opened the door for her, and she led the way down a short passage towards a small passenger lift. This was a self-operated affair, and when Kate had pressed the necessary button it ground slowly upwards. A spiral staircase followed its shaft. I counted two turns of the stairs but there was no floor other than the top where we stepped out of the lift into a small hall.

Kate ushered me through a doorway into a large and comfortably furnished lounge. Although the armchairs and divan were covered in a bright multicoloured chintz of the same material as the long curtains drawn across the window, there was nothing delicately feminine about the room. The chairs were smoking-room size, there were sporting prints on the walls, and the far end of the room was ranged with shelf after shelf of books.

"Sit down," she invited me. "I guess you could use another drink, seeing that I interrupted your little session with Clarissa."

She crossed to a cabinet, brought out glasses and a decanter with a siphon, which she placed on a small occasional table at the side of the chair I had chosen. She knew enough to let me pour. The whisky was the same smoothly excellent brand I had tasted downstairs.

"You know something, Mr. Pendleton?" she asked, with her warm alluring smile after we had pledged each other. I raised my eyebrows, and she went on: "There's something phoney about you. I don't know what it is exactly but I've got a kinda feeling you're not entirely what you make out to be. I guess I'm right at that."

"How so?" I countered.

She ran her crimson-nailed fingers lightly up and down the arm of her chair.

"I can read men. You're a guy without a care in the world. You've got plenty of assurance, and plenty of money. You're plenty fit. On top of that you call upon me within two hours of our meeting, and it's not because you've fallen for my eyes or figure. What's the answer, Mr. Pendleton?"

"May I call you Kate?" I asked.

"Sure. Most everybody does."

"Thank you. The answer is, Kate, that I'm not Pendleton. Mind you, there is a Mr. Pendleton and, with his permission, I took his place tonight. My name is John Chadwick, and I'm what is popularly known as a private dick. That doesn't surprise you."

"No. I figured it was something like that. You're a poor actor, John Chadwick. You sat there with a twinkle in your eye when you thought no person was watching you."

Kate laughed. "What's Mr. Swinton going to say when he learns about you? He'll get tough, Mr. Chadwick."

"Ah. Swinton," I said. "D'you trust him, Kate? You say you can read men. What of George Swinton?"

She frowned, took a box of cigarettes from under the table and pushed them towards me before replying.

"He's hard, that guy. I wouldn't want him for an enemy. I trust him to see this thing through because it suits his own purpose, but for no other reason. What's bothering you about him?"

"I don't know—exactly. There's one or two things I don't

like about the whole set-up. Maybe if I was really Pendleton
I'd be enthusiastic, like Ellery was tonight, and the doctor
too, if only he could have forgotten his profession. But as an
impartial judge there's something about it . . . a little too pat
. . . a little too easy . . . that worries me. How did Ward come
to leave that book lying around? If it comes to that how did
he come to pick on a shrewd and hard nut like Swinton for a
victim? Ellery, Pendleton and the doctor—yes. Miss Piper and
you, Kate—yes. But Swinton—an obvious egotist, a blow to
whose pride would mean far more than a drain on his pocket
—no. There is one more thing I found odd. Ward has an
accomplice, a woman, who has been nosing out his material
for him. Swinton has completely ignored this accomplice,
beyond a casual mention when he neglected even to hint that
it was a woman. I found that strange. Suppose we capture
Ward, does that automatically render his accomplice powerless? It might, but I don't think it safe to presume as much.
I'd like to get a line on this woman accomplice. Will you be
offended if I ask you whether or not you've met the girl?"

Kate found a table lighter and put the flame to the end of
a cigarette before replying. She relaxed in her chair.

"Not a bit, Mr. Chadwick. The girl was in my employ—here
in this flat, not the club. As a matter of fact I figured that she
herself was Bilter. Maybe I should have guessed she had some
male assistance, eh?"

"Maybe," I grinned. "What was her name?"

"Helen Rice."

"That's the girl. She was calling herself Ella Price when
she was sweeping the Pendleton bedchambers. Not at all a
subtle variation. How long ago was she working for you?"

"Six months."

"As recently as that? Sounds promising. Did you have any
knowledge of her apart from her capabilities as a servant?
Where she lived? Anything like that?"

"Sure. I didn't take kindly to blackmail any more than
our friend Swinton. I employed a private dick myself to try
and find the girl."

"Who was he? I like to know of the success or failure of
any rival."

"A man named Newman."

"I know him. Has an office in Oxford Street. Not bad—but . . ."

"Not up to the standard of John Chadwick, I guess," Kate drawled. "You sure hate yourself, John. But then . . . most men do. Newman was a nice little guy. He traced the girl but she was too quick for him. She dodged off before he could tackle her and he couldn't find her again. I have her last known address if it's of any use to you."

"I'd like it," I said.

Kate got up and moved with her customary flowing grace from the room. Seen from the depths of an armchair she looked taller and more statuesque than ever. I wondered not for the first time what secret of hers it was that Ward's accomplice had found. Something to do with her divorce, or nationality, I supposed. Owning this club and requiring a police licence to run it she was an admirable subject for blackmail. If it was her livelihood—she must have sunk quite a bit of capital into it—then anything unsavoury in her own background might prove disastrous if made public.

Whilst she was gone I finished my whisky. On the assumption that she had paid wholesale prices for it I felt safe in pouring myself another. I took more soda with this one. Added to those I had consumed with the inspiring Clarissa I was approaching my quota and feeling reasonably rosy.

Kate came back with a slip of paper.

"Newman traced her to this address," she told me. "It's a guest house. What you'd call a boarding house. D'you aim to follow your own investigation, John?"

"I do."

"Does that mean you're going to pass up Swinton next Tuesday?"

"No. I shall be there."

Kate sat down again, brushing out the beautiful skirt of her dress as she did so.

"If you go investigating before then, isn't that liable to queer things for Swinton?" When I made no reply she said quickly, almost anxiously, "You don't like that guy, do you?"

"No, Kate, I don't. For one thing there is only one person

he has any regard for—and that's himself. You noticed that·
He'll need watching on that account. If anything goes wrong
he'll ditch the lot of you without a qualm of conscience, if by
so doing he can make himself safe. For another—he's the type
that will underestimate an opponent. A professional blackmailer like Ward, unless he has grown careless with success,
can't be trapped by such a simple plan as Swinton's. You need
more subtle methods. Tracking down his accomplice for
instance might lead us to learning something about Ward that
might help. I hope you know what you have taken on, Kate,
by offering your flat as a dumping ground for the man. It won't
be pleasant, and it may lead to trouble."

"Sure. I'm used to trouble," she said a trifle bitterly, "I
was raised on it. This guy Ward can't be any worse than some
I've met and handled. In a way I'm fair game for his sort.
If I'm careless enough, and fool enough, to let them get something on me, then—O.K. I pay, and like it. But folks like little
Alice Piper and the doctor, and maybe Captain Ellery—
ordinary honest-to-goodness folks who've tripped once and
have to go on paying for it out of all proportion—they're
different. I don't suppose there's anything criminal in their
make-up at all. I guess the Piper's got an illegitimate child
somewhere, and can't afford to have the fact known—maybe
to her employers. . . ."

"And the doctor?" I asked. "What's your guess about
him?"

"He as good as admitted that it was unprofessional
conduct. A woman, I guess. Some dames go all goofy about
those dark and hairy types. Don't ask me about Ellery. I
couldn't place him. He looks as though he might deserve
anything that's come to him." Kate paused, and I took the
opportunity to put in quickly:

"Do you?"

She looked at me, and her great eyes were clouded for a
moment with memories. There was pain in them, and everything else that goes with sorrow. But in a flash they had
brightened again to their usual glint of half humour, half bold
defiance.

"I'm afraid I do," she sighed. "I had to fill in a great many forms and answer a heap of personal questions before I was allowed to run this place as a club. Some of the answers I gave were not strictly true, John. I took the chance. I like this country. It's my country, though a year ago I'd not seen it since I was four years old. That damned woman, Helen Rice, went through my private papers. She used skeleton keys, John. She was well equipped. If what she filched goes to the Foreign Office, or Home Office, or whatever department deals with such things, I'll be out on my neck plenty quick. So believe me I don't mind taking a bit of trouble over this guy Ward. It won't be so difficult. This flat is kind of high and isolated. He can holler all day, and bang on the floor all night—no one will hear him. Come over here a moment."

Mrs. Malone got up from her chair, and crossing quickly to the curtains swished one of them to the side. It had been covering a door that gave onto a small stone balcony.

"There's a fire escape," she explained, "an iron staircase zigzags down the wall of the building into the yard. You can bring him up that way. I'll have old Bates open the doors of the yard, and close them as soon as you've brought the car in. There'll be room for the car. It's not really what you'd call a yard—just a bay where the trucks back in to drop off goods at the service entrance. But it has a couple of high wooden gates that are shut at nights."

"Old Bates," I said, "is he the ancient in charge of the Gents' Cloaks? Looks like a bat?"

"Yeah. That's him."

"Sure you can trust him, Kate? He seemed to me to possess a quite out-of-the-ordinary frame of mind. As though he didn't care a damn whom he spoke to, or what he said."

Kate chuckled.

"I trust him, John. He's an old soldier. I took him on when he was up against it, though he wouldn't admit as much. He's grateful to me, and I like him. He works hard and puts in long hours."

"You can't be too careful," I said. "Not in a job like this. I squared him easily enough to get into your club tonight. Others might do the same for other reasons."

"That was different," Kate defended him stoutly. "The regulations regarding the admittance of new members are farcical, anyway. No. Bates is O.K. If he let you in that easily then I can trust you too. That's how I feel about old Bates. He can size up a man quicker than I can do it—and that's something. I wish I could size up a woman just as quick," she added ruefully.

"Well . . . let's hope Ward capitulates as soon as we get him here. Supposing you have to keep him, where will you put him?"

"I'll show you."

She led me into the hall of the flat, and opened a door at its far end. On the other side was a small cell-like room with no window, and only a square foot of grating over a ventilator to break the smoothness of its yellow distempered walls. The furniture was at a minimum: a plain uncomfortable-looking bed, a chest of drawers with a mirror on it, one cane-bottomed chair, and that was all. The floor was covered in a shiny print linoleum with a rush mat alongside the bed.

"Too good for him," I commented. "What is under this room?"

"Another—empty. This flat is on two floors. I bought the place off a French *restaurateur*. He had six children. I don't need the lower floor, and the elevator brings you only to the top one. Satisfied? I'll have old Bates put some bolts on the outside of this door."

"As a matter of fact, it couldn't be better," I said. "But I still think you're taking a nasty risk."

"With Swinton after Ward," she replied sensibly, "the risk is general whether I like it or not. I might as well join in and help lessen it by a fraction at least. That's how I feel about it. I'm not worried, John. I want my property out of Ward's safe, and this plan of Swinton's seems to me to be as good a way as any of getting it."

"Maybe," I said. "I feel sure he will approve of the layout. I'd be greatly obliged, Kate, if when he calls on you tomorrow evening you will keep up the pretence of my being Pendleton, and not let him know that I called tonight. Will you do that for me?"

"Of course—though I can't see any sense in your remaining Pendleton—not if you're out to help us."

"I'm out to help," I told her emphatically. "But in my own way, which I think may go a great deal farther than Swinton's. I don't trust him."

We had moved back into the lounge whilst talking, and Kate sank down into her chair again. She began her little dance with her fingers on the broad arm of the chair. She was frowning slightly.

"I wish you'd stop harping on that," she complained. "Outside of this plan he has for taking Ward off our backs I wouldn't go a hundred per cent on him myself, and when you start throwing doubts . . . Maybe you should find out a bit more about him first, eh? You could do that easily enough?"

"I know as much as it is possible to learn from outside sources—now. He's pretty well set up. He's managing director of a firm called Rabal Products. In addition he's a director of Radleys, the toffee makers. He's a nephew of the owner. A man of his type ought not to be the victim of a blackmailer, and if he is he should be important enough to be able to take the police into his confidence without himself coming to any harm as a consequence. It suggests that Swinton's secret—the hold Ward has over him—does not bear looking into. I don't much like the idea of catching one criminal and unwittingly furthering the interests of another. Swinton's an odd bird, Kate. I don't think this has anything to do with his being blackmailed, or his plan at all, but it's interesting if only because it explains my distrust of him, and incidentally how I came into the picture."

I told her of what had happened at Selsey.

She arched delicate and incredulous eyebrows.

"Say! It's fantastic!" she exclaimed. "What's he want with sea-water in his bath? Maybe he's got a hobby or something, eh? You read about these guys experimenting with plankton as a food."

"I doubt if the waters around Selsey Bill offer much scope for that sort of thing," I returned, dryly. "Anyway, it has me guessing. But you may be on the right track. He's just bought a seagoing dinghy in which he goes fishing at nights. He could be a student of marine biology in his spare time. It would explain why he had to go all the way to the coast to get away from any possible counter-spying by Ward. Perhaps he has a tank on order but is such an enthusiast he has to use the bath till the tank is delivered. But he's oddly shy about it."

After that our conversation became general. Then Kate looked at her watch and declared that she was due to sing a number, and would I care to listen?

I did that. I also had an excellent supper in the company of the charming Clarissa. I was able to see Kate again before I left, when I impressed upon her once more the necessity for absolute secrecy concerning my true identity.

I don't think she saw the necessity but she promised most faithfully to keep the secret, which was all that mattered.

I got back to the flat and my lonely bed at about one o'clock in the morning, feeling very pleased with myself.

CHAPTER VII

SWINTON had left Selsey by the time I arrived there on Saturday morning. Since I knew that he was due to call upon Kate at the Can Can Club that evening the problem of keeping myself unobserved by him did not present itself till the Sunday. Fortunately the weather remained brilliant and I was able to adopt the scanty garb of a pair of bathing trunks for the day. These, in conjunction with a pair of outsize sunglasses and the macrocarpa hedge, were all the disguise and screening I needed.

Swinton himself obliged by pushing off in his dinghy in the morning, puttering rapidly out to sea, and not returning till the late afternoon. I watched him come back, and if he caught any fish he must have thrown them back into the sea, for he certainly brought nothing ashore but a fishing-rod that still looked surprisingly new and unused. The man certainly was an enigma. Having been out to sea in an open boat during the heat of a cloudless day one would have expected him to

F

appear frizzled by the sun, but his face carried its normal healthy pink hue, and except for being a little red round the neck he might have been sitting in a summer-house all day.

"I think he's shy," Freda said. "I suspect that as soon as he has reached a safe distance from shore he puts on one of those floppy sun hats. I'm sure there's a simple explanation for all these activities you choose to make so sinister, John. Are we going for our walk this evening?"

"Westwards, darling," I answered. "I cannot parade the lanes in bathing trunks on a Sunday evening, and I dare not be seen passing the front of Kohinoor in my normal garb for fear of being recognized by Swinton. I shall sneak out of the extreme western end of our own garden."

"Montmorency won't go westwards," Freda said, firmly. "You know the bungalow on the corner—the one with the funny little stone gnomes on its lawn? Montmorency misbehaved himself on one of the gnomes and was chased by a man with a stick. Now he won't go that way."

"He will for me," I said, "and like it!"

On Monday morning Swinton left to catch his usual train, and though I would liked to have made a similar early start I thought it prudent to travel by a later one.

As soon as I reached the office I got Slater on the telephone and he came round about twenty minutes later.

"Edward Ward," I said, "that's the name of our black-mailer, Del. D'you know him?"

He thought hard for a moment or two, his scrubby eye-brows pulled down in a scowl. Finally he shook his head. "Doesn't ring a bell," he said. "I'll make some inquiries. Only man I know of that name is reckoned to be a 'fence'."

"This one," I told him, "is a big gross fellow. I don't think he can be Spirelza."

"No," he said, absently. He was searching his extraordinary memory with its store of names and crooked professions. "I'll make inquiries," he said again.

"Do that. Whilst you're on the subject you might check some locations for me. This bloke Ward, whatever else he may be, is a dutiful son. He visits his mother who lives not far from Stoke Mandeville. Let me get the Ordnance Map."

I fished it from its pile in the cupboard, and saw, as soon as I had it open, that Swinton had made a faithful reproduction of it. I pointed out the spot that should be Mrs. Ward's cottage, and Slater said that he would go along and check up.

"Discreetly, Del," I urged. "Don't spoil our plan for Tuesday night. We are going to nab Mr. Ward as he leaves. . . ." I gave him a rough outline of Swinton's plan.

"Stone the crows!" he said. "D'you think it will work? Sounds too easy for my likin' and that's a fact. If you was a blackmailer, guv, with 'alf a dozen suckers after your blood you wouldn't visit no lonely spots in the country. You'd stick to the built-up areas and walk in the middle of the road. I've never 'eard the likes of this, Mr. Chadwick. How the hell this feller Swinton got a list of names and addresses of Ward's customers to begin with beats me. You watch your step, guv'nor. There's somethin' screwy in this set-up. You mark my words!"

"I will, Del. I most certainly will. It is one of the reasons why I want you to check up. Is there a Mr. Ward? Has he got a mother, and does she reside in the indicated spot? Anything you can find about Ward at the same time will be useful. But be careful, Del. Swinton is a forceful, go-ahead, stick-at-nothing type, who by sheer persistence and a bit of luck has got the low-down on Ward without the man being wise to it. The idea of a bunch of blackmail victims ganging up on their oppressor appeals to me. As I see it the outcome will prove something in the nature of a stalemate. Ward will stick in his toes, admit nothing—do nothing. In the end I think his victims will be forced to go to the police *en masse* hoping to gain anonymity in numbers—or something of the sort."

"I'll do what I can," Slater promised. "There ain't much time. I'll report tomorrow afternoon. That'll give you an hour or two to play with if I learn anything that'll make you want to change your plans."

"Thanks, Del. But tread delicately—like Agag."

He said that he'd never heard of Agag but that he would watch his step all the same.

When he had gone I looked up the number in the book and

rang the Can Can Club. The instrument was answered by old Bates, who told me in his usual disrespectful manner that Mrs. Malone was out. I gave him my number and asked him to be good enough to get her to ring me as soon as she came in. He said he would in a grudging sort of voice as though he would more than likely forget all about it, but he didn't, and twenty minutes later she came through.

"Say! It's you, John. You never left your name. I guess you want to know what Swinton thought of the place."

"I didn't ring you to ask that, but now you come to mention it, what did he think of it?"

"Oh! Swell! He was tickled pink. You know something, John? That guy likes me. I'm his type—he says."

"Is he yours? That's more to the point, Kate."

"No man is. I hate 'em all, brother. Just for the time being. Why did you ring me, John?"

"I omitted to ask you for a description of the girl—Helen Rice. I could get one from Pendleton but he's not seen her for two years. What's she like, Kate?"

"Well . . . I'd say she was a good deal older than she looks, which is twenty-five. I reckon she's more like thirty-five."

"You'll have to do better than that, Kate," I chided her. "I'm one of the despised sex. The way girls make up and dress these days—anything between sixteen and thirty-six you need a lie detector to get at the truth. What does she look like? Height, weight, eyes, etc."

"Spoken like a cop," she said. "The girl's dark haired, and when I saw her last she wore it with an old-fashioned fringe. She's not tall. She might be an inch over five feet, and a wee bit on the plump side. Quite a pretty girl, really. Nice blue eyes with long lashes. As a matter of fact I always used to reckon that when she was in her service uniform she looked like the maid in a French farce. How's that?"

"Fine," I said. "Fine. By the way, did you happen to mention her to Swinton?"

"I did too. I asked him if she'd been involved in his case. He said, 'No. Nothing like that.' I got the idea he didn't like the subject."

"Well, thanks a lot, Kate. I'll be seeing you—tomorrow night."

"I hope," she said. "I'll have the decanter out. I figure you'll need it. 'Bye, John."

I put down the telephone, and got out the slip of paper she had given me that contained the last known address of Miss Helen Rice. It was in Kensington. After locking the office and stepping downstairs to the street, I was lucky enough to find an empty taxi, and within twenty minutes was standing outside No. 20 Fernside Road.

The house was prosperous looking, gleaming with new cream paint. Each window displayed a net curtain of the same shade; each curtain was meticulously arranged to hang like its fellow. Somebody had put in so much work hearthstoning the steps up to the front door I felt ashamed to step on them. A maid answered my ring, and when I had stated my business she asked me inside, and said she would fetch Mrs. Cameron. The hall of the house was as clean and as polished as a hospital ward. In a vague sort of way it even smelt like one. I guessed that the boarders in such an establishment never called it home. They wiped their feet when they came in. They were careful with their cigarette ash, and if they splashed in the bathroom they heard all about it.

Mrs. Cameron, when at last she appeared at the top of the freshly vacuumed staircase, looked to be a slim blonde of about twenty-five. She made a slow and elegant descent, pointing and poising her dainty feet on every step. As she came nearer so progressively I added to her age till, when she had reached the bottom stair where she stayed with her painted face on a level with my chin, I saw that she was in reality about fifty-five. The appearance of youth apart from her figure was all hideously false. The yellow hair was a tight mass of peroxided curls. The white teeth revealed in a charmless smile were as false as china eggs. At close quarters the lavishly applied cosmetics could not disguise the ageing contours of the tired face. She had beady eyes that glittered like a street walker's. The woman repelled me.

"Ai'm told," said Mrs. Cameron, in an accent as false as her face, "that you wish to speak to me."

"I'm trying to trace a Miss Helen Rice who was staying in your house about six months ago. Do you remember her, Mrs. Cameron?"

"Ai dimly remember her," she answered.

"Do you know what has happened to her? Where, for instance, she went after leaving you?"

"Ai'm terribly afraid ai do not. She left no address."

I was prepared for that, but I'd had to ask the question.

"I'm not surprised," I went on. "I've been wondering whether or not some of your other guests who were here at the time know anything of her?"

"Ai cannot raightly say. Ai believe Miss Delooze said at dinner one night that she had seen the Miss Rice who was here. Where exactly ai cannot say. Miss Delooze had been on holiday to the seaside."

"Is Miss Delooze still with you? I'd like to see her."

Mrs. Cameron fluttered the thin mascara spikes that served her for eyelashes.

"That is frankly not possible, unless you care to go to Blackpool. Miss Delooze is on tour. The profession you know. Actually, she is an assistant to a magician. Ai cannot raightly say when she will be back, though I clearly understood her to say that she required her room from last Monday."

"Meaning that she may be back at any moment?"

"Definitely."

Mrs. Cameron's carmined lips snapped off the last answer with an emphasis that suggested she was looking forward to seeing Miss Delooze on a matter of business. The unoccupied room, probably.

I thanked her, and as soon as I got outside took in a strong gulp of good old Kensington air. The woman had certainly given me the shivers. I wondered what the boarders called her. Adverb Annie, maybe. She'd shown a marked predilection for qualifying her verbs.

Back at the office I toyed with the idea of asking Chief Inspector Mackintosh or Sergeant Williams if they had something in their records on Edward Ward. Then I thought: "Supposing they have? They'll be interested. Williams knows that I'm after a blackmailer and he might feel inclined to start some premature investigation that will queer our pitch. Leave it. Slater may dig out something."

Swinton didn't use Kohinoor that night. Freda told me that he had apparently given Miss Arnett the run of his boat. The lady, garbed only in her scarlet Bikini, had been cruising up and down the shore all the afternoon.

I left it late getting to town the next day for it was certain that I would not be back the same night. I expected to find Slater waiting for me, but it was tea-time—the janitor had actually brought me in a cup of his foul brew—before he arrived.

"It's a true bill, guv'nor," he exclaimed, sinking into the one easy chair the office contained and stretching out his legs thankfully. "Edward Ward is the name, and Mrs. Ward is the old lady 'oo lives in the cottage. It's a quiet spot, all right. Little old lane off the main road—so narrow you can't turn a car till you reach the next road junction, if there is one. Path runs through the woods to the cottage. Tumble down old place. If 'e's such a devoted son you'd think he'd give the old girl a bit o' cash to get the roof patched."

I handed him a drink, which he took with a grin.

"Thanks, guv. Skin off!" He took a man-sized gulp at it.

"Learn anything about Ward himself?"

"A little. Not enough time to get much, and I was being careful. Ward lives in Palmers Green, all alone in a big old Victorian 'ouse. Local mystery man. . . ."

"Then he could be our blackmailer?"

"Could be? Don't you think he is, guv'nor?"

"Swinton says he is. I'm merely trying to check on Swinton. I don't actually disbelieve him. What do you think?"

Slater pushed back his bowler with a characteristic gesture.

"I dunno, guv. He suits the part. But while I was taking a gander at the house in Palmers Green—nothing mysterious about that. It's listed in the Post Office Directory—I saw a bloke come out and I thought I knew 'im. Didn't get a real look at 'im, you understand, but 'e looked like a man named Mike Slocum. If it was, Mr. Ward does other jobs besides blackmail, or else 'e's contemplating a moonlight flit out of the country. Slocum is in the currency racket. A contact man.

You want a couple of 'undred quids'-worth of Swiss francs you see Mr. Slocum and give 'im the sterling along with your address-to-be in Switzerland. In due course, after you've got there, a bloke calls on you with the Swiss francs. Neat, eh? You don't 'ave to smuggle it. They do it for you, and take their cut in the rate. Works the other way too if needs be."

"Can't see that it helps," I said. "Ward may be thinking of an expensive holiday abroad. He can afford it by all accounts. Anything else, Del?"

"Nope. I daren't get too nosey. . . ."

"I'm glad you didn't." I paused. "Think our plan will work tonight, Del?"

"If you mean, will you be able to nab Ward, I'll say—I shouldn't be surprised. It's an ideal spot, guv, for a bit o' dirty work, and no mistake. Wonder is to me that Ward hasn't realized it. That's the bit that sticks in my gullet. A bloke like 'im—livin' on other people's secrets—expecting any day for someone to catch up on 'im—you'd think he'd be as wary where 'e puts a foot as any old fox—but—no! Not this bloke Ward. Every Tuesday night, regular as clockwork accordin' to what you say, he walks about a hundred yards through a dark and lonely wood." Slater wagged his head. "It don't make sense, guv, to me. And that's a fact!"

There was nothing to keep me at the office after Slater had gone. I spent the time mooning about the flat, had a late dinner, and walked up Oxford Street to the Marble Arch. The time was a minute after nine when I turned into the Edgware Road. The daylight was softening, and the neon lights were beginning to glow, pale shadows of the brilliant reds and blues to come.

The Humber was there, as Swinton had promised. He himself was waiting at its wheel with Ellery already installed in the seat beside him. The captain grinned when he saw me and leaning back flipped open a rear door. I got in.

"Glad to see you, Pendleton," Swinton observed. He was wearing his black homburg and a lightweight nearly black overcoat. Ellery had chosen a doggy-looking cap and check patterned tweeds for the occasion. The cap didn't suit him, or his long inquiring nose.

"You'll be glad to know that Mrs. Malone's flat should prove an excellent one for our purpose," Swinton went on over his shoulder. "Also—Ward has caught his train. Unfortunately, he saw me at Baker Street. I'm sure that he didn't think I was spying on him. The point is that the glance he gave me was one of recognition, which means that he knows me. I was hoping that the opposite was the case, since he had taken the trouble to remain anonymous himself."

"Probably knows us all," Ellery returned lightly. "I can't see that it matters. Going to wait for the doctor? I'll bet you a pound he fails to turn up."

"Why shouldn't he?" I asked.

Ellery gave his bleating laugh.

"Scared," he said. "Going to take the bet?"

"I don't want to rob you. Whatever you may think of Gribble he's a man who, if he has said he will come, will undoubtedly do so. He's the type. Probably how he came to lay himself open to blackmail in the first place."

Ellery twisted himself round his seat the better to address me.

"You know, Pendleton," he said, "I've been speculating on what it was that put us all paying forfeits to Bilter——"

"Ward," Swinton corrected him.

"All right—Ward. I had the devil of a job pinning something on you, Pendleton. Couldn't think what it was in your case. In the end I was rather clever about it. You're the big craggy type all the women fall for. Poor dears can't help themselves. I reckon you're a bigamist, Pendleton."

The car's interior was filled with his hee-hawing laughter.

"Take some advice from me this early in the evening, Captain Ellery," I replied grimly, "though what the devil you were ever a captain of is beyond me. Keep your ugly mouth shut! Or someone will shut it for you."

"What the hell?" he cried. "Can't you take a joke?"

"Every time," I retorted. "But that was not a joke. It wasn't even intended for one. . . ."

"Pendleton is right," Swinton put in. "Keep your remarks to yourself, Ellery. I want no quarrelling."

At that moment Doctor Gribble tapped on the window glass

with impatient fingers. I opened the nearside door and he slipped in beside me.

"Sorry I'm late," he apologized.

Swinton told him of Mrs. Malone's flat and the incident with Ward, pulled on his gloves, pressed the starter, and we were away.

The journey was uneventful. Swinton drove slowly and carefully; too much so for Ellery, who made pointed remarks about travelling faster in a hearse.

"Many a good scheme has been ruined by careless driving," Swinton said, with an edge to his voice. "I don't intend it to happen with this one."

I think that he would have told Ellery flatly to keep quiet if he had not realized, like me, that the captain's suddenly acquired garrulity was a form of nerves.

The doctor said little, but I could see in spite of the rapidly gathering darkness in the back of the car that he was tensed with the prospect of the uncertainty ahead. Would the scheme work? What if Ward was armed? There were a hundred and one different things to go wrong. Nobody realized it better than I—whose role was really one of spectator. For the doctor, the only man of the four of us with a profession to consider, it must have been purgatory.

Full darkness had descended by the time Swinton stopped the car alongside a telephone call box on the main road outside Stoke Mandeville.

"It is now," he said, consulting his wrist-watch by the light of the dash, "five minutes past ten. Ward's train leaves at ten-forty, and his car leaves its garage to pick him up at roughlyten-twenty. If one of you will be so good as to telephone this number"—he produced a slip of paper and held it up between finger and thumb—"the number of the garage to say that the car is not required since Mr. Ward has decided to stay the night in his mother's cottage, the timing will not seem out of order. You, Pendleton?"

I wanted to tell him to do it himself, but Swinton was a compelling sort of person, and it was not a particularly onerous duty. I took the slip of paper bearing the number and got out of the car.

The country air was cool and sweet after the close atmosphere of the car smelling strongly of cigarette smoke, leather upholstery and petrol. The night was still, and not really dark with the stars showing faintly through a thin haze of cloud. In the distance some sheep were bleating, and the plaintive sound seemed to be coming from incredibly far away.

The telephoning was a simple business. A voice said, "Shapley's Garage," and I said: "Mr. Ward asked me to 'phone you. His mother is not very well and he has decided to stay the night. He won't require the car that takes him back to the station."

"What about the morning, sir?"

"He didn't say anything to me about that. I dare say he'll ring you himself."

"Right. Thank you for ringing, sir." That was that.

There was some wrangling in process when I got back into the car. Ellery was saying: "For Heaven's sake, Doctor! The man is a blackmailer. What the hell do you want to do with him? Wet-nurse him?" I guessed that Gribble had brought up his stipulation against the use of violence again.

"It will not be necessary," Swinton said. "At the same time, Doctor Gribble, I must remind you that from now on you are under my orders. Captain Ellery will bear me out when I say that there can only be one command. All right, Pendleton?"

"Entirely successful," I reported, dutifully.

"Then we'll go. The lane where the car waits for Ward is very narrow and we have to travel some way along it before we can turn."

The Humber moved smoothly along the main road for about half a mile, then Swinton turned into a narrow lane. He drove slowly and quietly. The headlights carved strips of livid green from the hedgerows on either side.

We travelled steadily for ten minutes until, reaching a T road, Swinton stopped the car, reversed it skilfully, and moved back the way we had come. When the lane entered a wood he slowed to a crawl and finally stopped.

He switched out the headlights, leaving the sidelamps burning.

"This is the spot," he said, crisply. "Will you please all get out, and make as little noise as possible?"

He had pulled the Humber as close to the trees on the nearside as possible.

I followed the doctor out of the car. Beneath the trees it was intensely dark but I could just discern the entrance to a track into the wood.

"All right, gentlemen." Swinton had joined us from the driving seat. "Our man will come down this path in about seven or eight minutes' time. I dare say that normally the interior light of the car is left on, but I propose to leave it doused. Too much illumination may enable him to spot us before we are ready for him." Swinton was keeping his voice low. If any local rustic happened to be passing at that moment we must have aroused suspicion. Huddled in a dark group, with a leader giving directions in a voice a shade above a whisper, we could not have seemed more villainous had we been hatching a second Gunpowder Plot. "Unfortunately," Swinton went on, "Ward saw me earlier this evening, and so I think that you, Ellery, since you are wearing a cap, had better wait by the car. Have the rear door open, and take this torch. It is new and very bright. When he gets close enough for you to see the shape of him—and remember he is a vast and gross individual—I want you to shine it full in his face. That will dazzle him, and in this way I think he will step into the car suspecting nothing. Is that perfectly clear?"

"Of course," said Ellery, his tone of voice implying that he had found offence in the suggestion that it should have been otherwise. He tested the mechanism of the torch, shielding its rays with the cloth of his jacket.

"We three," said Swinton, "will wait by the entrance to the track. You, Pendleton, with the doctor over here . . ." He led me by the sleeve to the bole of a giant beech. ". . . and I shall be on the other side. As soon as Ward is in the car follow him in as quickly and as silently as possible. All right, then. And, gentlemen—absolutely no noise at all. Complete silence. We shall never get another chance if this fails!"

He waited for a moment to let the import of his last remark sink in, and then he moved silently away, his bulk melting into the pitchy blackness on the other side of the track.

The doctor had followed me, and together we moved round the giant beech and leant our backs against its smooth bark. "All very melodramatic," I heard him whisper. "But what the devil do we do with the man once he is in the car?"

"Nothing," I whispered back. "As soon as it is moving he'll have no option but to come with us. We ought to be able to frighten him into keeping quiet before we reach a main road."

The doctor muttered something I didn't hear and lapsed into silence. But the night was so quiet I could hear his gentle breathing.

We waited. The strange hush of the wood was faintly disquieting. When I turned my head I could see Ellery's figure immobile against the reflection of the car's side lights. Though I strained my eyes I could see no sign of Swinton. He might have been whisked a thousand miles away. You had to hand it to Swinton, I thought. His organizing was as near perfect as he could make it. Chance alone could wreck it. And chance had a playful habit of doing just such a trick. For all we knew a boy and his girl might even then be using the wood for some rustic love-making. The lane was isolated but public. It carried occasional traffic. A passing car with its headlights glaring at the precise moment when Ward arrived would undoubtedly reveal Ellery, at any rate, as a complete stranger. And what sort of a man was Ward? Would he not realize immediately that someone had caught up with him? And would he not then fight as viciously as any other animal caught in a trap? Swinton seemed strangely complacent and trusting on this part of his plan; that once in the car Ward and victory were ours.

The minutes dragged slowly. The doctor, less used to this sort of thing than I was, fidgeted a great deal. Ellery, safe in the assumption that his presence alone could be revealed, coughed noisily once or twice. A small car came down the lane and squeezed past the stationary Humber. The light from its lamps cast queer jumping shadows along the fringe of the wood whilst the doctor and I crouched like squirrels behind the beech. The noise of the car's motor sounded unnaturally loud as it beat away in the distance.

When it had gone the pall of silence descended again. Was Ward ever coming? I found myself getting restless. The damned wood seemed to blanket every sound save those that had travelled a distance, like the barely discernible whistle of a far-off train, or the faint scratch of a motor-horn way off on the main road.

Then quite suddenly and alarmingly close, from what seemed the very depths of the wood, we heard the bass rumble of a man's voice. I peered down the black void of the path seeing nothing, till, jerking and bobbing, and at odd intervals, I caught glimpses of a moving light. It came nearer and pretty soon I could identify it as a torchlight focused at a man's feet. He came closer. The path curved and I lost him for a second or two. It straightened out, and now I could see him closely. Nearer. The circle of his light on the leaf-strewn ground grew bigger. At its base I could see a couple of ponderous legs moving heavily and slowly.

This then must be Edward Ward.

CHAPTER VIII

HE CAME on quite unsuspecting until he was nearly level with our beech, and then he stopped, but he kept his torchlight on the ground. I think it was the absence of the car's interior light that worried him for a moment.

"That you, Shapley?" he growled in his deep voice.

I give Ellery full marks for the way he played up without a moment's hesitation.

"Yes. This way, sir," he called, in a voice that contrived to lose its normal educated accents. He switched on his own powerful torch and swung its beam into the empty car. Ward grunted and moved forward. Then Ellery, as he had been directed, swung the torchlight full into the man's vast moon-like face. I'd moved instinctively towards the car myself, for it was essential that once Ward entered it we followed on the instant. I saw what happened.

Ward knew that he was trapped the moment the fierce light caught him. His big pouchy face was masked in fear, for following the light came the swish of a descending sap. He opened his mouth to yell but he was too late. His large wide-brimmed hat was crushed onto his head. For a second he stood swaying in the light like some great stricken animal, his head hunched as though it had been driven into his shoulders, then, without a sound save for the thud of his weight on the path, he dropped and rolled on his side.

Swinton's brutal voice reached us immediately.

"Right! Get him in the car. Ellery! Switch off that light!"

The captain obeyed, but Ward's own torch was still alight on the ground beneath him, and slivers of yellow light crept out from under his bulk.

"Damn you, Swinton! I said there was to be no violence."

The doctor, his voice thick with rage, was already crouching over the fallen man's head, his hands exploring and probing.

"Never mind that. Get him in the car!"

"You'll wait till I've examined him."

"For God's sake, Doc.! Suppose a car comes along." This was Ellery. "We—we daren't show a light."

"I don't need one. Swinton—if you've killed this man, you'll hang for it!"

"My dear Doctor!" Swinton was himself again, but his voice was as cold and as menacing as an iceberg. "I would have required a pole-axe. The man is stunned. Will you please hurry? If we are caught with Ward in that state it will mean disaster for all of us."

Reluctantly it seemed the doctor scrambled to his feet.

"I can find no depression of the skull. But, Swinton . . ."

"Later, Doctor. You and Ellery take an arm. Pendleton and I will manage his legs."

Somehow we got that inert bulk into the back of the car. The man's weight was twice any man's of normal size, and for one horrible moment he jammed in the doorway. We worked in silence except for the harsh sound of our breathing and the creak of the car's laden springs. The sweat rolled from me, and but for the fact that three of us could be said to have had more than average strength, I doubt if we would have done it.

Swinton found his hat and his still burning torch, and took them with him into the front of the car. Five minutes later we were on the main road and bowling smoothly towards London.

Fortunately the Humber was a big and wide car so that Ward could be accomodated on the floor once his legs had been drawn up. He lay on his side with his head almost touching Gribble's feet. Every now and again, whenever some passing light or street lamp made it possible, the doctor leant down, and felt his pulse, or rolled back an eyelid. He seemed to have recovered from his momentary fury at Swinton's use of violence but I was not surprised when he brought it up again.

"I never had the slightest intention of doing anything else but bang him on the head," Swinton remarked calmly, without taking his eyes from the road. "For Heaven's sake use a little realism, Doctor. The man's a criminal. He's robbed me of hundreds of pounds. Do you imagine he can bring a charge of assault against us?"

"You took a hellish risk," Gribble snarled. "I saw you hit him. Luckily for you, and for us as well, the man must have an abnormally thick cranium. Had it been abnormally thin you would have killed him. Can't you realize what a mess we would have been in?"

"Don't worry, Doc. We are doing fine. Can you bring him round as soon as we get to Mrs. Malone's club? We are going into the yard at the back, and Ward has to go up the fire escape to her flat. We can't possibly carry him up there. He must go up under his own steam."

The doctor laughed harshly.

"The man's concussed. I can't bring him round from that as though he was in a faint. You'll just have to wait. You may be lucky. You may not. He may be like this for hours."

"Hours?" Ellery jerked round in his seat as though he'd been shot. "For God's sake, Doc.! You don't mean that?"

"I do mean it," Gribble said. He was getting a certain amount of satisfaction in driving home the point that Swinton had been too clever, but if Ellery was concerned over it Swinton was not.

"He'll come round," he said calmly. "The trouble with you, Doctor, is that you are basing your premise on only half the facts. You don't know what I hit him with. I do."

Swinton drove carefully, never taking his eyes from the road while he was talking.

I didn't like Swinton, and I was liking him less as the night progressed for there had been a risk in clouting Ward and Swinton had involved us all without so much as a by-your-leave, but I had to give him a certain amount of grudging admiration. There is a science in sapping a man, and Swinton, by his cool assumption that Ward would soon come round, showed that he had studied that detail as carefully as he had arranged everything else. The doctor knew it and relapsed into an infuriated silence.

Then, as though to vindicate Swinton, Ward regained consciousness. By that time we were half-way down the Edgware Road.

Ward groaned loudly above the noise of the car, and stirred his bulk against the confines of the matted floor. He quickly realized what was happening to him, and treated us to a rumble of invective. Then he made an effort to get up. The doctor would have helped him if I'd not stopped him. He seemed incapable of realizing that in his present role he must put aside the promptings of his profession.

"Let him be, Doc.!" I snapped. "You can treat him if you must when we get to the club." Not without difficulty I got a foot on Ward's gigantic and heaving posterior, and pushed him flat. I bent over him. In spite of his bulk and the indignity of his position he managed to turn his head. In the dim light from the vapour lamps over the street I could see his little piggy eyes glaring at me malevolently like some old tusker's from a trap.

"Listen, Ward!" I said, with as much menace as I could muster. "If you have any sense you'll stay quiet, or take another tap on the head that will keep you that way. Nobody loves you here, and don't forget it!"

"Who put you up to this?" he rumbled. "By God! I'll make the bastard pay, and the whole damned lot of you. Who split? You . . ." He winced. His head was giving him hell,

G

and until that moment his indignation had been so great he could ignore it. Now it was catching up with him. He groaned and lay still. He stayed that way till we reached the club.

I'd made it my business to keep my eyes on Ward's bulk, for I was not trusting the man, and in consequence I saw little of our progress, beyond noting the moment when we reached Oxford Street. The traffic there was too thick to be comfortable. Swinton cleverly kept the car in one of the middle lanes, but unless some nosey parker chose deliberately to peer into the car's interior during the involuntary halts at the lights there was little chance of Ward being seen. Nevertheless I breathed a sigh of relief when we turned into a narrow and darker street, and a minute later into Kate's diminutive back yard, into which the car fitted almost like a bullet into the breech of a gun. No sooner had the car stopped than I heard a scraping sound, and a glance out of the rear window showed that the high wooden doors were being closed behind us.

Mrs. Malone was keeping to her part of the plan, and that was old Bates closing the doors.

Swinton was out of the car as soon as it had stopped. I expected to hear his orders, but instead he said something to Ellery in a low voice and then melted into the darkness of the yard.

Ellery came round to the rear door.

"All right," he said. "Let's have him out. Swinton's gone up to warn Mrs. Malone."

I found that strange. It wasn't like Swinton suddenly to delegate his command, and Mrs. Malone needed no warning, but I said nothing.

We got Ward out of the car; not that he required any prompting. He stood in the dim light of the yard—the tiny place was nothing but a gap in a huddle of buildings whose windows were showing no lights—and swayed drunkenly whilst he pawed his head with one ham-like hand. Then he peered at each one of us in turn, including old Bates who had added his grinning face to the assembly.

"I don't know any of yer," Ward growled. "What's the meaning of this business? There'll be trouble——"

"Later, old man," Ellery cut in briskly. The bottom of the

fire escape from Kate's flat debouched almost on to the nose
of the parked Humber. Ellery indicated it with a sweep of
his hand. "You're going up those stairs, and we shall be
behind you. Nothing more is going to happen to you while you
behave yourself, and do as I say. Just keep still for a moment,
will you?" With a few swift patting motions the captain made
certain that Ward was carrying no lethal weapon, while the
captive grunted either in fury or amazement.

"What do you think I am?" he rumbled. "You sure you've
got the right man?"

"Tolerably so," Ellery said. "But I'm taking no chances.
Off you go, Mr. Ward—straight on and up the stairs. There
might even be a drink at the top—who knows?"

Ward shrugged. "You're crazy!" he growled, and taking a
step towards the staircase, hauled his bulk on to it. Ellery
followed, then the doctor, and I brought up the rear. Old Bates
plucked me by the sleeve as I put a foot on the bottom step.

"Keep yer fingers crossed, son," he advised, with a wicked
chuckle. "That weren't built to take elephants!"

We made slow progress, and Bates's warning was by no
means out of place, for the whole staircase creaked alarmingly
at times as though it would come away from its wall and hurl
the lot of us into the yard below. Ward had evidently made up
his mind that resistance was useless, but the climb was distres-
sing to a man of his bulk. I could hear him grumbling and
swearing. When at last we reached the balcony outside the
french windows of Kate's lounge he was sucking in breath as
noisily as a bicycle pump fills a tyre.

We filed into the lounge. Kate, wearing a white fur coatee
over an evening dress of a pleasing green, was waiting for us.
The only illumination was a small and parchment-shaded
reading lamp glowing from the mantelpiece against which she
was leaning. There was no sign of Swinton. It was obvious
that for some reason he thought it best, since Ward had
spotted him earlier in the evening, to keep out of the man's
sight till we were properly ready to deal with him, though
what was to be gained by remaining anonymous at this stage
I could not imagine. Ward had admitted that he knew none
of us, and I found that vaguely disturbing. To add to my

discomfort the man stopped as soon as he caught sight of Kate, and with obvious bewilderment said:

"Madam, I have been assaulted and kidnapped by these men. I don't know——"

"You will!" Kate cut him off, and silenced his further muttering with a look of utter disdain.

"Take him right through, boys. Room at the end of the hall with the bolts on the door."

Ward shrugged, and would have protested, but Ellery kneed him in the back and he lumbered through the open doorway into the hall. When he saw the tiny dimensions of the room where he was to stay he bellowed with fury. Ellery and I gave him a shove that sent him sprawling with a discordant jangle of springs onto the bed, slammed and bolted the door.

It was not long before he was banging on it with his fists, raising an unholy racket. Ellery looked alarmed but Kate, who had followed us as far as the hall, said:

"Don't worry. No one'll hear him. Come on into the lounge and have a drink."

"That's a great idea, Mrs. Malone." Ellery brightened perceptibly. Ward had stopped his futile banging by the time we had followed Kate back into the lounge.

Gribble, who had stayed there, scowled at us ferociously.

"Where's Swinton?" he barked. "It's time we put an end to this farce."

"Aw, come on, Doctor—relax," Kate drawled. "Mr. Swinton has gone down to turn his car round. I sent him down my back stairs whilst you were using the fire escape. What'll you boys drink? Whisky?"

"Why does he want to turn the car round?" Gribble persisted. He appealed to me and Ellery in turn. "I distrust Swinton. I think he let us down, hitting Ward as he did. It might have had the most disastrous consequences."

"But it didn't," Ellery snapped. "For God's sake forget you're a doctor, and remember that Swinton is getting you out of a jam. You medicos are all the same—even in the Army —regard everyone outside your own profession as brainless idiots. Swinton is turning the car round now to save time.

It's conceivable that Ward will be missed—as early as this maybe. Once we've taken his keys we have to get to his house and open his safe. There'll be no time to lose."

"I hope it's as simple as it sounds," the doctor retorted sourly. "But why is Swinton avoiding being seen by Ward? I suppose he imagines that by doing so he can escape the consequences if things go wrong?"

"You'd better ask him," Ellery said. I could see that he was getting thoroughly tired of the doctor, and to a certain extent I sympathized with him. The tip of Ellery's long nose was fairly quivering with the restraint he was putting on himself.

Kate, who had been pouring out drinks, handed them round. Gribble's hairy hand shook slightly as he took his off the tray, but the fire died out of his deep-set eyes as he thanked her and said: "This is very good of you, Mrs. Malone. I'm sorry if I appear in the least ungrateful."

"Not a bit, Doctor. You go ahead and let off steam. It's been a nervy business—even waiting for you to arrive. Help yourself to soda or water."

The whisky was the same good stuff I'd had on my first visit to the flat, and Kate, as though to remind me of it, and unseen by the others, gave me a broad wink as I downed it. I grinned and moving over to the curtained windows twitched one aside. Swinton had turned the car, and the gates to the yard were now open. I expected him to come up the fire escape but he didn't, he came in by the door and he was a long time coming. When at last he appeared there was sweat on his forehead, and though he forced a smile it was nothing but a grimace, for his eyes were as hard as sin. Was the great man beginning to feel the strain of the evening after all?

Kate welcomed him with a drink, for which he thanked her and downed it immediately.

"I don't think we should waste any time," he said. "If Ward realizes quickly that the game is up, hands over his keys, and tells us all we wish to know, the name of his accomplice or accomplices, that sort of thing, we may yet be able to spare Mrs. Malone the doubtful pleasure of his company for the night."

"So far," I told him, "Ward hasn't the slightest idea of what it's all about. He's not recognized any one of us."

Swinton took out a spotless handkerchief and dabbed at his forehead.

"So much the better. It is one of the reasons why I took care not to be seen by him. Obviously it has never entered his head that his victims have ganged up on him for the simple reason that he considers it impossible for them to be known to each other. May we bring him in here, Mrs. Malone?"

"Surely. Give him a drink if it will help—only if it will help though, Mr. Swinton."

"It won't be necessary, Mrs. Malone. Let's get him in."

We trooped into the hall. Ellery was the first to reach the bolted door. There was no sound from inside the room as though Ward had realized the futility of trying to burst out, but when Ellery released the topmost of the three bolts the door sagged outwards. It was then that I noticed that the middle bolt had never been shot. We'd probably missed it in our excitement. Only the bottom bolt was holding, and the door's latch.

"Blighter's shoving on it," Ellery muttered. "All right, Ward," he called, "we're opening up."

He eased back the bottom bolt with an effort because of the pressure on it. The latch gave way and the door burst open almost knocking Ellery aside.

Ward was on his knees in the doorway, one gigantic paw clamped against the inner doorpost. For the fraction of a second he stared at us with blank and glazing eyes, then toppled over slowly on his side, his outstretched arm landing with a thwack from the palm of his hand on the floor.

"Christ!" Ellery exclaimed.

Kate, who had followed us out, gave a little squeal of alarm, and Swinton, pushing to the front, barked:

"Take a look at him, Doctor. Quickly!"

Gribble was over the man in a flash, groping for his pulse, fingers of his free hand automatically loosening the collar round the bulging neck. For a few seconds he worked. When he looked up his eyes were burning and his mouth was set like a closed trap. Slowly he got to his feet, dusted the knees of his trousers.

"Well, Doctor?"

"I can do nothing," Gribble said distinctly. "The man is dead!"

"Oh, no!" Kate's voice was indescribably shocked and came in a hoarse agonized whisper. Again she said "No!" whilst she stared at Ward's body with dilated eyes. The rouge stood out clearly in big red patches on her cheeks.

"Are you sure, Doc.?" Ellery's reaction took the shape of bewilderment.

"Of course I'm sure!" Gribble snapped. "We can do nothing except call the police."

"Now . . . just a moment." Swinton came to the fore. "Let's not panic. What was it, Doctor? Heart failure?"

"I imagine so. An autopsy will determine the cause of death. He was a likely subject. All that weight. Fatty degeneration of the heart, I dare say. Clumping him on the head and making him climb a fire escape will not have helped—nor the strain of finding himself a prisoner. If you will show me a telephone, Mrs. Malone, I will telephone for the police and an ambulance."

Kate had recovered herself. The natural colour was back in her cheeks blending with the make-up. She had drawn herself to her full height, and her eyes were ranging speculatively from one to the other of us.

"Now take it easy, Doc.," she drawled. "If that guy's found dead in my flat over my club it's not going to do me any good even if he died naturally with nobody helping him. There'll be an inquest and a heap of police investigation. My affairs won't bear that. Before you go bawling for the cops let's talk things over, eh? What do you say, Mr. Swinton?"

"I say it's an admirable suggestion, Mrs. Malone. We must not lose sight of our objective. Ward's death is of course an unforeseen complication but I fail to see why it should be insurmountable."

"A complication!" the doctor flared. "Is that all you can find to say about it, Swinton? It's disastrous for all of us.

We brought him here. In a way we shall be held responsible. We must inform the police immediately!"

Ellery swivelled his long nose and pointed it menacingly at Gribble.

"For God's sake stop bleating about a policeman!" he snapped. "And look a bit farther than your own damned profession. With Ward dead it's more than ever necessary to get that stuff out of his safe." He turned to Swinton.

"We'll take his keys, get over to his house, open the safe and then report his death. Who is to be the wiser?"

"You get him out of here first," Kate said, belligerently. "You boys brought him here. I guess you can take him away again. Dump him somewhere. That's what they do in the States. What's there to worry about? He died naturally. He could have had a seizure any place."

"I must protest." Gribble was white with emotion. "I refuse to be embroiled further in this. What you propose is outside the law. I shall——"

"You'll what?" Swinton grasped him by an arm and swung him round. "You'll do what, Doctor Gribble? I'll tell you. You'll do precisely what I and the rest of us decide. Is that clear? If not I personally shall see that the evidence of your illegal operations, or whatever it was brought you into this, is put before the Medical Council."

We were seeing the real Swinton now; hard, ruthless and somehow merciless. There was a cruel curve to his mouth, and he fairly shook the doctor till he quailed in his grasp. Gribble was not a big man, nor was he physically a coward, but he saw in Swinton for the first time something he didn't understand; a man of sheer determination, blind to reason, a man who would win at all costs. That, and the true realization of the meaning of Swinton's threat, had the doctor beaten. When Swinton released him he stood away and he cursed him, but he made no further protest.

Swinton turned on me.

"And you, Pendleton? You've been strangely silent. Are you going to be squeamish?"

"Do I look it?" I asked. "And don't adopt a bullying tone with me, Swinton, or lay a hand on me. If you do I'll hit you so hard you'll look deader than Ward. I'll play along with you because it suits my purpose, and Mrs. Malone's, and Ellery's, and the doc.'s, only he doesn't see it our way. What are you going to do with Ward, always provided we can get him down the fire escape? As a corpse he'll be twice as heavy."

Swinton would have made me a corpse myself the way he glared at me when I threatened him. What hurt him was the realization that I could probably do what I had threatened. But he didn't allow his emotions to override his common sense.

"Once we have opened the safe and secured what we want, Ward can be dumped anywhere by the roadside. He can then be found five minutes after we have left him for all it matters to us. That means he must stay here whilst we go to his house in Palmers Green. . . ."

"No!" Mrs. Malone cried. "You get him out of here first!"

"If we do," Swinton replied, "we must put him somewhere where he is unlikely to be found for some time. We cannot guarantee that getting into his house and opening the safe will be a simple or speedy process. . . ."

"All the more reason why he can't stay here," Kate told him flatly. "Get him out of here, and hurry!"

"Very well then." Swinton shrugged his shoulders, and looked for a moment helplessly at the men in the party. "But I hope you realize, Mrs. Malone, that it will delay us getting at his safe. Will you telephone down to your man Bates and tell him to close the doors to the yard? I had him open them again. Then get him into the house. I don't think he ought to know that Ward is dead." Swinton turned to us. "In the meantime we'll have his keys."

As soon as Kate had disappeared he bent over Ward's body and in less than a minute had extracted a sizeable bunch of keys on a long silver chain.

"There we are, gentlemen!" he exclaimed, singling out one long key from the bunch. "This one fits a Ratner safe." He slipped them into his own pocket. "Now get yourselves set for some arduous and distasteful work. This mound of flesh has to be moved, and we have to do it—unaided."

"Suppose we move him into the lounge for a start?" Ellery

suggested. "He's got to go out by the way he came in. Ready, Doc. ?"

"I do this under protest," Gribble said, tight-lipped. "I want you to witness that my position in this affair has been forced on me."

"So it has," Ellery said. "So has mine. You should have thought of the consequences before you hid a body under the surgery floor or whatever indiscretion you were fool enough to commit. But who am I to preach? I borrowed a brother officer's cheque book. We're all crooks together. Grab a leg, old man!"

The doctor spluttered at Ellery's levity but he joined in with the rest of us. Between us we could just lift Ward's body clear of the floor and move it with infinite labour into the lounge, where we dumped it thankfully by the doors to the balcony. It was a ghastly business and the thought of the fire escape outside made me sweat.

When Bates—I could imagine his blistering comments on the order—had once again shut the doors to the yard, and taken himself indoors, we began our descent. Fortunately the rear of all the adjacent premises was in complete darkness, but the night sky of London's West End always reflects a certain amount of light from the glare of its main streets, and it seemed to me, lifting and straining one slow step at a time, that we must be plainly visible to anyone who cared to look our way as they passed the gap in the buildings that constituted Kate's back yard. The fire escape groaned and creaked, threatening partition from the wall, as we lifted and bumped and slithered our grotesque burden down to the yard below.

We got it there at last, took a breather, then manhandled it into the car.

Gribble muttered something about *rigor mortis* and the necessity for removing the body before this set in or it might be impossible to get it out again.

"Where are we going?" Ellery demanded, his chest heaving for breath. None of us was in much better shape.

"I know a spot back of Epsom Downs," Swinton answered, "where he may never be found—certainly not for a day or two at any rate."

"That's a hell of a way with a corpse on the back seat," Ellery grumbled.

"We can't risk him being found before we're certain of clearing that safe. There's stuff in his pocket that will identify him within a minute of being found. Once his identity has been established they'll have a policeman calling at his house within another ten minutes. Bloody fine fools we shall look unlocking his safe with a bobby peering over our shoulders. I think it will be safer to have him sitting properly in the middle of the back seat with Pendleton and the doctor on either side."

"Thanks," I rejoined, "I'd sooner drive."

"I'm driving," Swinton said, and moved to open the yard gates.

But that was the way it worked out. We put Ward's hat on his head, for it was a wide-brimmed affair and shaded the waxy hues of his dead fat face. Maybe it had been purchased for just that reason whilst he had been alive. But however carefully or delicately we put it on, it was distressingly obvious that he had not put it on himself.

In the brief moment we waited for Swinton to get behind the wheel I had time to think: "This serves you right for not minding your own business, Chadwick. You could be at Selsey now . . . just going to bed. . . ."

My reflections were cut short as Swinton started the car and turned out of the yard. The car swayed slightly, and I had to brace myself against the clammy uncontrolled weight of the shifting corpse.

CHAPTER IX

THE journey, of course, was completely without incident. It is practically impossible for any passer by, disinterested as he must be, to observe at night that of three men seated in the back of a moving motor-car the middle one of the three is dead. We ought to have realized that but we didn't, and to me at any rate, and certainly to Doctor Gribble on the other side of the corpse, the journey was one of taut nerves and sweating apprehension. Every stop, every slowing in the smooth beat of the motor, the glimpse of a passing patrol car, meant another tightening of the rack on which our nerves were stretched. Once we had passed over Westminster Bridge it was not so bad, but before that the traffic delays were frequent and I expected to hear at any moment some shouted denunciation from the pavements crowded as ever in spite of the late hour.

I recognized the route as far as the road to the Downs but thereafter I was lost. I remember we waited a long time to cross an arterial road, then entered a long and winding lane that dipped into a valley, and almost immediately began to climb again through woodland. Half-way up the ascent Swinton stopped the Humber. When I got out I saw that he had drawn the car off the lane onto a track through the woods so that it was screened effectively from any passing vehicle. He switched off all lights as soon as he stopped the motor but there was a thin inverted crescent of a late moon hanging in the eastern sky, and this gave a faint metallic sheen of light to our immediate surroundings.

"I know this spot," Swinton said. "There is a big dell not very far into the woods—rather like a huge hole. If we can manage to get him that far I don't think it likely that he will be found quickly—not until the week-end, and perhaps not then unless some hikers get off the beaten tracks. Ready? Let's have him out."

Rigor was not sufficiently advanced to delay this process. It was horrible enough without our having to labour over stiffening limbs. Desperation lent us strength as it had done before. Once we had the inert bulk clear of the ground we proceeded in a series of short sharp rushes that at times had all the elements of panic. In a way the terrain was responsible for this. Swinton struck off into the woods, and apart from the darkness and our incontrollable burden, we had to contend with saplings that whipped us nastily as we forced our way through them, and threatened to tear the unwilling corpse from our frenzied grasp. The uneven ground was for ever setting us at odd angles to each other so that we were constantly lifting instead of holding and carrying. This put an intolerable strain on the arms. The physical effort required was enormous, and Ellery, who was so much older than any of us, began to breathe with a whistling effect much the same as Ward had done on the fire escape, so that I had the crazy idea that he might collapse on us just the same as Ward had done, thereby presenting us with yet another corpse. Swinton called a halt after fifty yards that had seemed like five hundred, and went forward to reconnoitre. He was back in no time.

"We're practically there," he gasped on his return. "Another ten yards." He got a grip on the leg he had abandoned. For some reason the corpse was proceeding feet first. "Ready?" he rasped. "Let's go."

The final distance was accomplished in a last rush that nearly precipitated the bearer party as well as the body into a vast hole in the woods. There were trees growing at its bottom. The thin moonlight glinted on the leaves of their topmost branches.

We stopped on the edge of the sheer slope. Swinton switched on his torch to look for a place reasonably free of undergrowth, and as luck would have it we had but a bare yard to move him to one side before we tipped him over. He rolled down the slope, then some projecting limb of a tree caught him so that he performed a grotesque cartwheel. For a moment only his eyes stared glassily in the light of the torch and then he was gone. His hat was on the edge and Ellery kicked it contemptuously after him. The crash of his arrival came up to us faintly. Without a word we stumbled tiredly back to the car.

Little was said on the return journey. The doctor sat slumped in a corner chain-smoking cigarettes. We had, of course, left the most obvious tracks through the woods, and I think Gribble was brooding on the possible consequences for a doctor who had acquiesced in the removal of a body after death, even though death had been from natural causes. I didn't feel too happy about it myself, for if I was to go on playing detective it was essential that I should keep in well with the authorities. For some reason, too, apart from my share in the unauthorized pall-bearing, I was vaguely uneasy about the whole thing. Again I believed it to be Swinton. The man was uncannily prepared for everything—even for the disposal of an apparently unplanned corpse. The spot he had chosen had been a good one from our point of view; the avoidance of immediate discovery. Swinton had taken about a minute to think it up.

He and Ellery conversed briefly, but I was too tired to pay much attention to them.

When we had crossed Westminster Bridge, Swinton halted the car in Victoria Street.

"Our next objective," he announced, "is Ward's house in Palmers Green, and the opening of his safe."

"Let's hope, after all our exertions so far, that he keeps what we want in that safe and not in the strong-room of some local bank," I pointed out.

"I happen to know—in fact I made it my business to find out," Swinton replied, "that Ward does not use a bank. Have any of you considered how this next job should be approached?"

"Damn the man!" I thought. "Is there any angle of this business he has not studied or for which he is not prepared?"

Aloud I said, somewhat nettled, "Obviously, in view of Ward's death, and the fact that we have hidden his body, we cannot very well drive up to his house and troop in through his front door. . . ."

"Exactly! We shall be seen—late as it is. The actual entry should be made by one man—or at the most two. I propose to go myself and since I do not disillusion myself into thinking that you all trust me I suggest that one of you comes with me. The others can either wait in the car, which I shall park some distance from Ward's house, or drop off now and await our return to the Can Can Club. Mrs. Malone will be glad to know that we have successfully disposed of Ward. If that meets with your approval who is it to be? With all due respect to the doctor and his profession I think he has committed himself sufficientiy for one night. Which leaves you, Captain Ellery, or you, Pendleton."

"Toss you for it," Ellery said languidly, and producing a coin spun it briefly. I called, hoping fervently that I had called wrongly. If the doctor had committed himself sufficiently for a man of his profession, then so had I; particularly should something go wrong, and so far we'd had all the luck.

Ellery peered at the coin he had caught, holding it in the dim light from the dash.

"Tails! You lose," he said.

"Good!" cried Swinton, not disguising his pleasure that Ellery was going and not I. Evidently my threat to him in Kate's flat still rankled. "Would you mind getting out here? It will save me a good deal of time if you can make your own way to Mrs. Malone's. With any luck we shall see you there in about an hour to ninety minutes' time—possibly less. All right, Ellery?"

The doctor and I got out, called a soft "Good Luck", and Swinton drove off immediately.

Gribble glanced at his watch.

"I suppose that I must see this thing through," he muttered, "though I would just as soon go home. God! How I hate that man Swinton! Had the matter rested solely between him and me, and not involved you others, I would have done the sensible thing with Ward and called the police when we found him dead. I've a nasty feeling that no good will come of disposing of that body. Shall we split a taxi? I'm dog tired."

We found a cab and fifteen minutes later Mrs. Malone was taking us up to her flat above the club.

"You'll have to excuse me," she explained. "We're closing pretty soon and I'm needed downstairs. You boys look as though you've been through the mill. Help yourselves to drinks. I'll send up old Bates with sandwiches. Say!" she added with a fervour that betrayed her conviction. "Was I glad to see that car move out of the yard. I've had some pretty nasty jolts in my time but that guy rolling out of the room dead when you loosed off that bottom bolt—Boy! That really jolted me. See you later, eh? We'll have a chat."

The doctor and I settled down into easy chairs with a generous measure of Kate's excellent whisky to soothe us. It succeeded with me, though I doubt if it did the same for Gribble. He sat and brooded over the night's activities, seeing himself in more trouble with every thought. It was very quiet in the flat, and it was difficult to imagine that only an hour or so ago Ward's grotesque body had sprawled on the carpet by the windows whilst we'd braced ourselves for the task of getting him down the fire escape.

"Doc.," I said softly, more for the sake of conversation than anything—his complete introversion was getting on my nerves—"there's been one possible flaw right the way through Swinton's planning. He's made no provision for dealing with Ward's accomplice. I know for a fact that he has one—a woman. She got the goods on Mrs. Malone, and on Pen—me, that is. Of course," I went on hurriedly, to cover the slip I'd made, "if Swinton comes back with all the evidence Ward's accomplice is powerless anyway, but—it leaves an end," I finished lamely. Gribble was looking at me with an odd expression in his deep-set eyes.

"You were going to say 'on Pendleton', I think. Which suggests immediately that you are not he." No doubt he saw a momentary look of dismay on my face for he snapped: "What's been going on? Who are you?"

I told him, adding the usual objurgation for him not to let Swinton know, and he shrugged his shoulders.

"I can't see that it matters—now. Yes. There was a woman accomplice in my case. Her name was Ellen Gryce. You know her?"

"I know of her. She's called herself Ella Price and Helen Rice. I'd like to trace her so that I can make certain she can no longer cause trouble. After all she must know all your secrets even if she has passed on the documentary evidence to Ward. Tricky business—blackmail. It doesn't always require supporting proof. Mere knowledge can be enough to turn the screw on some poor devil. You remember little Miss Piper? We thought—that is Kate Malone, who knows I'm not Pendleton, and I—that Miss Piper probably has an illegitimate child which she must, perhaps because of her job, keep a secret from the world. Well—there's an instance for you. The knowledge alone passed on might be enough to cause Miss Piper untold anguish. How are you placed, Doc.?"

He took a sip at his whisky and nursed the glass in his hand.

"I'm not sure," he said slowly. "My profession of a medico makes me easy meat. I cannot afford to have mud slung.

Some of it always sticks. There are of course some letters which would prove their case to the hilt. If Swinton brings them back—well and good. . . ."

"What do you mean, if he brings them back? He'd better, Doc. I know his hide-out on the coast. As a matter of fact I'm his neighbour, though he's never known it. If he tries any funny stuff on his own account I'll jump on him quickly enough."

Gribble smiled faintly.

"That's reassuring at any rate," he replied, "because, just now, whilst we were relaxing in silence, I was going over in my mind's eye the whole of the evening's proceedings, and I recalled an item the significance of which had escaped me till that moment. I'm surprised that you, a private detective, had not spotted it. But I'll come back to that later. I was about to tell you how I became involved in blackmail. I feel that I can trust you."

His last sentence was by way of being a question. Reflecting that I must have been mistaken about the effect of the whisky on him, for he was now becoming almost garrulous, I nodded.

"Certainly," I said.

"It concerns chiefly my young brother, and not me. I have never been interested in women except from a biological point of view. I am unmarried." The doctor settled back between the wings of his chair, so that with the lone table lamp away to one side I could no longer see his face but only his whisky glass, which he continued to support on his knees steadying it with his thin, strong-looking fingers. His precise voice, however, lost none of its resonance and I could hear him clearly.

"My brother," he went on, "was living with me at the time I engaged this girl Ellen Gryce as a general domestic help. She was an attractive wench, besides being well spoken and intelligent. I suppose, in the light of subsequent events, that I ought to have wondered what the devil she was up to working as a domestic, but then—I was glad to have her because she made an admirable stand-in for my receptionist. This is a sordid story, er—Chadwick. I dare say it's not alone in that. My young brother became intimate with the girl. As usual the whole thing had a diabolical timing. She was three months

H

pregnant when I heard about it, and he had just landed a job —an excellent job which would not have been his for five minutes if the truth about his relations with the girl had become known. So—they came to me. The girl was willing. I operated on her in my own surgery, and quite successfully, but, of course, she left my employ. A month later came the first demand note, threatening me with a court action. I hadn't a chance. My fool of a young brother had written her the most intimate letters. I paid. Without the letters I might have stood a chance. If I get them back I'll take the chance— now, though I'm not sure that I would have done so at the time."

"Yes. But I'll have to find that girl. She's got to realize that if she ever tried anything of the sort again on anybody at all she'll be behind bars within a week."

"Agreed." The doctor sat up again. "If it comes to a matter of identification," he went on dryly, "I can tell you that she has a big heart-shaped mole on her midriff."

"Thanks," I drawled, "I would prefer it to be in a more accessible spot——"

I broke off as, after a perfunctory and token knock, old Bates marched in bearing a plateful of succulent-looking sandwiches.

" 'Ere you are!" he said. "On the 'ouse! Chicken this side. 'Am on that. All right too. I had a couple on the way up, so you don't 'ave to tip me."

"Pity," I grinned. "Put 'em down there. How long before Mrs. Malone is free to join us?"

"Ten minutes. Where's Fatso?"

"Bates," I said, "I don't know how well you know Mrs. Malone, but she has a high regard for you. If you feel the same way towards her forget you saw a fat man on the fire escape. Forget that he ever came near this place. Understand?"

The twinkle was in his little birdlike eyes, but it vanished when he saw that I was not joking.

"I get you," he said. "I never saw the bloke." He set down the plate of sandwiches and marched out.

The doctor and I waded into the food, and were just finishing the last of the ham when Mrs. Malone returned.

"That's another night done," she exclaimed. "Gee! I'm tired. Must be all the excitement we had earlier." She glanced at the French clock on the mantelpiece. "About time our friend Swinton came along. Sit down, boys. Don't stand on ceremony with me. I'll change into something more comfortable. Be right back."

"Time is getting on," Gribble admitted. "Nearly an hour and a half since we left Swinton in Victoria Street. How long ought they to take?"

"Doc.," I said, "I'm as anxious as you are. The whole business—even Ward's untimely demise—has gone so smoothly I keep wondering when we're going to strike the snag. It could be right at the end. Ward might have had someone staying with him this week—that sort of thing. By the way, what was the point I missed? You said you'd come back to it later."

"Yes. It worries me. If Swinton becomes overdue it will worry me even more. You remember that we all trooped out to fetch Ward, and Ellery unlocked the bolts on the door?"

"Of course. Ward fell out—an obvious corpse at that, come to think of it, though naturally I hoped otherwise. But I'm not likely to forget it. What are you getting at, Doc.?"

"The bolts on the door. Only two had been shot."

"That's so. I noticed it myself. I put it down to excitement. Ellery and I locked him in. I remember shooting the bottom one and presumed that Ellery had seen to the middle one. I dare say he was thinking that I had done it."

Gribble shook his head.

"He shot the middle bolt. I saw him do it—at least I'm tolerably certain I saw him. I followed you out," he went on, seeing protest in my eyes. "I was behind Mrs. Malone. I watched from the door of the lounge and was back in here before you had turned round after locking the door. I'm damned certain Ellery shot both the top and middle bolts, though thinking on it continually tends to blurr the mental image. If he did, you know what it means?"

I felt a creepy feeling of alarm stirring along my backbone.

"Hell, yes! The bolt could not have moved itself. Whoever moved it probably unlocked the lot to get into the room, and coming out shot only two of the bolts. But who?"

"Who but Swinton!" the doctor snapped through gritted teeth. "He looked in on Ward on his way up from the yard after turning the car."

"Yes," I said softly. "Five minutes later we found Ward dead. There's something here I don't understand, Doc. Nor do I like it. Swinton looked uncommonly grim when he came in, and there was sweat on his forehead. He'd taken great care that Ward should not see him, but he deliberately looked in on the man—and the shock of it was sufficient to bring on a fatal attack of heart failure. That doesn't suggest that the relationship between the two was merely Blackmailer and Victim."

"If it was heart failure," the doctor said, quietly.

"God's grief, Doc.!" I bawled at him harshly. "You yourself said it was!"

"My dear chap—please." He made a deprecating gesture with one hand. He was patently anguished. "I made a most cursory examination. Doctors are limited in their immediate powers to make such decisions. I was concerned mostly to find that the man was in fact dead, and that I could do nothing for him. Had I had immediate access to drugs I would have made an attempt at resuscitation—a shot of adrenalin, but it was useless. Only an autopsy can find the true cause of death, and perhaps not even that. There are poisons that cause all the symptoms of heart failure. . . ."

"Cyanide, eh?"

"I don't think it was that. It certainly causes great depression of the heart, but you can usually smell the stuff. I had in mind something like curare. It's rare, but it can be obtained. Then there are a number of like——"

"They're not taken by mouth are they, Doc.?" I cut in. "You'd have to use a hypodermic?"

"Something like it. The merest scratch infected with the poison——"

"Let's have a look at that room!" I interrupted, jumping to my feet. He followed me out of the lounge, and in the hall we bumped into Kate. She'd changed into a wrap of soft clinging stuff that made her look positively voluptuous. She was wearing bedroom slippers. She saw at once from our expressions that something had happened.

"What in hell is eating you?" she demanded bluntly.

We explained about the bolts and asked for her confirmation that Ellery had shot both the top and middle ones, but she was unable to remember clearly.

The three of us went into the room that had held Ward for so brief a time. We found nothing. The place looked as bare and as uninteresting to me as it had done before Ward had set eyes on it. I don't know what we expected to find. It was probably an unconscious urge to be doing something to make an antidote to the vague fears that were besetting us once we had entertained the idea that Swinton had called in on Ward and caused his death, either deliberately or accidentally, by his mere presence.

"They ought to be here by now," Gribble said, as soon as we were back in the lounge.

The minutes dragged. Kate had left instructions with Bates for the old man to wait up and let in Swinton and Ellery when they returned. The situation was not improved when after half an hour had crawled by old Bates came up to the flat and asked permission to go to bed. By that time I was convinced that something serious had happened, and recalling my earliest convictions that Swinton was a wrong 'un, I was beginning to think that it was no accident. That I had made a dreadful mistake.

"Let him go to bed, Kate," I advised, when she looked questioningly at me. "I'm not waiting for them to come any longer. I'm going after them."

"I don't like this," she said, when she had seen Bates into the lift. She looked very tired, but unlike many women when under a strain, she looked no older and the natural vitality that made her so attractive was unimpaired.

"This is going to give me the shivers," she went on, sinking back into an armchair. Her long healthy limbs were clearly outlined under her wrap. "Say something, Doc. What d'you think has happened?"

Gribble drew fiercely on what was possibly his thirtieth cigarette of the long night.

"I can only repeat, Kate—I don't trust Swinton. I never have. If anything untoward has happened it will be as a result of his planning. What are you going to do, Chadwick?" he asked, turning to me.

"First. Telephone. I want to know the exact location of Ward's house. May I use your 'phone, Kate?"

"Surely. You'll have to go downstairs. I've only a house 'phone up here. Bates will show you."

I found Bates, the office, and the telephone in quick order and dialled Slater's number. I let the instrument ring remorselessly until I had him out of bed.

"Cor stone the bleedin' crows!" I heard his protest. "You started a milk round or somethin'?"

"Listen, Del," I said, "things have gone wrong. I want the exact location of Ward's house, and I want it quickly."

"I said there was somethin' screwy about that set-up. . . ."

"You did," I admitted. "You certainly did, and I just as certainly ignored it. All right. That's agreed. Now where the hell is that house?"

He gave it me. I banged down the receiver and a minute later was back in Kate's lounge.

"Are you coming, Doc.? I'm off to Palmers Green."

"Isn't it a little like shutting the stable door after the horse has bolted?" he asked, easing himself out of his chair.

"A little, but if Swinton is playing some game of his own, what has happened to Ellery? I'd be prepared to believe the gallant captain capable of many things, but I don't believe he would rat on us. If Swinton is on the level then they may both be in a jam and need help. Hope we can find a cab easily. Wish to God I had my car here."

"Like to use mine?" Kate asked. "It's garaged in some mews round the block. I'll fetch the keys."

She went out and came back with her handbag from which she extracted the keys.

"Mayton Mews," she said, "along Priden Street. Garage is No. 4 and the car is a Sunbeam Talbot. Take it easily, John. I'm kinda fond of my little car. You'll let me know what's happening? Uncertainty is worse than knowing we're sunk."

"We're not sunk," I said. "Don't forget I know Swinton's hide-out on the coast. I'll return the car in the morning. And thanks a lot, Kate. Ready, Doc.?"

He had found his hat, and I picked up my own from a table where Kate had put it. She came down and saw us off.

Gribble shook hands with her at the doors of the club. He seemed reluctant to let go of her slim fingers.

"You've been a tremendous help . . . Kate," he said in his curiously resonant voice. "If there is anything I can do for you at any time . . . you'll let me know? Promise me that?"

"Why—that's real nice of you, Doc. Sure I'll let you know."

Mrs. Malone's voice sounded strangely soft and confused; the sort of voice that goes with a blush. The light was too bad for me to check on that.

"A splendid woman," Gribble said to me as we hurried along the length of Priden Street, "and very lovely, don't you think?"

"Swell," I agreed. "You could do a lot worse, Doc."

I expected him to make some snorting noise of derision. Instead he said gravely as though the idea was being treated on its merits and finding favour:

"Yes. I believe I could."

We had no bother in finding Kate's car and after I had been driving it for five minutes I could understand why she was fond of it. I drove it hard through the deserted streets, and it went like the wind.

The doctor, away from Kate and what must have been an expanding influence on him, relapsed into his taciturn self and said little or nothing during the journey.

Slater had given me implicit directions for finding Ward's house which was situated in a road known as Micheldene Avenue. Once off the main road I had to click on the head-lights, for the street lamps, save for those at the ends or corners of the network of residential roads, had been turned off at midnight.

It was galling to have to stop for the doctor to get out and decipher the names on the street boards, but we had to do it when it became evident that Slater had slipped up in his directions. There was nobody to ask about the way, and even if there had been I doubt if we would have taken advantage of the fact. Not knowing what we would find it might have been to our advantage not to advertise our destination.

We came upon Micheldene Avenue at last. Ward's house, which was about half-way down it, according to Slater, was called The Pines, and was numbered fifty-one.

I sent the car crawling along as quietly as possible and when I had gone far enough at a rough guess, stopped and switched off the motor. We got out and stood on the pavement.

The silence after the noise of our moving was staggering. There was no breeze. The long avenue, save for a lone gas lamp, a tiny circle of greenish yellow, at its far end, was in complete darkness. The big detached houses, square and solid bastions of respectability, looked cold and forbidding in the thin moonlight. The night air was pungent with the harsh smell of laurel growing in a thicket in the front garden of the house by which we had stopped. It was not the house we wanted, but we were able to decipher the number on the gate-post of its gravelled drive. It was forty-eight. This meant that Ward's was on the other side of the road. We crossed over, leaving the car where it was. Here the moon was behind the houses, and their fronts were featureless, dark blurrs against the lighter star-studded sky. It was odd to think that each of these houses, with the exception of Ward's, contained sleeping humans. The place so still and quiet. Even our cautious steps along the pavement clattered alarmingly.

Gribble spent some time trying to make out the number of the house we had crossed to, and decided finally that its number was not displayed. We moved along to the next one. Far away on a main road a late motor-cyclist opened his throttle with a ripple of distant sound. It was the only noise we had heard since we'd stopped.

"Forty-nine," the doctor observed, after stooping to peer closely at the next set of gateposts. "Damned if I know which way they run. It's either the one we've just passed, or the next."

It was the next, and from where we stood at the bottom

of the short gravel sweep to its front doors, as characterless as any of them.

"I'm going to have a look round, Doc. Don't know what I shall find. I don't know what I expect to find. Looks as though our friends have come and gone. Judging by the solid way in which the entire neighbourhood is sleeping they must have found it surprisingly easy."

"Then what has happened to them?" Gribble asked. "Do you realize that it took us barely twenty minutes to get here, even allowing for finding the place?"

"They came earlier when the traffic was still fairly heavy, and Swinton would have observed the thirty limit. I didn't. Still . . . they could have done the journey four times in the time."

"I suppose there is no doubt that this is Ward's house?" The doctor sounded tired and irritable. I felt much the same. Finding the house undisturbed, the neighbourhood wrapped in its usual respectable slumber, with no sight of Swinton's Humber parked anywhere about, was something of an anti-climax.

"If it is fifty-one Micheldene Avenue, Palmers Green, then it's Ward's," I returned. "Come on, Doc. Let's prowl round a bit."

We opened a big carriage gate, and crept through onto the gravel drive. This, like so many others in the road, was bordered by clumps of laurel, and after about ten yards gave way to a big square stretch of gravel in front of the house. We crossed this, then, with the doctor mounting guard, I climbed the three steps to the front door. Using my hand-kerchief as a shield against finger-prints I tried opening it. I couldn't move it a fraction of an inch. It might have been a door in the Bastille it was that solid.

I rejoined the doctor, and together we moved round the side of the house along a badly tiled path to the back regions. We could see better here for the late moon gave us light. There were a number of out-houses in the form of sheds, and a shaggy lawn straggling away towards a line of trees. Beyond these, presumably in the next road, someone had left on a bathroom light, and it was shining vividly in a bright yellow square.

The back door was locked. We tried some french windows and these too were locked.

"Doc.," I said, "I'm going home to bed. I can't guess at what has happened. Whether or not they've been and gone. Whether or not they failed to get as far. I'll find Swinton in the morning. But chasing our hunches round this place no longer appeals. Let's go."

"It's so damned late," he agreed.

We went back the way we had come, cutting straight along the edges of the square to the short drive. It was pitch black on this side of the house, and I heard rather than saw the doctor stumble awkwardly.

"Christ!" he swore viciously, for I think it frightened him momentarily. "What the . . . wait a minute, Chadwick!"

"What is it, Doc.?" I asked softly. Something had rattled him badly.

"Caught my foot," he hissed. "It felt for all the world like . . . By God! It is—a man's shoe, and leg. Chadwick, there's a body here!"

If he'd punched me on the jaw he couldn't have jolted me so effectively. I got over it in a moment though.

"We'll have to chance a light, Doc." I dragged out my matches. The burst of flame dazzled us for a moment till I shielded it clumsily, and the dancing flame gave us a sight of the ground. There was a body there all right. A long lean body in check-patterned tweeds, and I didn't need the sight of the thin greying hair or the long nose to identify it. We had found Ellery.

CHAPTER X

ELLERY was not dead, though he was not far from it, according to the doctor, unless something was done for him very quickly.

Gribble made his examination by the light of matches, and poor as the illumination was it was sufficient to reveal the fact that the captain had been hit hard on the head by the much publicized blunt instrument. This had been no scientific sapping such as Swinton had used to stun Ward but a blow struck with something akin to the butt of a gun. Ellery's skull had been crushed in, and the splintered bone was pressing on the brain. The man needed a hospital and the operating table to stand a chance of survival.

"I'll go and find a telephone, Doc."

"Do that. I'll stay with him. Wait a bit. Did I see a rug on the back seat of Kate's car?"

"There may be. I don't recall——"

"Fetch it, will you? It will help to keep him warm. He ought not to be lying here exposed for longer than absolutely necessary."

I crossed the road. There was a rug on the back seat and I took it back to him. He arranged it carefully round the unconscious man.

"This is going to be awkward, Doc.," I ventured, "particularly when Ward's body is found—as it will be sooner or later. Any ideas? I mean—we shall be asked what we are doing here. Ellery won't be able to speak—anyway."

The match I had struck to give him light burnt my fingers and I flipped it away. I sensed rather than saw the doctor get to his feet, then I felt his arm on mine.

"Get an ambulance first. They won't come unless they know the police have been informed so you'd better 'phone them as well. I'll think of something while you're gone. But I cannot leave this man. You needn't come back. Say that I stopped you passing, and asked you to 'phone. I shall say that I have friends in the neighbourhood and was passing when I heard him groan. . . ."

"Hell, Doc.! That won't hold water. What friends? Where were you going this time of night? There's no transport. . . ."

"I'll bluff them. After all, I'm a respectably registered doctor."

"No. No. It won't do. For Christ's sake think hard, Doc. Have you any friends in this part of the world? Even farther out of London?"

"You must get that ambulance, Chadwick. I'll think up something."

He sounded adamant. I knew that I would have to return after telephoning. The police would be asking searching questions needing smooth answers, and the doctor was not the one to provide them. He was an honest man caught up in the intricacies of a plot he didn't understand. There was a hell of a lot I didn't understand myself; in particular—where was Swinton? Until I understood a great deal more I was not prepared to come into the open with the truth about Ward. I thought that under pressure the doctor would adopt an attitude of tell and be damned. He was inclined to assume—as the unfortunate Ellery had been the first to note—that his profession of doctor, except where his own unprofessional conduct had been concerned, made him rather a superior person who should not be bothered with the troubles that beset lesser mortals. I reckoned that the average detective-constable would suspect the worst within five minutes of questioning Gribble.

These thoughts danced through my mind as I crossed to Kate's car, and drove off in search of a telephone box. I found one at the end of the road.

The telephoning was amazingly simple. I dialled 999 and asked for an ambulance. As the doctor had forecast they wanted to know if the police had been informed, and I said Yes, got back to the exchange, and spoke to the local police. They asked the usual questions, chiefly personal, and then came round to the injured man. On the strength that half a truth is better than none I told them his name and how and where we had found him, that I'd had a doctor friend with me who was doing what he could for the man till an ambulance got there. This seemed to reassure them, and I had time to think that there was something to be said for Gribble's exalted opinion of his profession after all. The police said they'd be round to 51 Micheldene Avenue within a short time and that they expected me to be there. I rang off. On an impulse I shovelled in three pennies and dialled Kate's number. Bates answered, and I told him to fetch Mrs. Malone just as quickly as he knew how. I needn't have bothered for she came on the line within seconds. She must have been sitting up waiting for a ring.

I told her what happened and cut short her cries of woe.

"Listen, Kate. I've told the police we know Ellery. They would have guessed that anyway, because under no circumstances could he have been found by two strangers passing down the road in a car—and it's your car, Kate, and that let's you in because they'll check on the number. I'm going to tell them we got drinking with Ellery in your club. You, the doctor and I are close friends—you've known us a long time. Pass that on to Bates in case they question him. Ellery you've known by name only. You met him elsewhere and asked him to drop in sometime. Now listen to this, Kate. I've got a sister-in-law who lives in Hertford, and I'm going to say that we left your place round about half ten this evening after borrowing your car in order to call in on her. She's an actress and is never home till late, anyway. I hope to Heaven I can get her to play ball with us. I think I can. She's a good sport. But here's the point. Ellery asked us to drop him off in Palmers Green at Ward's address. We don't know why. He simply said he had business there. He also asked us to pick him up on our way back however late we were, because he expected his business there to keep him late. That's all we know about him. . . ."

"Sounds—plausible," Kate said.

"Plausible!" I cried. "It's as flimsy as tissue paper and it's horrible. But it's all I can think of. Now I must go. I'll ring you later."

There was no sign of the ambulance or the police when I got back to Ward's house. The whole neighbourhood was as tightly wrapped in sleep as when we had arrived. In a vague way I resented this because my own mind was in a tumult and it seemed impossible that the whole dark avenue of big brooding houses should be so implacably undisturbed. Actually, apart from the car, we had made no noise, and Ward's immediate neighbours were probably used to him receiving visitors at odd hours.

The glow of a cigarette guided me towards Gribble, who appeared to be squatting on his haunches beside Ellery.

"Are they coming?" he asked. "You seem to have been a long time though I dare say you've been quick. God! I'm tired, Chadwick."

"Me too. But we're not finished yet, Doc. I've thought up a yarn, and I've told it to Kate. All I hope is that the night telephone operator, after being thoroughly awakened by my 999 call, didn't relieve the tedium by listening in on my subsequent call to Kate." I told him the yarn I had thought up.

"I can go one better than that," he commented. "My young brother lives in Bedford. It is a fact that every now and again I treat him for ligament trouble in his knee." He thought for a moment. "I like the idea of saying that Ellery asked us for a lift to this place, and also asked us to pick him up on the way back. It accounts for our presence here. Suppose we stick to your yarn about the three of us being in Kate's club? Would it not ring more truthfully to say that a telephone call from my brother was relayed to me there asking me to run out to Bedford to fix his knee, because he has an important job on tomorrow that cannot be delayed? It will account for the lateness of our starting from Kate's. We can say that they were some time learning that I was spending the evening in the Can Can Club."

"Go on, Doc.," I prompted. "I like it so far."

"The rest, I think, can tally with yours. Kate offered her car. You came along for the sake of companionship. Ellery begged a lift."

"Can you fix your brother to tell the same tale?"

"Easily." Gribble laughed mirthlessly. "He owes me the benefit of a few lies for getting me into this infernal mess. I'll telephone him just as soon as I get the chance. You'll remember to correct your story with Kate?"

"You bet. I think it will work, Doc. At least long enough to get after Swinton."

"Ah! Swinton," he repeated. "I think Swinton——"

But whatever it was the doctor had to say about that gentleman had to be postponed for a car, driven at speed, came tearing into Micheldene Avenue. A spotlight sprayed the houses with its beam. I went out into the road, and the police patrol car screamed to a stop on my signal.

"Are you the chap who 'phoned?" they demanded. Doors slammed as they got out. "What's been happening here?"

"I'll tell you. What about the ambulance?"

"On its way. We passed it a mile back. Where's the injured man?"

I led the way into the garden and introduced the doctor.

"Anyone at home?" The sergeant in charge had produced a handlamp, and flashed it over the front of the house.

"Apparently not. We knocked, because we expected to pick him up to give him a lift to the West End. Walking back to the car the doctor here stumbled across his leg. We've not moved him."

The sergeant played his light over Ellery's recumbent form, then stooped to examine his head, without however touching him.

"What hit him, Doctor?"

"Something heavy and reasonably sharp."

"Butt of a gun?"

"It could have been."

Further speculation on this interesting subject was cut short by the arrival of the ambulance, and the speedy removal of Ellery.

"Now, gentlemen," the sergeant said, hooking his lamp on to his tunic and producing a notebook, "I'll take your statements if you please. Doctor?"

Gribble spun the yarn quite smoothly. I simply corroborated all he had said.

"Have you any idea of the name of the party on whom this man Ellery proposed to call?"

"No," I put in quickly, though the sergeant had asked the question of the doctor. "He never mentioned it. Nor his business. I got the idea, somehow, that his call was not by appointment."

"How d'you get that idea?"

"Well, he asked us to pick him up on the way back. We said that we were bound to be very late, and he said something about that being the reason for asking. I got the idea that he intended to camp on the doorstep here till the owner showed up, and that he didn't expect him till late."

"Was that your opinion, Doctor?"

"Yes. I remember that the house was in darkness when we dropped him off."

"Do you usually go out of your way to oblige a stranger?"

"He wasn't exactly a stranger, Sergeant. We'd met him earlier in the evening. He seemed a pleasant enough type, and a gentleman. Nor," Gribble added with emphasis, "were we going far out of our way. No farther than from here to the main road."

The sergeant seemed to realize the sense of that. He asked us a number of additional questions which were mere elaborations of those that had gone before. Finally, after warning us that we must expect further questioning from the police, he let us go. The doctor picked up Kate's rug and we made for the car. As we drove off I noticed that the police were already marching up to the front door of one of Ward's neighbours. I would have cheerfully bet them a fiver they'd learn little of Edward Ward from them.

We were half-way back to the West End before I deemed it safe to stop at a telephone box.

Gribble by this time was either sunk deep in gloomy thought or was half asleep.

"Come on, Doc.," I roused him. "You've some telephoning to do."

"Now?" he demanded.

"Definitely. We've burnt our boats with that yarn to the law. It's our story and we're going to stick to it. Your brother must be dragged from his bed and warned. I want to get after Swinton just as soon as I can. If, when the Bedford police call upon your young brother, he asks them what the hell they are talking about, I shall not be able to get after Swinton because I shall be in a cell—and so will you. Rouse him, Doctor, and if you've no small change reverse the charges."

It was a slow business. The junior Gribble was apparently a heavy sleeper to whom a telephone bell ringing in the small hours, if he heard it at all, was a fair subject for cursing and nothing more. The doctor despaired of ever getting him. I think he was so tired himself he was feeling dangerously sympathetic. When he assured me that the chances of his brother sleeping away from his own flat in Bedford were extremely slender I kept him and an obliging operator at the continual ringing, and finally his brother answered.

Gribble was pretty sharp with him, pointed out exactly the consequences of his failing to support our story and even instructed him exactly what to put on his knee.

After that contacting Kate was a comparatively simple business. I told her little beyond the correction in our story, said that I would return the car in the morning and rang off.

By that time we were both so tired we could have slept in the car where it was. Apart from our physical efforts earlier in the evening the more recent mental efforts required in thinking up a story that would pass muster, and making certain that we missed none of its implications, had proved equally as exhausting.

I dropped the doctor off at his house in Maida Vale, drove round to the flat, put Kate's car away in our own garage and fairly staggered up to bed. I reckoned with luck that I would get possibly three hours' sleep. When I would get the next and where was problematical.

The family alarum clock was at Selsey with Freda so I had to ask·the exchange to call me. This they did, and it seemed barely five minutes after my head had hit the pillow that they were doing so.

I got up, not without effort, set the percolator going, had a cold bath and a shave, made the coffee with tinned milk, drank three cups and felt reasonably fit.

It is amazing what sleep will do for the brain. Before going to bed I had been incapable of thinking properly on what had happened to Ellery, and why. Maybe I had been too busy concocting a story that would keep the doctor and me temporarily clear of trouble. The fact remains that as I started rummaging through the cupboards seeking more tins for breakfast I saw quite clearly what had happened to Ellery. Swinton had hit him. Whether it was before he had let himself into Ward's house, or immediately afterwards, was really beside the point. It had probably been afterwards because Ward's safe, though it had yielded something entirely rewarding from Swinton's point of view, had contained nothing of the slightest use to Ellery or any other blackmail victim.

I

I thought I was beginning to see daylight. It seemed to me that Swinton, whether or not he was a blackmail victim, had been engaged in a private vendetta against Ward. The very size of the man had precluded him from handling him by himself. Somehow he had obtained a list of Ward's victims and hit upon the idea of hoodwinking them into helping him. He had admitted that to have paid some hired bullies to do the job would have been laying himself open to further trouble.

"Wait a bit, Chadwick," I told myself. "Swinton's name was in that little black book he produced. He must have been a fellow victim for all the names were in the same handwriting, though he could have written them into the book himself. Maybe he did. He took care to disguise his hand when he sent out the invitations to meet in a Chelsea pub!"

I thought at first that I had something in that idea. Then I realized that Swinton's business address had been in the book—an address which tallied with the one Patey had dug out. If Swinton had set out deliberately to make himself appear a fellow victim he would have put in some fictitious address and certainly not his business one. What the hell was the man playing at? Was it conceivable that he had murdered Ward? I sweated at the thought of it. The idea of a murderer getting me, even unwittingly, to assist in the disposal of his victim's body, put a queasy feeling in my stomach. Sooner or later I would have to confess to my part of pallbearer. It was going to be bad enough if Ward had died of natural causes. If he'd been murdered . . .

I made some toast and opened a tin of beans. Needless to say they were not particularly appetizing, hungry as I was.

When I had finished I got through to Selsey on the telephone. Mrs. Mulraney answered the call with a strident "'Allo!" that strained the capacity of the instrument. She told me to hold on, which I did. I heard her clumping her way to the bottom of the stairs, and her shriek of "Mrs. Chadwick!" Somewhere in the background dear old Montmorency had found something to bark at. The cheerful normality of it all tugged at my heartstrings, and when Freda came on with "Darling, I've missed you!" I could have wept with the cussedness of it. Damn and blast my infernal nosey-parkering!

All I looked like getting out of it was a charge of accessary after the fact.

We chatted about this and that for a bit and then I said: "Is Swinton at home? He would have arrived back in the early hours. It's vitally important, darling. Can you make certain? Knock on his front door if necessary. Send Mrs. Mulraney. She'll make enough noise to rouse him."

It was early in the day to be making neighbourly calls, but Freda managed it. Swinton was not at home, nor was his car in the garage.

"He wasn't home Monday evening," Freda said, "nor yesterday—Tuesday morning. His girl friend Helen Arnett has not been around lately either. Maybe he's run off with her."

"I don't think so, darling," I said with a smile.

I arranged for Freda to telephone the office and leave a message with the private exchange in the block should I not be there. She would telephone as soon as Swinton showed up.

I dumped the remains of my breakfast in the kitchen sink —Freda's domestic help had condescended to look in now and again whilst we were away at Selsey and the sight of dirty plates in a supposedly empty house would probably give her hysterics—but I had no time to worry on her account.

I got Kate's car out of the garage, drove it to Priden Street, and put it away in the Mews. Then I walked along to the Can Can Club. Old Bates answered my ringing after I had done so much of it my thumb had grown sore. I wasn't very popular with him or his mistress, who was still in bed when I stepped out of the lift into the hall of her flat.

"Lawd's sakes!" she called out after I had announced myself by banging on her bedroom door. "What is it, John? The police?"

"Not yet," I said. "But any minute now. I must talk to you, Kate."

"Well . . . make yourself useful while I get up. Go and put the kettle on."

I went along to her tiny kitchen and plugged in the electric kettle. It boiled pretty quickly. I'd found the teapot and had the stuff brewing by the time Kate came along. She may have been short of sleep but she didn't look it. She was as cool and as fresh as dew. A plain summer frock revealing the soft roundness of her arms—Kate had really beautiful limbs—and her hair hastily brushed instead of set took about ten years off her age.

"My!" I exclaimed. "Sweet and twenty this morning. If only Doc. Gribble could see you now!"

"Oh, don't talk rot, John!" But there was only a half smile on her face, and her big brown eyes were serious. "What do you think of the doc.?" she asked me.

"The doc.'s all right," I said. "He rallied round last night and lied like a veteran. I like him. He's one of those men who grow on you. None of this mess he is in is on his own account, Kate. Did you know that? Getting his younger brother out of a jam put him into it."

"I was afraid you'd like him," she sighed.

"Afraid?" I queried. "What d'you mean?"

"I trust your judgment that's all. The doc.'s a nice man under his forbidding exterior. I don't want him getting goofy about me. I'm a divorced woman."

"Aw. Come off it, Kate! How can he help it? If I wasn't married to the nicest girl in the world I'd be chasing you myself. Besides, d'you think for a moment that sort of thing would weigh with the doc.? Not on your life. I'll tell you what, Kate. You rather like the doctor yourself and it's shaken you a bit. You thought you'd got over that sort of thing. . . ."

Kate thrust a cup of tea into my hand.

"Drink that, and shut up!" she said. "At least, keep your private detecting for Swinton. You'll need all your imagined powers of deduction to find him, I guess."

"I might at that," I agreed, and took a sip of the scalding tea. "I think it was he who slugged Ellery," I went on. "I'm beginning to get ideas about Swinton, Kate. Ideas that I've come back to because I thought he was a wrong 'un the first time I set eyes on him. Subsequent events sidetracked me but now . . . He's had us for a gang of suckers. I'm not certain of the exact set-up but the basic fact is plain. He wanted help to deal with Ward so that he could get into his house and open his safe. He dared not employ some professional thugs in case they in turn put the screw on him. He dared not waylay Ward by himself, knock him out and pinch his keys, leaving Ward unconscious. The chances were that Ward might have been found, and the police calling at his house before Swinton could get there. You must remember that Swinton, big as he is, could not have even dragged a man of Ward's weight as far as the nearest bushes in order to conceal the body. He had to have help, and he hit on the idea of calling all Ward's victims together in order to get it. I'm certain that he never had the slightest intention of helping anybody but himself. He got what he wanted from Ward's safe, and when Ellery went for him because there was nothing else in the safe of the slightest use to the remaining victims Swinton slugged him and drove off."

"Nice feller," Kate commented bitterly.

"I'll find him though," I said. "He probably imagines himself to be perfectly safe in his hide-out at Selsey. He's got an awful shock coming to him when he discovers that I'm his neighbour. Freda—my wife—will telephone me as soon as he arrives home."

"Is that going to help us any?" Kate asked. "Aren't we back where we started? If there was nothing in Ward's safe . . . Say, John!" she went on, dismay in her voice, "we can't be sure now that Ward was our blackmailer. Not if Swinton was using us to work off some private feud with the guy. Come to think of it Ward didn't act like a blackmailer. He didn't know any one of us. He must have known Swinton pretty badly to be frightened into a heart attack. . . ."

"And Swinton took care to keep out of his sight till he was snugged down behind a bolted door," I put in. "But Swinton knows a hell of a lot about the blackmailing, Kate. He must do. How else could he have obtained a list of victims? He was listed as one. That was his business address in the little black book. I'd found that out before I went to the meeting."

"Then maybe he's keeping the evidence on us to make certain that we play ball over Ward's death, eh? Maybe that's his game."

"Maybe. If it is it suggests that Ward's death was no accident. The doc. himself was not happy about it. He says

there are poisons that can produce all the outward effects of
heart failure."

Kate dropped her cup back into its saucer with a nervous
crash.

"For crying out loud!" she wailed, "this gets worse and
worse. Murder! You'd better do something, John. And do it
quick. I wasn't too happy thinking of the police coming here
asking questions about Ellery. . . ."

"You needn't worry on that score," I soothed her. "Stick
to our story. You met Ellery in a Chelsea pub the other
night. . . . That's perfectly true, isn't it?" I went through the
story again with her. "The police will take your statement.
Later on they'll probably send round a typed copy for you to
sign, and that will be all. Ellery won't die. The doc. said last
night that if it had been a killing blow he would have died
before we found him. He has some bone pressing on his
brain which they'll remedy on the operating table, and he'll
recover."

"What about Ward?" she demanded, refusing to be
mollified. "There'll be loads of publicity when he's found.
That damned Helen Rice will guess something happened to
him. She'll be snooping round again. Somebody may have
noticed him on the fire escape. . . ."

"Now don't go imagining things, Kate," I pleaded.
"Nobody but Bates knows of his arrival here, and I warned
Bates to say that he had never seen him."

"Did you ever get a line on that girl?"

"Helen Rice? No. One of her fellow boarders is reputed to
have seen her at the seaside somewhere. I don't know where.
The boarder was not available for questioning."

I made a mental note to repeat that inquiry. What was the
fellow boarder's name—the assistant to the magician? Miss
Delooze. That was it. Be as well to get tracks on Ward's
female accomplice whatever the outcome of events.

I finished my tea, handed Kate her keys, told her to keep
her pecker up, and left. She came downstairs with me, and as
we were passing the office heard her telephone ring. I said a
hasty "So long!" as she turned into the office. I'd made a
quick bet with myself about that telephone ringing and so I

lingered. I heard her lift the receiver and then coo: "Why, Doc.! This is nice. Sure I'm up! John Chadwick came back with the car. . . ."

I hurried out, having won my bet.

The use of Kate's car the previous night had brought home forcibly how essential it was when things really started happening to have transport on hand. I'd always had a car of my own, a sporty Midget, till the continued use of Freda's opulent saloon coinciding with the slow disintegration of the M.G. through sheer age had induced me to sell it, and not replace it. Now, with Freda miles away, I needed a car.

I recalled a car-hire firm with whom I had done business in the past, and took a cab to their premises in Mayfair. The holiday season is not the best time to hire a drive-yourself car at a moment's notice, but on this occasion I was lucky. I came out at the wheel of a nearly new Zephyr, and drove it round to the office.

Here I fully expected to find Freda's message awaiting me but nothing had come in.

I began to champ a bit. I needed quick action because before long my position would become intolerable. The police would have learnt very quickly that the house outside which Ellery had been found belonged to Ward, and they would be looking for him, and it was unlikely that he would be found easily. Whilst I imagined—perhaps wrongly—that I might be excused a little subterfuge in the interest of my client, or as I now had to admit, my several clients, I had no possible excuse for keeping close lipped concerning Ward's death and the disposal of his body. Once the hunt for him was properly on then I would have to tell. But if there was a chance of catching Swinton and making him talk, then I thought I ought to take it, for it was just possible that the doctor and Kate, and Pendleton and Miss Piper, might be kept out of the exposure they feared.

I picked up the 'phone again and asked the girl if any message had come in. She seemed surprised that I had not gone out. Although nothing had been heard of Selsey she said that a Mr. Pendleton had 'phoned and been told that I was out. He was going to ring later.

I hadn't the slightest desire to speak to Pendleton though I was not surprised that he had rung.

"I really am going out this time," I told the girl. "It's the Selsey message I want. I'll be asking you again as soon as I come in if I don't ring you from outside."

I had no real desire to go out, but two things were driving me to it. The idea of making lengthy explanations to Pendleton at this stage set my teeth on edge, and the prospect of telling more lies to the police to whom I had given my office address the previous night was even more distasteful. I would have to keep moving. Then I thought: "Why not call at Swinton's place of business? It would be just like him to be sitting enthroned in his managing director's chair carrying on as though nothing had happened." If he was in, which I very much doubted would be the case, he would have some plausible explanation for the whole thing, and by some alchemy of his own contrive to shift the blame onto Ellery. That is, if he still thought I was Pendleton, but on this occasion he was going to deal with Chadwick.

It took me some time to get to the Goswell Road through the thick of the early morning traffic, and by the time I had identified Rabal Products Ltd. as being housed in a magnificent post-war building of gleaming white stone I had come to the conclusion that the whole project was a complete waste of effort. I parked the car in a nearby lot, walked back to the building and took a lift to the third floor where Rabal Products Ltd. had offices of a splendour rarely seen outside of a film.

A young lady receptionist of undeniable charm, and a painted freshness that matched the building's, asked me my business. I said that I needed badly to see Mr. George Swinton, that I had no appointment, but if she would be good enough to take in my card I thought he would dispense with that formality. I handed over my card which said "John Chadwick, Private Inquiry Agent" fully expecting her to state immediately that Mr. Swinton was not there.

She said instead, "Will you take a seat?" and indicated an armchair of such sumptuous depth that once in it I doubted my ability ever to get out of it. Her high heels took the girl away down the long corridor and I watched her go. Her hips had quite a fascinating sway.

I fingered some magazines on a mahogany table while the bustle that was Rabal Products Ltd. in action went on behind the tall glass screens that surrounded the reception area.

The girl came back She was only slightly apologetic.

"Mr. Swinton can spare you a few minutes only, Mr. Chadwick. He has an appointment soon."

"That's fine," I said. "That's dandy. A few minutes is all I need." I meant it. After the sculduggery of the previous night, in which Swinton had played the major part, it riled me to find him next morning blandly carrying on business, happily oblivious to the distress and fears he had caused others.

As I followed the girl down the corridor I was mentally bracing myself. Swinton was going to get the edge of my tongue. Swinton was going to talk and talk fast. If he didn't . . . I'd not lost my temper in a long time, but this morning it would need very little of Mr. George Swinton for me to lose it entirely. The damned brazen effrontery of the man! Or had I been badly mistaken in presuming that it had been he who had slugged Ellery?

I felt sure that I would find him inhabiting the most sumptuous office in this most sumptuous building. I hoped that he would not endeavour to bluff me, or put over the big business man's act, for I was not in the mood. It would be a pity to lose control, give him the slug on the jaw he deserved, thereafter to be summarily ejected from this palace of industry.

It *was* a nice office. My guide closed the heavy mahogany door behind me, said, "Mr. John Chadwick" in disapproving tones, and took herself away through another door. I glanced across a miniature sea of red carpet towards a handsome flat-topped desk set across one corner of the room. Sitting at the desk was a little bald-headed man. He was wearing rimless glasses that flashed in the morning light from the tall windows.

"Some mistake!" I snapped. "I was to see Mr. George Swinton."

The little man took off his glasses, and wiped the lenses with a snowy handkerchief he plucked from a breast pocket.

"I am Mr. George Swinton," he said, importantly.

CHAPTER XI

IT WAS possible, though I've always flattered myself that I can keep my emotions from mirroring themselves in my face, that I was so dumbfounded I looked momentarily weak. At any rate the little man said rather hastily, "Won't you sit down?" He didn't press the point when I did nothing except stand where I was while the implications behind the discovery I had made raced through my mind.

"Let me see," the little man picked up my card, hooked his spectacles into place with a practised gesture, and read it, I suspected, for the first time. "Private Inquiry Agent?" he said, his voice rising. "I can conceive of no situation in our business that calls for the services of a private detective."

By this time my wits had sorted themselves out and I was catching up on them.

"No?" I echoed. "How about the private affairs of the managing director, Mr. George Swinton?"

"Still less," he said, but his eyes, magnified by the lenses, were as nervous as a rabbit's. He looked too as though at any moment he would emulate that animal by turning to bolt for a hole.

"Why are you here?" he demanded.

"Primarily because a man I am seeking has been using your name and business address." He appeared to be on the verge of making another false denial, so I said quickly: "I think you'd better hear me out, Mr. Swinton. A few days back a man using your name convened a meeting of people, strangers to each other but with one thing in common—they were all victims of the same blackmailer. He claimed that the purpose of the meeting was to get help from his fellow victims to put in action a plan he had made for taking this blackmailer by force, and making him see the error of his ways. This man had a near plausible explanation of his possessing a little black book in which were recorded the names and addresses of the blackmailer's victims. Yours, which he said was his, was amongst them. The suggestion fell on fertile ground because none of the victims had ever met the blackmailer, whom they had known only by the name he had used—Bilter. The evidence of their indiscretions had been obtained, almost probably in each case, by a female accomplice. I won't weary you with the details of the plan or how, from the point of view of the other victims, it miscarried, but it seems probable now that it was nothing but a successful attempt on the part of the man using your name to hi-jack the business. You can guess what that will mean. Do you still maintain that you are not being blackmailed?"

During my recital beads of perspiration had appeared on his domed forehead. He proceeded to dab these away using the same handkerchief he had previously used on his spectacles. In business when up against a difficulty delaying tactics must have been second nature with him and they rallied to him now.

"Really . . . this is all very disconcerting . . . I must have time——"

"There is no time," I cut in brutally. "The damage has been done." He winced at that, and I went on: "If it's any help to you, I'll tell you how I came into it." I did so, but it failed to make him look any better. If anything he had now paled perceptibly, probably because he had not listened to a word of my last peroration, and instead had been turning over in his mind the possible consequences of the blackmailing business changing ownership, and finding them bad.

"I'm out to help," I told him. "I've met some of the victims and they're normally decent honest folk paying an entirely disproportionate price for some stupid moral lapse or other. They don't want their dirty linen flaunted for all to see. If I can get my hands on this pseudo George Swinton I may be able to stop it, but it's got to be soon. During a mix-up one man was badly hurt, and the police are now active. If it suits their purpose not to do so they won't study the feelings of a blackmailer's victims."

"No. No. Of course not." He picked up my card again as

though he had come to some decision. "I feel I must trust you, Mr. Chadwick. Normally . . . a delicate matter such as this . . . I should require references. But much of what you have said . . . I feel sure that you will use discretion. Yes. I am being blackmailed," he finished with a rush, "by a man calling himself Bilter. But is the knowledge of any help to you?"

I found it difficult to believe that this diffident, stammering and perspiring little man could be the controller of such a prosperous-looking business as Rabal Products Ltd. In the mood I was in I almost said as much.

"Isn't it obvious, Mr. Swinton," I asked with asperity, "that if the man who chose to take your name in order to represent himself as a victim did so deliberately, then he took your identity with a purpose? Having done so he could not ask you to the meeting. Perhaps he chose your identity because he didn't want you at the meeting. In other words you might have recognized him." I described the pseudo Swinton to him with as much detail as I could muster but he shook his head.

"I meet many men who might answer to that description in business," he said, "but none of them fit the description exactly, and in my private life I can think of no acquaintance who resembles it even vaguely."

"Can you think of any other reason why this man should choose to avoid you, or perhaps have no wish for you to meet your fellow victims?"

"I . . . I don't think so. There is one point, however, in respect of which I feel sure I must differ from the . . . er . . . others."

He paused, and looked even more embarrassed and flustered than before.

"Go on please, Mr. Swinton," I urged.

"You mentioned earlier a female accomplice."

"That's so. She has been used by the blackmailer to get the evidence on his victims. The same applied in your case presumably?"

"Not exactly." He allowed a ghost of a smile to twitch the corners of his mouth. "Please don't think that they hold over me documentary evidence of some crime or other. Nothing of the sort. As a matter of fact I doubt if their threat, put into practice, would have the effect they imagine. There is, of course, a faint chance, and since it would mean my being cut out of a will involving something like a hundred and fifty thousand pounds I prefer to pay rather than take the slightest chance."

Recalling Patey's miniature biography on the real George Swinton I supposed him to be referring to his aunt, the Toffee Queen. I couldn't blame him there, but he was getting away from the point.

"You were speaking of the girl," I pointed out.

"*I* was?" he asked. "It was you who mentioned her. But I do know all about her, Mr. Chadwick, and I suppose in all our interests I should tell you—though the subject is one I normally avoid at all costs. I want your solemn assurance that anything I tell you will go no farther than your own ears."

I was about to give him this when there came a perfunctory knock on the door and the girl receptionist came in.

"Mr. Midwinter is here, Mr. Swinton," she piped, in faintly reproaching tones.

"Then Mr. Midwinter must wait!" the little man barked immediately, thereby assuring me that in matters relating to Rabal Products Ltd. he was a vastly different individual from the one I had imagined. When the girl had gone I said:

"What I hear about you, personally, will be kept to myself. But, naturally, I must tell others that you have been impersonated."

"Good! Er—I do wish you'd sit down," he burst out, petulantly. "You're rather tall, and I do so hate peering up at people."

All this I fancied was to delay the fatal moment when he would have to tell me something that he would have much sooner forgotten, so I humoured him by taking the padded chair by the side of his desk.

"That's better. Smoke?" He pushed a silver box of giant Perfectos towards me. I helped myself and we each lit up.

"Well now—this girl. I may as well get it off my chest. She's my daughter. My . . . er—bastard daughter."

"Indeed?" I said. It was a mild comment considering the information burst in my intelligence with all the shock produced by a fair-sized bomb. But I was getting used to shocks, and the commotion quickly subsided leaving the mildly exhilarating thought that at last I was to learn the truth about the girl, who all along I had considered might be the key to this business.

"A long, long time ago, Mr. Chadwick," he resumed, "I was associated intimately with a woman who in due course had a child of which I was the father." He made a deprecating gesture with his hands. "I was young—not then twenty-one. I won't bore you with the details. The woman was not—what shall I say? . . . Tremendous importance was placed on such things in those days—she was not my class. My parents arranged the whole thing discreetly through their solicitors and I paid a paternity order on the child until she was sixteen. That was that. I'd never even seen the child."

He paused. With the embarrassing part done he could afford to look more comfortable.

"About three years ago," he went on, "a girl came to work at this office. She was not specially employed—the female staff are always coming and going. She was just one of many. I have nothing to do with the staff, anyway, but in this instance I did notice this particular new girl because she bore an uncanny resemblance to her mother at that age. I inquired her name, but it meant nothing to me because it was not her real name, and I immediately lost interest, putting it down to coincidence.

"The girl was bright and worked well. After a few months she was given a certain amount of confidential work to do—work which would have entailed her learning a good bit about the directors and myself. She probably did a good deal of prying on her own account. We are closely associated with Radleys the toffee people. I am on the board, and my aunt, from whom I hope to inherit, owns a controlling interest in Radleys' stock. It would not have been difficult for the girl to have learnt all this.

"She left us quite abruptly. It meant nothing to me at the time, but about a week or two later I received a letter purporting to come from a man named Bilter demanding money. Unless it was paid the full details of my bastard daughter were to be sent to my aunt." Again he spread out his fingers. "Well—the demand was not great. My aunt is very aged, and whatever her reactions regarding her will the information would have undoubtedly caused the old lady great distress, and so I paid. It was no bluff. I had undoubtedly been employing my own daughter in my own office."

He stopped and waited for my comments. I let him wait for a moment or two. He was a smooth old hypocrite if ever there was one. I liked the part about causing the old lady great distress. The old girl was worth about a quarter of a million and that was all there was to it. His story was as sordid as Pendleton's. Come to think of it Sex played a magnificent part behind the scenes in the greater part of this business, but then so it does behind most blackmail efforts. They always stink.

"What is the girl's name?" I asked him.

"She was registered in her mother's name of Ward. She is Helen Ward. Her mother was Phyllis Ward."

"Ward, eh?" I repeated. "I'm beginning to see daylight. The blackmailer for whom we set the trap was named Edward Ward. Do you know him?"

"I think perhaps he is the girl's uncle. I remember her mother had a brother who was a bad lot. He'd been to prison at an early age. I cannot recall his Christian name. He was younger than his sister. A fat and repulsive youth."

"That'll be him," I said, and got to my feet, crushing out the remains of the Perfecto in a glass ash-tray the size of a fruit dish as I did so. "I'll keep you posted, Mr. Swinton. If it comes to a showdown I shall do my utmost to keep your name out of it."

"Er . . . thank you. I need hardly mention that . . . er . . . any success you achieve in that direction will be amply rewarded, but . . . of course . . . I shall expect you to use absolute discretion."

For a moment I toyed with the idea of telling him exactly what to do with his ample reward, then I reflected that Money was a God for him and millions like him and left it unsaid. We shook hands solemnly, and I departed.

On the way out I passed a thin hatchet-faced gentleman

struggling out of the armchair with the pretty receptionist hovering by. He scowled at me. I said, "All yours, Mr. Midwinter," and went out of the building.

I drove the Zephyr back to the office block, and passed hurriedly to turn into a side street farther down the road. No one is allowed to park outside the office for longer than it takes to purchase a packet of cigarettes at the tobacconist's on the ground floor, but it was not this that made me drive past. Parked squarely beside the entrance to the block was a big blue squad car, and it needed no guess on my part to know that its occupants were at that moment knocking on the locked door of my office.

I drew in to the kerb and sat for a while, fingers tapping on the steering wheel, while I thought things over. When questioned the previous night I had made a point of not telling the sergeant that I was a Private Inquiry Agent. The knowledge would have only made him suspicious, and caused an even longer delay before the doctor and I were allowed to leave. But that knowledge, once the police had called at my office, was now theirs, and if, as I had strongly suspected all along, Ward had a police record they were bound to assume that my discovery of a slugged Captain Ellery outside Ward's house in the small hours was tied up with my Private Inquiry work. In addition Detective-Sergeant Williams knew that I had been looking for a blackmailer. There was no guarantee that Headquarters were engaged in the matter as yet save for a routine request for records, but it would surely not be long before they were.

I felt pretty miserable about the whole thing. I loathed the idea of obstructing the police, but once I told them the truth my chances of doing anything for the doctor and Kate and the rest of the victims were as good as gone. I had to get to Swinton (I kept thinking of him as that though of course he was not Swinton at all) before the police found him if I was to have any sort of chance at all. I decided to compromise. If I kept on the move, which I was at perfect liberty to do, then it might be some time before they looked for me in earnest, and it would heighten the impression that my relationship with the Ellery affair was entirely accidental.

So I moved on, but not very far, for I stopped at the first public telephone box I came to and put in a call to the office exchange. No call had come in from Selsey. I think the girl wanted to tell me that the police were there, but I slammed the receiver down before she could say any more.

I moved on again, and taking a chance that the police had already called on Kate, I drove round to Priden Street. Old Bates let me in.

"What 'ave you been up to?" he wanted to know. "Place 'as been full of bleedin' bluebottles—askin' questions."

"They ask you any?" I said sharply.

"Me? No. Not likely! They know an old soldier when they see one. Waste of time, son. I mind me own business. That's all I ever tell 'em."

"Just as well. Mrs. Malone in?"

"She is. Know yer way, don't yer?"

I took the lift up to Kate's flat, and was only mildly surprised to find Gribble there. He had not as yet acquired a proprietary air but he looked considerably more at home than he had done the previous evening.

"Hallo, Doc.," I greeted him. "No patients this morning?"

"A few at surgery. A few more to be seen on my round. Fortunately there is nothing serious amongst the lot of them. I've made inquiries concerning Ellery."

"How is he?"

"Fair. They operated early this morning—quite successfully. His general condition is not too good. That's not surprising. He must have been lying there for an hour or two before we found him."

"How long before he is able to talk?"

Gribble spread out his hands.

"Say, rather—before they allow him to talk. I would insist upon at least twenty-four hours, but if the police are adamant . . ."

"I see what you mean. If Ward's body is found they'll have a bobby by the bedside shaking his shoulder. If not they'll bide by the doctor's ruling. I reckon I'll get a few hours' grace at least."

The doc.'s formidable eyebrows came down in a frown.

K

"How do you mean?"

I sank myself into one of Kate's chairs and then had to hoist myself out again as she came in.

"Hallo, John. The cops have been. Did Tony tell you?"

Tony, I thought. No wonder the doc. looked comfortable.

"He was telling me about Ellery. Bates obliged with the news concerning the cops. How did it go?"

"Pretty well, I'd say. I made a statement after a lot of questions, and then I signed what they'd written down."

"They interrupted me at surgery," Gribble cut in. "I signed a typed version of last night's statement. All very pleasant and respectful. Have you seen them yet?"

"No. I dodged 'em. The point being," I went on, seeing their puzzled expressions, "that they now know that I'm a private dick. Also, I was round at Scotland Yard badgering them for information on possible suspects before I had attended that meeting in Chelsea, or met you people. They're bound to suspect that my relationship with the Ellery affair is professional. And—quite frankly—I'm bound to tell them if they ask me. I can't afford to get in bad with them. Whilst it is only Ellery being banged on the head that concerns them I'll risk stalling them, but once Ward is found—then the balloon goes up, and I shall tell the truth, and nothing but the truth. In the meantime I might locate Swinton—and talking of the devil, just listen to this. . . ."

I recounted what I had discovered by my call on Rabal Products, telling them everything except why the real Swinton was being blackmailed and his relationship to the girl. I'd thought I might enjoy their joint expressions of amazement but in fact their consternation was pitiful.

"Then who is the man?" Gribble snapped.

"I don't know, Doc. It's virtually unimportant. 'Where is the man?' is more my slogan. I pin my hopes on Selsey. My wife is in the house next door, and she's telephoning as soon as he gets there. Trouble is—I can't be certain that he will go back there, or I'd be down there now."

"You know something, John?" Kate put in. "I still don't think that fat guy Ward was our blackmailer. He didn't know a single one of us."

"Yet the girl—Ella Price . . . Helen Rice . . . Ellen Gryce—is really his niece, Helen Ward."

"Can you be sure of that, John?"

"Reasonably so." I thought, with a small pang of guilt, that I had omitted to ask the real Swinton for a description of his bastard daughter, but it would have been stretching coincidence too far to suggest that there was another woman concerned in the blackmail racket. Besides, little Swinton was a man in his fifties and the girl had been born before he was twenty-one. I had Kate's word for it that Helen Rice, at any rate, had been in her thirties. It tallied.

"I can't think why she bothered to change her Christian name," Kate observed, apropos of nothing.

"It was near enough to Helen every time," I said.

Then I thought: "Helen! God's Grief! Helen!" and aloud I said: "I've got to be off. I've just thought of something. See you later, maybe."

"Come to lunch, then," Kate offered. "I'm getting so damned jittery I just can't bear to be left alone. Doc.'s going off on his rounds."

"I'll try hard," I replied. "But if Swinton arrives in Selsey I shan't wait for lunch. So long!"

But Big Swinton—as I was now thinking of him—had not arrived in Selsey. I telephoned Freda as soon as I got out of the Can Can Club and had parked the Zephyr in a spot where it was less likely to attract the attention of the police.

"But, John," Freda said, and I could tell even over a wire that she was excited, "something else has happened. Helen Arnett, his girl friend from the Marine Hotel, is missing. It's official. She's not been seen since Monday night. The hotel people have reported to the local police. There are all sorts of wild rumours flying round."

"You mean she's just walked out of the hotel and bilked them?"

"That may be it, of course. But she was last seen wearing only a Bikini. You remember she was using Swinton's boat on Monday afternoon—cruising up and down the shore for hours. I told you about it."

"But surely she was seen after that?"

"I suppose so. She certainly didn't fall out of the boat. I saw her mooring it."

"Then where did she go?" I asked.

"John, darling! How on earth do I know? I was mildly interested in the woman because you've been so suspicious of Swinton, but I didn't watch her every footfall. What has Swinton been doing to make you so anxious about him?"

"Plenty!" I said. I was tolerably sure on that point. "He's a crook. His name is not Swinton, anyway. It's one he borrowed. I don't know what his real name is—yet. I've got to find him, but it looks rather as though he and his girl friend have performed a long-arranged moonlight flit. Let me think now—Swinton was not down at Selsey on Monday night, was he?"

"We didn't think so, dear."

"Now what d'you mean by that? He went up to town on the early train on Monday morning. I caught the later one in order to avoid him. He wasn't back by the time we turned in just before midnight, and his car was not there the next morning."

"Yesterday morning," Freda said.

"So it was, but so much has happened since it's difficult to realize it. Where's the snag, sweetheart?"

"Only that Mrs. Mulraney went visiting in Siddlesham Monday night, and caught the last bus back to Selsey. She says she saw Swinton get off the bus at the Crown in the village."

"Wow!" I exclaimed. "That's interesting. So he could have had a tryst with Miss Arnett the night she disappeared."

"In her Bikini?" Freda said.

"Well. Maybe. I suppose Mrs. Mulraney really did see him? The bus, presumably, would have been the last one from Chichester."

"She volunteered the information, John. I didn't ask her for it. In her own scandalmongering way she's as nosey as you are."

I laughed.

"That one hurt, darling. You wait till I reach you."

"Well . . . hurry, John. I'm getting lonely."

I said that I would be ringing again before long, and hung up.

I left the Zephyr in the parking lot, and went by Underground to Kensington. No. 20 Fernside Road was just as immaculate as it had been when I had seen it last, and the same serving girl answered my ring.

"Is Miss Delooze at home?" I asked. Perhaps I ought to have asked for Mrs. Cameron since she was the landlady, but the idea of another interview with that false horror made my flesh creep.

"She's out," the girl said. "Sorry," she added as an afterthought.

"But is she in residence? I mean she has returned from Blackpool, or wherever it was she was performing?"

"Oh yes. Come back Monday. Blackpool it was. Did you wish to see her?"

"That was the idea," I admitted, as patiently as I could.

"Well . . . I expect she'll be in for lunch. Or you might see her in the High Street. She's gone shopping."

"What time do you serve lunch?"

"One o'clock. She won't be late. None of 'em are."

"Then I'll telephone if I may. Can you give me the number?"

She gave it me. I thanked her and left.

There was nowhere else to go but Kate's flat, particularly as she had invited me to lunch. I was running a risk of encountering the police by so doing since it would no doubt occur to them that I might be found there. Still, I clung to the idea that they would not be seeking me in earnest as yet. They'd had my statement, which tallied with Gribble's, and he was an eminently respectable doctor of whom they could not possibly entertain the slightest suspicion. Until Ward's body was found I was reasonably free of a man-hunt.

I was beginning to think of Ward's carelessly dumped corpse as something of a menace. The horrible shape of it, sprawled in a heap at the bottom of that dell in the Epsom woods, loomed largely in the background of my mind. The thought of its discovery was hanging over me like a Sword of Damocles. It imparted a sense of urgency to my every movement; an urgency I could do nothing to meet. More than once I asked myself what I was doing mixed up in such a situation. I owed nothing to the other participants. I could yet save myself some unpleasant moments by reporting the full facts to the police and letting the others go hang. But some perverse illogical quality in my make-up made me stick it. Maybe it was only conceit, or just plain obstinacy. I clung hard to the belief that if once I could find the pseudo Swindon I could straighten things out, at least to the satisfaction of Kate, the doctor, and their fellow victims.

Kate had gone out by the time I arrived back at the club. Old Bates let me go up to her flat, however, and there I was joined about half an hour later by the doctor, who had completed his rounds and, like me, had returned for lunch. Like me, also, he had been doing some hard thinking on his journey.

"I'm worried about Ward's body," he said, as soon as he had put himself into a chair. "And so is Kate. She puts on a couldn't-care-less front every now and again but at heart she's worried stiff. We ought to do something about it. Our statement to the police is going to be shot full of holes as soon as Ellery is allowed to talk, anyway."

"Is it, Doc.? The captain's no fool. He'll take refuge in the time-honoured excuse of all those for whom it is perhaps unwise to speak at all after an accident. He won't remember. He got a bang on the head. He'll probably remember shaving himself that morning, or some other homely act of the day, and not a thing since. I'm not worrying much about the captain. If he thinks by telling the truth there's a chance of his own indiscretion coming to light he'll say nothing. But it's up to you, Doc. And Kate. If you want the whole damned thing reported—say so. I'll not stand in your way."

Gribble frowned.

"It's not I, Chadwick. Honestly. If it had rested with me I would have reported Ward's death as soon as we found him. But Kate is hopelessly involved. She's not told me why she is being blackmailed, but she has told me that if her secret is made public she'll be as good as ruined. She'll lose this club at any rate. I believe it has something to do with her ex-husband. Kate is a decent sort, Chadwick. Whilst there is the slightest chance of this thing being settled without all our secrets coming to light—let us carry on as we are."

"Supposing Big Swinton killed Ward? What then? Do you still think murder may have been done?"

The doctor pulled out a cigarette and took a light from Kate's table lighter.

"In a way I'm certain it was. We can be reasonably sure that Swinton looked in on him whilst we were here in the lounge waiting for him to come in after turning the car. He must have done that with a purpose. For all we know he intended to murder him. What I think actually happened is that he found Ward in the throes of an attack, realized it for what it was, and deliberately said nothing about it, which amounts to the same thing."

"Possibly, Doc. But if he killed him then he must have employed a poison of sorts for there was no obvious wound on Ward's body. If it was poison then it must have been administered externally because he could never have forced Ward to swallow it. But he could have jabbed him suddenly with a hypodermic or its equivalent. It sounds far-fetched but then you've got to remember that Big Swinton had this business planned to the last detail a long way ahead."

"Except that bringing him to Kate's flat was almost a last-minute detail," the doctor demurred.

"Maybe. But if you work on the assumption that Swinton had planned to murder Ward, and use his blackmail victims to help him dispose of the body, you can see that the last-minute substitution of this flat for his hide-out in Selsey was no real obstacle. Had Kate not offered her flat I think this would have happened. After Ward had been stunned and put in the car Swinton would have asked one of us to drive, and himself got in the back with Ward. Don't forget we should have been faced with a drive to Selsey, and the route could have been very close to those woods where we dumped Ward. Approaching them Swinton would either have made some excuse for stopping, or else he would have jabbed Ward where he was in the back of the car, having first distracted your attention, or whose ever it was in the back of the car with him.

"Swinton thought up that spot for the disposal of Ward far too easily, Doc.," I concluded. "He had it ready, and waiting."

"You may be right at that," Gribble agreed grudgingly. "I remember I thought at the time how ridiculously quick he was thinking it up. I don't much like the sound of it, Chadwick. I hope you're wrong—hopelessly wrong."

"There is only one way to find out. If he did kill Ward by injecting some paralysing poison then the mark would show on the skin. On his hand or neck, or face?"

"Almost certainly. It would depend to some extent on the poison used. What are you hinting at?"

"Nothing like making sure, Doc. Suppose we take a run down to those woods this afternoon? The body must be there still."

"Are you crazy?"

"I'm not sure. Maybe I am. But I want to know whether or not Ward was murdered. If he was——"

"Supposing we are seen? If we are caught handling the body won't we be in a worse position than ever?"

"Not necessarily. We can always say that we were prepared to report it as soon as we were able to get to a telephone. If Ward was murdered that is precisely what I shall do. That's what is worrying me. We can't keep murder under our hats, Doc. A natural death, for a day or two—yes. But murder—no."

"I don't like it," he said.

"But you'll come?"

He glowered at me, drawing fiercely on his cigarette in one quick drag; a gesture which I was rapidly coming to regard as characteristic of him.

"I suppose so. This business will ruin me. I might as well have told Bilter to go to hell in the first place. The result could not have been worse."

I said nothing to that, and soon afterwards Kate came in. She had lunch scheduled for one o'clock. At ten minutes to the hour I begged leave to use her telephone, and went down to the office.

It took me barely thirty seconds to dial the number of Mrs. Cameron's boarding establishment, and ask to speak to

Miss Delooze. In another minute she was on the line. I was beginning to get ideas at last on the true meaning of everything that had happened to date, and the answer I would get from Miss Delooze would either go a long way to support those ideas or scatter them like chaff. My mouth was dry from excitement as I explained the reason for my call.

"Oh, yes," she said, "Mrs. Cameron told me that a detective had been asking about Miss Rice. Yes. I did see her. She was riding a horse. I'm almost certain it was her—she, I mean. It was at Selsey. That's right. Selsey Bill."

"Thank you very much, Miss Delooze," I said, and put down the receiver.

I had the answer I'd wanted. Wanted? I was not so sure about that. Feared would have been a better word.

CHAPTER XII

IT WAS a quarter to three when, with Gribble as my passenger, I pulled the Zephyr off the road, and parked it on almost the identical spot occupied by the Humber on the previous night.

Finding our way to Fletton Woods had been a comparatively simple matter. On our way out of London I had stopped at a book shop and purchased an Ordnance Map. A minute's study of this had been sufficient to identify the arterial road we had waited some time to cross, before entering the narrow lane which had led us a winding way into a valley and then climbed again through woodland. These woods formed part of the private estate of a place called Fletton House, which in turn took its name from the village of Fletton on the other side of the hill.

The doctor climbed reluctantly out of the car.

"I was almost asleep," he said.

It was in fact an afternoon for sleep. The sun was beating down through a thin haze that took the freshness from the sky and lent it a whitish look, as though it was one huge reflecting bowl. The world seemed airless. The crowding woods were so still they might have been painted on a canvas background. Nothing stirred in them. Nature itself was taking a siesta all save one lone wood pigeon cooing to himself in a sleepy monotone.

The doctor yawned and stretched widely, thought of the task ahead and pulled down his expressive brows into a scowl. He looked around.

"Vastly different by daylight, John," he observed. My Christian name had crept into his conversation over lunch. "How the blazes did we manage to get him through that lot?"

"Desperation," I answered lightly. "I thought we must have left a track like an elephant, but all that bracken and stuff, and the saplings, are remarkably resilient."

"Still . . . you can just make out the way we went. See here," he went on, bending over the ferns on the edge of the track that struck off into the woods, "there's a broken one, and there's another."

He pointed them out to me, and I felt a sudden quickening of interest.

"Looks a bit fresh, Doc. This one is still oozing sap. I'm no expert woodsman, but wouldn't you say this was more recent than last night? Say this morning? See how the stalk is all bruised and wet?"

He straightened up, and groped for the inevitable cigarette, a sure sign that he was thinking hard.

"Maybe. I can't confirm it, not being a botanist. Supposing it was made this morning? Do you think some idle nosey parker has followed our tracks and found him?"

"Not a nosey parker, Doc. The place would be stiff with police cars by now. Besides, he would have had to come off the lane and onto the track, and even then he would have had to be searching deliberately."

"But an expert countryman—a gamekeeper perhaps . . ."

"If there is any game. There's no fencing. There was once. Nothing but a few rotting staves now. See any Notice to Trespassers?"

The doctor walked back down the track to the lane, then came back shaking his head.

"Doesn't mean to say that there aren't any placed at strategic points around the woods."

"No. I still think someone went in there this morning," I declared. "Either he never bothered to look in the dell, or . . ."

"Or what?" Gribble snapped.

"Or he knew what to expect."

"You mean . . ."

"Big Swinton," I said.

The doctor tightened his mouth and glared at the woods as though they themselves had some secret to offer. Certainly their utter stillness gave them a brooding and faintly mysterious air.

"Why should he come back?"

"I don't know, Doc. Unless he had some idea of further concealing the body. He might just be able to budge it by himself. We'd better find out. Ready?"

He said he was ready, lit his cigarette, and followed me into the woods.

In daylight the going was comparatively easy for we could pick our way round thickets of saplings, and clumps of bramble, or banks of bracken, through which we had blundered with the corpse in the dark. In places the tracks we had made were still obvious, but more than once I noticed an odd single track which I thought was so much more recent than the others. The conviction that Big Swinton had for some reason returned to visit the body of Ward grew stronger.

It took us not more than three minutes to reach the lip of the giant hole in the ground, and seeing it for the first time in daylight we studied it curiously. In the first place it was a hole and not, as I had suspected, a cliff edge. The woods were on the side of a hill, and I could see through the top tracery of trees growing from the sides and bottom of the hole the opposite rim. It was about twelve feet below us, and the hole at its top was about thirty feet across. Its length from where we were standing was impossible to judge, and I realized that it was not so much a hole as a slit in the hillside. Yet it was not a crack or fissure, for the lip on which we were standing curved downwards on either side to meet its oppoiste number curving upwards.

The drop in front of us was almost sheer. Probably in the

corners where the lips joined the slope was gentle towards a bottom centre. The true shape of this queer depression was more than likely resembling the wedge-shaped cut that a woodman's axe will make in the trunk of a tree as he directs his axe, striking first slightly downwards and then slightly upwards.

"Curious spot," Gribble remarked. "Not all chalk either. Great lumps of rock in places."

The sides were festooned with brambles, and trees growing outwards with their trunks curving upwards at curious angles.

I moved along the edge a short distance.

"I think this is where we tipped him over, Doc. A sort of clear shoot downwards except for that tree near the bottom. You remember he performed a cartwheel? Must have been that root there he caught."

The doctor came along and leaning outwards peered down. "I can't see a sign of him," he said.

"Nor I. Didn't expect to from here. Too much under-growth. Suppose we go down? If we move along to the corner there we should be able to climb down easily."

I led the way along the rim to a miniature valley where the lips joined. The place was a tumble of ancient moss-covered boulders, fouled with piles of bramble, but the slope to the bottom was much less sheer, as I had thought.

We found a corner where we could start the descent, and threaded our way downwards towards the centre. It was noticeably cooler in the shadow of the rocks, but curiously enough the place was the home of countless insects, and they were soon buzzing round our heads in threatening clouds. Where there was no rock, or chalk outcrop green with un-disturbed age, the ground was soggy. In these spots some foul leprous-looking fungi, shaped like long gas mantles, had thrust themselves upwards. Their stink was abominable. I paused to follow the doctor's example and light a cigarette, hoping it would relieve the smell and the flies.

The bottom of the hole was narrow and long, rather like the base of a canyon, and though there were trees growing there, its floor was nothing but a soggy mass of dead leaves. There was no grass or bushes, or even bramble, probably because the sun's rays never reached it. The trunks of the trees went up smoothly for several feet before they threw out branches, and in places the thick roots writhed along the surface before they buried themselves in soft ground between the rock. It was a queer dead sort of place. The air had the clammy coolness of a tomb.

The doctor and I moved slowly along between the trees expecting to see the body of Ward slumped behind some concealing trunk or ledge of rock. The ground was by no means flat, probably because through the ages miniature falls of chalk and rock had tumbled onto it. When the walls began to narrow we knew that we had passed the spot where Ward should have fallen, and we retraced our steps thinking that the body must have been trapped by the profusion of bushes and small trees growing out of the wall at higher level.

"I should have thought we would have found him here." Gribble stopped and squinted upwards. "It's just possible that when he cartwheeled he was thrown over to the right. Maybe he lodged in those saplings there."

"Not a chance, Doc. He was too heavy. No. He hit bottom all right. See these dead leaves scuffed up? This is where he was."

"Was? D'you mean the body has been removed? Good God, man! It would need a small army of men complete with block and tackle to hoist that corpse out of here!"

"Yet it's gone," I said. "No mistake about it. His hat as well. Ellery kicked that over the edge after him. Remember?"

"Yes. Who's done this, John? And how?"

"Big Swinton, I dare say. But the corpse can't be far off, Doc. If he exerted all his strength, and he has plenty, he could just about drag it." I bent over to peer closely at the ground. "That's just what he has done, Doc.," I said excitedly. "And he has taken pains to conceal the tracks he made. See there." Very lightly with my finger-tips I began brushing away the top layer of dead leaves below me. "Look, Doc.! That groove. Wouldn't that fit a hip? Say he turned it on its side . . ."

"You're right, John. I think he must have buried the body. What else could he have done? Within a yard or two of here, I dare say."

We began to follow the groove made by the dragged body. The concealment had been painstakingly done, but although in the dim light of the hole it was adequate to hide what had been happening from any casual eye, to us, who had come seeking the body, it became increasingly obvious as we moved along.

Swinton must have exerted enormous effort, but what really staggered us was the fact that although we followed the marks of his prodigious dragging right across the bottom of the place we found no grave. The distance was about fifteen feet and at that particular spot it sloped downwards to the opposite wall, though that never occurred to us at the time. The marks finished against a big moss-covered boulder.

"Christ!" the doctor swore. "It's uncanny. What the devil did he do with it—here—at this spot? Hoist it up the wall?"

"No, Doc. It's behind this rock."

"But he could never have moved that by himself."

"I think he did—with the aid of a crowbar. See—round the bottom of it. The moss has been torn away. Come to think of it those smaller rocks at the top don't look as though they fell into that position naturally."

Gribble scrambled awkwardly over the big boulder till he was standing on it leaning forward on his hands against the heap of smaller stones.

"There's a natural gulley here," he said, looking down at me. There was so much sweat on his face he might have been dragging Ward across the ground himself. He began throwing out some of the smaller stones, grunting with the effort.

"No, Doc.," I urged. "Come down. We might be able to shift the big fellow between us. The rest will tumble down then."

He scrambled back, and getting a grip, each of us on the same side we gave the giant boulder all we had. We might have been pushing on Gibraltar for all the impression we made.

"How the hell could Swinton have done this by himself?" Gribble panted irritably when we paused for breath.

"If he had a lever he could have moved an even bigger weight. I've seen two men put a tram back on the rails using

one fair-sized crowbar. Wonder if he jettisoned the thing anywhere around?"

"Not a hope," the doctor said. "Too much like evidence.
Suppose we try again? I think it must be a question of pushing
or pulling at the right angle. I rather think we were
pushing the blasted thing up against something instead of
sort of rolling it clear. Now if I get over there with my back
to the bank I can get a good shove on it with my feet. Think
you can get a purchase to pull?"

We tried again. This time we moved it slightly. We had a
short rest, and then tackled it again. Another move. Then
it stuck and stuck hard.

Gribble swore at it, and so did I. He began to shift his
position, moving round to the top centre of the boulder. He
put a foot on one of the smaller stones heaped there. Quite
suddenly his foot sank, and the whole pile moved down against
his leg. He withdrew it with difficulty, and jumped down to
rub his shin vigorously.

"That hurt!" he said. "We must have shifted the rock
farther than we thought for the pile behind it to sink as much."

"Maybe, Doc. But don't get up there again. I think there's
a hole below this lot. Those stones settled in like the grains of
sand in the neck of an egg timer, till they jammed. If we can
budge this big brute again the whole damned heap may drop
in. You ready?"

He hopped around flexing his leg till the pain had gone,
and then we tackled the task once more. We heaved and
strained till the sweat poured from us. The thing would sway
and settle back again. It was not, of course, absolutely round,
and its shape at the bottom was presenting us with something
akin to a step to overcome.

We moved it at last, however, just in time before fatigue
and cracking muscles made it impossible. As it rolled so the
stones behind began to shift, slowly at first, then with gathering
momentum, rustling eerily, till with a final miniature roar they
disappeared with a rush, leaving a haze of dust to mark their
going.

One on either side of the big boulder we leaned over it to
look down on a wide slit in the rocky ground. It was shaped

not unlike an opened mouth with our boulder still poised over the nearer end half covering it. The sides of the opening were solid rock as far as the light went for us to see.

Without a word the doctor stooped, picked up a stone and tossed it into the opening. We listened intently. It chinked once against the side as it went down, and though we listened for a ridiculous length of time we never heard the stone land.

"Well, Doc.," I broke the silence, "that's where Ward is— down there. He could have got him in all right—head first. Can you imagine it? I bet he was here at the crack of dawn, dragging the body with God knows what effort, shifting this rock, and levering it back. . . ."

"But it must have taken him hours! All that stuff behind this boulder. He couldn't have been alone."

"He was. I fancy that all he had to do was to lever out this one. The rest of the stuff was there, considerably more of it than we saw—probably the result of a landslip above. When he moved the big one it started to fall in, then jammed, but it left an opening. He got the body into the opening, gave it a damned good shove and down it went with another shower of rocks and dirt to help it. The stuff jammed again, and he levered the big fellow back into position. As soon as we started to move it the stuff at the back started its slide again. I reckon that's how it happened."

"I suppose you're right. Will they ever be able to get the body out?"

"You tell me, Doc. Some adventurous soul will volunteer to go down on the end of a rope. A damned long rope. But it won't be me. Let's get out of here. I never want to see the blasted place again."

"Some sort of pot-hole, I suppose. Must have been the action of water on limestone originally. You realize, of course, that this means Swinton murdered Ward, just as plainly as though he had shot him in front of us?"

"I realize it, Doc.," I answered wearily. "I don't pretend to know how, except that I think you suspected it last night, but you were—I don't know how to put it. You were hoping so much to the contrary you refused to entertain your own suspicions."

I turned to move out of the place, but he put a hand on my arm. "John!" He sounded almost desperate. His dark eyes were haggard. There were tiny beads of sweat poised on his formidable bar of eyebrow. He was streaked with dirt and green mossy stains were splashed about his once nicely pressed flannel suit.

"I'm to blame," he said hoarsely. "I ought to have spotted it. I'm a doctor. I want you to make that point clear to the police. I never even searched his skin for a mark or puncture..."

"Oh! For God's sake, Doc.!" I was as filthy as he, and the prickling of sweat on my clothed body always induces a sort of frantic irritability in me. "Let's get out of here. We'll talk about it when we get to the car. What the hell do you want by making a martyr of yourself? Swinton fooled the lot of us."

We climbed tiredly out of the gully and retraced our steps through the woods to the spot where we had left the car.

"What now?" the doctor asked, before I started the motor. "The police?"

"Don't be in such a hurry, Doc. Ward is down a deep dark hole, and the man who put him there is now miles away with his girl friend. I want to think first. I've an idea it might be important not to rush matters and I can't see that there is any immediate advantage to be obtained by doing so. Let me cool off. Have another cigarette, won't you?"

"I'd sooner have a shower and a cup of tea," he said, ruefully.

"Might get the second wish," I commented, starting the motor. "We'll postpone the discussion till then."

It was good to be on the move again. The car had heated up inside while it was parked. We felt better as the air rushed in through the opened windows.

Over the hill was the village of Fletton. It wasn't much of a place. The building of the new arterial road through the valley had made a backwater of it and now it had a dilapidated air, except for rows of new council houses at one end, and these were as alien to the scene as an Army barracks, and just as hideous.

There were two pubs in the village and one of these had a sort of tea garden attached. We went in, and chose a rustic table in one corner. There was not much chance of our being overheard for, apart from a car load of obvious cockneys, behind whose jallopy I had parked the Zephyr, and a big Airedale dog cadging buns from the party, the place was empty.

A fat girl in a soiled apron and on legs that wobbled plodded out of the house, and took our order . . . plodded back again.

"I can't get at the truth behind Swinton and Ward," Gribble said suddenly, coming out of a reverie. "If it were not for the fact that the girl—Ellen Gryce, Helen Rice, or whatever the name is——"

"Helen Arnett at the moment."

"If she were not Ward's niece then I would say that Ward was not our blackmailer. Kate doesn't think so. He didn't act as though he was, though he did say once 'Who split on me?' or something like it. You maintain that Swinton—I can't think of him by any other name—is friendly with this girl?"

"She has been calling on him at Selsey. It looks rather as though they've gone off together somewhere."

"Supposing," the doctor went on, "the boot is on the other foot? Supposing Swinton is the blackmailer, and Ward was a victim who was catching up on him? How would that work out?"

"Could be, Doc. But a blackmailer doesn't kill a mutinous victim. It seems to me that Swinton planned this murder right the way through, and there must be a far more telling reason behind it. Hold on, here come Fat Orphan Annie with the tea."

She bumped the tray on the table, thereby disturbing the half-dozen wasps already feeding on the jam dish.

"Cakes are a tanner each," she informed us. "What you don't eat, you don't pay for. It's 'ot, ain't it?"

We agreed that it was hot. She flung cups, saucers, and plates around the table with a practised if somewhat grimy hand, and ambled away leaving us to ourselves.

Gribble poured out, and it was an excellent brew. We nibbled the bread-and-butter, leaving the jam for the wasps.

"At the moment, Doc.," I said, taking up our conversation

again, "I'm more concerned with finding Swinton. Anything strike you as peculiar about the spot we've just visited?"

"It must have originated through some freak condition of geological strata, but I don't quite see——"

"Aw! Come on, Doc.," I interrupted. "Surely it's obvious? How the blazes did Swinton learn of such a spot? He could never have found it by accident. The pit—yes. But not the pot-hole. Doesn't it suggest a great detail of local knowledge? The hole through the rock, hidden by a stone, and covered by a fall—probably occurring later—isn't that the sort of secret knowledge a small boy might have had?"

"Are you suggesting that such is the case with Swinton?"

"I am trying to suggest that Swinton, to use the only name by which we know him, may well be a native of these parts; that before he left for the big city to make his fortune by blackmail, chicanery and murder, he may have lived in this particularly uninspiring village of Fletton. It would explain his intense familiarity with Fletton Woods. I shall make a few inquiries. Can you spare the time, Doc., or would you like to get back?"

"I ought to be back for evening surgery," he answered, and added with a grin: "This afternoon's escapade has been done at the expense of a post-graduate lecture at University College. I've not missed much, but I would like to be back home by seven o'clock."

I realized only too well that the weakness in my idea, even if by some stroke of luck I had hit a bull's-eye with it, was the fact that Swinton, had he ever lived in these parts, had certainly not been known by the name of Swinton. What was the use of making inquiries without knowing the man's real name? But it was a hunch, and I was fond of it.

I still pinned my hopes on the house at Selsey for finding Swinton. Knowing that he must have been busy in the early hours I thought I could see the reason for his non-arrival. The man must have been on his feet all night, and had followed it with his exhausting work in the hole in Fletton Woods. Somewhere he was catching up on his sleep. He had shown himself to be a detailed planner. He had taken the house at Selsey for three months. He had left a boat there, and he seemed to have a hobby that embraced marine biology, or something of a similar nature. I suspected too that his own car, the big Austin, had been parked probably in Chichester to await his return. Or had that been hired like the Humber? Maybe he had been required to return the Austin before he could take the Humber, which might explain his arrival by bus on Monday night. It was beside the point. I felt tolerably sure that sooner or later he would be back in Selsey.

The doctor broke in on my thoughts. He had been doing some thinking on his own account, his practised fingers neatly dissecting a captured and jammy wasp with the aid of a cake knife, whilst his mind worked.

"John," he said, keeping his voice low, "the thought of Ward's body being pitched down that bottomless hole scared me stiff for a little while. It was, I think, the incontestable proof that he had been murdered, rather than the act. Now, I'm inclined to find it comforting. It will never be found by accident. Can you see what I'm driving at?"

"I think so, Doc. You mean the suspense of not knowing when it would be found, how soon the hue and cry would be raised, and how soon the police would be on your doorstep accusing you of making false statements, has all gone. You have a slight feeling of guilt, but that can be ignored."

"Yes. Need we report it immediately? Hasn't Swinton given us the chance to catch up with him?"

"Doc.," I said solemnly, "if you can shut your eyes to your bounden duty as a citizen for a few more hours then so can I, but by undue delay we put ourselves in horrible danger. Nobody but ourselves knows that Swinton murdered Ward. Nobody but ourselves knows that the body is in that hole. If we say nothing, and by some freakish chance it does come to light, the police could not be blamed in taking the view that there was a conspiracy to murder Ward, and that we are equally guilty with Swinton of his murder. You must remember that you failed to recognize his sudden death as such. I know you had every excuse for believing it to be heart failure, but— how will that sound as a story to the police? You—a doctor?"

"Then we must report it," he stated flatly.

"Yes. But let's risk a few more hours. What do you say to

this? We'll wait till tomorrow morning to get a line on Swinton. If we've learnt nothing then you and I will go round to Chief Inspector Mackintosh, whom I know, and tell the whole thing."

"All right," he agreed. "God! How I wish I'd never entangled myself in my younger brother's affairs. Let's get out of here, John. This dilapidated tea garden doesn't match my mood."

We paid off the fat girl, who insisted on counting her precious cakes though we had obviously not touched them, before she made out the bill.

"Where do you propose to start making your inquiries?" Gribble asked, as soon as we were in the car.

"I thought, perhaps, the local vicarage. Parsons usually have a comprehensive knowledge of their parishes."

"Why not at the house we saw on the map? Fletton House. Swinton, if your theory is correct, must have had at one time easy and frequent access to the woods. Although they are now derelict, fences gone and all that sort of thing, they must have once been part of a private estate when their use to the public would have been virtually barred."

"You mean that Swinton may have actually lived in Fletton House?"

"Possibly. Our one-time landed gentry are slowly being taxed out of existence, and it is difficult to imagine them turning to crime to make up their losses, but Swinton may have been connected with the house—his family employed there—which would have given him as a boy the run of the estate."

"Not bad thinking, Doc. I thought I was supposed to be the detective. Let's go. We passed some derelict gates and a lodge house on our way into the village."

The drive to Fletton House when we reached it some three minutes later did not offer any immediate prospect of further-ing the success of our inquiries, or even giving them a start. The place was most obviously ramshackle. One of the once noble entrance gates was missing, and the other was a giant framework of rust propped open against its stone pillar. The gargoyles that had once snarled defiance over the top of the gateposts were now weathered blurrs of decaying stone. The lodge itself appeared to be occupied, but in a sort of furtive fashion, for many of its windows were boarded, and the thatch was hanging from its eaves. No doubt its tenant had only squatter's rights.

I turned the car onto the weed-grown gravel, and drove slowly along, avoiding the encroaches of the laurel and rhododendron thickets as best I could. The drive was not a long one though it contrived to twist and turn successfully during its short distance. We emerged on to what had once been a broad gravel sweep in front of Fletton House.

"Hell!" the doctor exclaimed forcibly. "We're wasting our time. The place is a ruin."

Ruin it was. Half of its roof had fallen in, probably as a result of fire, for the timbers that had been left sticking out of the rubble like pins from a cushion were charred and black. One wing only had escaped destruction, and hope for this had long been abandoned. The glass in its tall windows gaped with jagged holes, and these themselves were fast becoming smothered under the sprawling mass of thriving green-leafed creeper.

"So much for that!" Gribble said, with a harsh laugh. I put a hand on his arm.

"Wait a bit, Doc. We've been observed. Who is this, d'you think?"

An old man, bent almost double on a stick, had come round the corner of the rubble, from where he had obviously watched our arrival, and was hobbling purposefully towards us across the open space.

CHAPTER XIII

THE old man was definitely hostile. His round and rheumy eyes, faded to a light blue with age, glared at us angrily.

"What d'ye want?" he piped. "This place is private. Didn't ye read the notice?"

I got out of the car, and so did the doctor. The old man

stood some distance off and treated us both to a fixed un-winking stare. He kept the stick in front of him as though at any moment he might be called upon to use it in order to warn off attackers.

"Take it easily, sir," I suggested. "Are you the owner?"

"No!" he snapped. "Caretaker!"

The idea that this pile of ruins required the services of a caretaker amused the doctor.

"But the place is a ruin!" he exclaimed.

"Ha! There's a lot of valuable stuff in there. Lead and such-like. Place is always bein' overrun by thieves and vandals. 'Sides, there's the stables and out'ouses. Nothing wrong with them. Nor the Dower 'Ouse." He pointed behind us with his stick to where another overgrown drive curved off into the woods. "That's down there," he said.

"Who owns it?" I asked him. "We've not come to pinch anything. But we'd like a little information if you'd be so good as to give it us."

The ancient tweaked the end of his thin nose with a sudden lightning movement, which combined with the fact that he never blinked, but kept his curious round stare upon us whilst he did so, was a trifle disconcerting.

"Be glad to. Whole estate belongs to McCready and Angus. Builders. Lunnon firm," he added gratuitously, possibly because he thought that the names might lead us to believe that they came from Glasgow.

"That's not quite what I meant," I replied. "We're more concerned with its history. Presumably the builders have bought it recently with the idea of developing it into a building estate when they get the chance. Can you go farther back than that?"

"Aye. Seventy year or more."

"That's a grand time," the doctor put in flatteringly.

He succeeded in mollifying the old chap completely.

"Aye. It is that, mister. I'm eighty-four. I see'd 'em building Fletton 'Ouse when I was a nipper. What d'ye think of that?"

We made suitable congratulatory noises, and he went on: "I mind the time when the whole county 'ud come to a ball at Fletton 'Ouse. There'd be a hunderd or more carriages waiting 'ere, and fillin' the drives. Wunnerful times they were, mister."

"But who was the owner?" the doctor asked. "The house, of course, must have taken its name from the village."

"So it did. 'Twas the Fitzgeralds as built it. Aye, and lived in it right up to the time of the last war." The old man pulled out a huge yellow handkerchief from an inside pocket of his tweed jacket, and wiped his eyes, which were perpetually watering. He covered this weakness by blowing his nose with an effective trumpeting sound. He seemed to have forgotten his first hostility, or perhaps our interest in the history of the place, which was something of a pet subject with him, had driven it from his mind. At any rate he appeared ready to go on answering questions without bothering about our authority for asking them.

"Irish, were they?" I remarked.

"Mebbe," he snapped, "but Loyal Irish. There was three Fitzgeralds killed in the 1914 war, and the last of 'em shot down over Germany in 1943. The Fighting Fitzgeralds they was called in these parts, and they were proud of it."

The old man spat on the ground. "They was good honest gentlemen. Weren't a mean one amongst 'em, nor their womenfolk."

"That's very interesting," the doctor murmured, "and now they've all gone?"

"All the men. There's three daughters married with families of their own. 'Twas the 1914 war did it. Old Aemon had four sons, and three of 'em was killed on the Western Front all unmarried, not much more'n boys. The fourth was in the Diplomatic Service. He couldn't get out of it or he'd 'a been in it, scrappin' with the rest. He married after the war, and it was his boy, Percy, was killed in the last lot."

There was nothing unusual in the story. It had happened to hundreds of families throughout the land, but hearing the old man recount it—he had obviously at one time been a family servant—whilst we stood beside the ruins of what once had been their home, gave it a poignancy that was easy to experience.

The old man went on giving us details of old Aemon and his lady, the surviving son of that era and his three still living married daughters. Receptive as I was I could not place Swinton as being even remotely connected with them. We asked him about the estate, and there was not much doubt that right up to the outbreak of the last war it had been a jealously guarded preserve. If the pseudo Swinton had at one time had the run of it then he must have been connected in some way with Fletton House.

"Who lived in the Dower House?" I asked him.

"Old Lady Fitzgerald, widow of Aemon's brother, Sir Denzil. That was up to the end of the first war. 'Twas empty for a bit, then some furiegn friends of Mr. Tom's, him that was in the Diplomatic Service, come to England away from the Revolution, and they lived there for years. I dunno what become of 'em."

"What revolution was that?" the doctor asked.

"Why—the Bolshies. The Russian. Mr. Tom was in Russia right up till the time of it."

"Russian eh?" I repeated, whilst an association of ideas ran through my mind with all the livening qualities of an electric current.

"Did these people have any children?"

"Aye. Three or four nippers. I can't rightly remember. There was two boys I mind."

"What was their name—the family name? The surname?"

The old man stared at me, whilst the water gathered in his faded eyes and began to run down his leathery cheeks.

"I don't remember that, mister. Some 'eathenish name it was."

I pressed him, and the doctor looked at me, completely baffled by my sudden interest after apparent boredom.

But the old man shook his head, and grew waspish when I urged him to greater efforts. I would have prompted him with the name that was ringing in my head, but I wanted proper confirmation and I was afraid that he would agree readily with anything I suggested for the sake of shutting me up.

"No good, Doc.," I said, wearily. "We'll have to go elsewhere."

He would have questioned me then, but I didn't want the old man to hear. I found a ten-shilling note, and passed it to the old chap. He was obviously grateful for he'd not expected it. Gribble gave him another, so that our departure struck an entirely different note from that of our arrival, with the old man touching his cap and positively beaming with gratitude.

"Why the sudden interest in the exiled Russians?" the doctor demanded.

"You'll see," I told him. "If I can only learn their name then I might have a line on Swinton. D'you remember seeing a church in the village?"

"Yes. Farther down the road—past the pub where we had tea. I remember seeing its spire. What on earth do you want with a church?"

"Not the church, Doc. But the vicarage or rectory—bound to be adjoining."

It was a rectory as it happened. The maidservant who answered the door put us right on that point. I asked the girl if the rector, whose name was Barnabus, according to the board in the churchyard, was of long standing, because if he was new there was no sense in disturbing him. She said that he'd been the rector as long as she could remember, and took in our names. She came back to say that he would be pleased to see us, and showed us into his study. It was a delightful spot, with a big bay window of diamond panes looking over a stretch of lawn as smooth as old silk. The greystone wall of the churchyard ran along one side, and I remember there were peach trees growing along it.

The Reverend Barnabus himself was a little disappointing. To match his mellowed old house he should have been round and rubicund. Instead he was tall and stooping, and his face was as grey as the church wall. He looked a sick man, except for his dark eyes, which were as bright and as lively as a boy's.

"What can I do for you, gentlemen? My maid omitted to tell me your names. Mine is Barnabus. Since you seem anxious about my length of service I can tell you that I have been rector here for twenty-five years." A smile touched his rather austere face and transformed it at once. "Won't you sit down?"

We introduced ourselves, and he said that he was delighted to make our acquaintance.

"I'm very anxious to learn the name of the family of exiled Russians who lived in the Dower House on the Fletton Estate," I told him. "The old caretaker there cannot remember it. They were a family whom Mr. Tom Fitzgerald brought back from Russia at the time of the Revolution."

"Yes, yes. I knew the Fitzgeralds of course—a very fine family." The rector had returned to his desk at which we had disturbed him. He leant forward and supported his bony chin on his clasped hands. "I don't know that I can remember the name myself. I'm very sorry, gentlemen. I can only excuse myself by pointing out that they were not Church of England. Nor indeed were the Fitzgeralds. They were Irish and Catholics. I am trying to think who can help you."

We waited whilst the rector racked his memory, still with his chin on his hands and his long back curved like a question mark.

"I can tell you this much," he said, after a pause. "The family were not Russians. They were, I believe, Roumanians, of whom the father was actually in the service of the Czars at the time of the Revolution. Don't ask me how I remember that much about them when I cannot recall the name. Nothing has been heard of them in Fletton since the early days of the war, and memory plays strange tricks. I can honestly say, however, that the knowledge of their Roumanian ancestry—it seems likely if they fled the Revolution they had Russian nationality—is here in my head. Why, when I cannot recall another thing about them, I honestly don't know."

He got up from the desk, and stood with his hands in his pockets, gazing thoughtfully out of the windows across his perfect lawn. Standing, his back was not so very much straighter than it was when he had been sitting.

Once again I was tempted to prompt, particularly with a so much more intelligent subject, but I needed definite confirmation. The average Englishman is contemptuously careless about foreign names, and one strange sound in the memory is very like another.

"The Fitzgeralds," the rector said, half out of the window,

"had their own chapel in Fletton House, and kept a resident priest. It was usually a youngster fresh from college, but of course he was administered by the local diocese. Now, let me see. . . . Father Hobley!" he exclaimed emphatically. "He was a great friend and frequent visitor to the Fitzgeralds. You could call upon him. He still lives in the Presbytery at Golhurst."

"Is that very far?" the doctor asked.

"About five miles."

We thanked the rector for his courtesy, and he regretted once more his inability to remember the name we wanted.

"Is there much more of this to be done?" Gribble asked, when after identifying Golhurst on the map I turned the car in that direction.

"Maybe," I said, not very encouragingly. "You get used to it in time. I used to be in the C.I.D. Most cases were one long round of inquiry. We may find Father Hobley at home. We may not. He may remember the exiled Russian's name. He may not. He may think of someone else who might know it. That person may live back here in Fletton. We'll get there eventually."

"I was thinking of evening surgery," he said, glancing at his watch.

Golhurst was a village of much the same size and nature as Fletton except that it was in a valley, and possessed, in addition to its church of Anglican Faith, a smaller and newer building for the Roman Catholics.

A severe-looking and elderly serving woman answered our ring at the Presbytery door. Father Hobley was resting. He was, we were told, a very old gentleman who tired easily. He was not normally roused from his afternoon's rest till seven o'clock. Could we not return at that hour or shortly afterwards?

The serving woman, by gently closing the door in our faces, made it distressingly plain that whether or not we cared to return later, she was not rousing Father Hobley straight away, and left us standing on the step.

"Come on, Doc.," I said, "I'll run you home. I had intended to go to Selsey tonight in any event. I can come this way and get the confirmation I need later."

On the way back we decided that it was only fair to inform

"Won't he have it in a safe?" the doctor countered. "You can't crack a safe, or can you?"

"No. But I don't think he has a safe in the house. He's renting it furnished. I think he relies upon his complete anonymity for security. After all it was pure chance that brought me into this, and he thinks I'm Pendleton."

It was obvious that they were not holding any high hopes for the success of the plan though they had brightened considerably at its mention. If Ward's death was to be reported in the morning, the fact that they had all been victims of a blackmailer was bound to be revealed, and from there it was an easy jump to a presumption that the reasons for their being blackmailed would also be revealed.

I thought that there was just a chance that this could be kept from the police, but only if there was no concrete evidence of it for them to find.

I left them then, still holding hands. Gribble's patients seemed to have been forgotten. An hour or so later I was once again knocking on the door of the Presbytery in Golhurst. It was then twenty minutes past seven.

Father Hobley was a very old priest, but there was nothing, as far as I could see, infirm about him. His face was as fat and as pink as a baby's, and he had a thatch of pure white hair under the biretta he was wearing. When at his invitation I had taken a chair near the window, and he turned towards the light, I saw that he had eyes of an intense blue nested in countless wrinkles. They were very kindly and wise old eyes, such as one might expect to see in a man who must have spent sixty years of his life in the service of the Church, listening to and offering counsel for the troubles that beset the human race.

"Will ye have a glass of wine, now?" he asked, in a soft Irish voice. "The housekeeper was after tellin' me that ye called whilst I was resting. Tis the least I can do to reward ye for yer wait."

"No, thank you, Father. It was not a wait. I had somewhere else to go. I won't keep you long. The rector at Fletton told me that he thought you could tell me the name of the Russian family that came to live in the Dower House at Fletton Park soon after the First World War."

"Sure, I remember them well, and the Fitzgeralds, God rest their souls! But they were not Russians, my son. 'Twas Roumania was the land of their origin. Didn't they make the smoothest plum brandy I ever tasted? Their name was Spirelza."

Spirelza! The name rang in my head. Here was confirmation indeed.

"You know them, my son?" It was only half a question. The old priest had watched my reception of the name.

"I think I know one. He would be a son—a boy of six or seven years when they arrived."

"There were two boys. Anton was the elder. A good lad, who enlisted as a soldier in the last war and was killed in Libya. The younger . . ."

"Sergius?" I asked.

"Yes, Sergius." Father Hobley's white woolly eyebrows came down into a frown.

"What happened to him, Father?"

"I can't tell ye, but whatever it was it wouldn't surprise me. May the Holy Saints forgive me, but he was a devil!"

The old priest was obviously distressed by a memory that was painful to him. I would like to have known what it was but one cannot expect a priest to pass on something that he may have learnt only by reason of his cloth. I let it go. After all I had the name, and that was all I wanted. Father Hobley could not have known anything worse about Sergius Spirelza than I knew myself.

I stayed chatting to him for several minutes for it was not often the chance of meeting such a benign and utterly selfless character as the old priest came my way.

When I came to say good-bye he failed to respond immediately, then he said solemnly:

"My son, you came to me asking for the name of Spirelza. You've told me that you know Sergius Spirelza, and I think you are seeking him. You are an honest man, and it may be that the sins of Sergius Spirelza are due to be paid. Will ye take my blessing before ye depart?"

I am not a particularly religious man and such creed as I

have been taught was not his. He gave me the blessing, and made no comment that I stood instead of knelt.

I thanked him, shook his warm hand and continued my journey to Selsey in a particularly thoughtful frame of mind.

It was dark when I arrived, a darkness made almost impenetrable by a sea mist clinging like wool to the lamps of the car. The first sound I heard when at last I stopped the motor in the drive of Freda's house was the fog warning off the Isle of Wight. It made me shiver. Then as I approached the front door Montmorency sent up a joyous welcome, and the front door rattled as he hurled himself at it.

The next moment Freda had opened it, and almost fell into my arms as soon as she saw it was me.

"John, darling. Thank God you've come!"

"Why? What's happened?"

"Nothing. Nothing at all. It's just this damned fog . . . and . . . and I've been so lonely. . . ."

I put that right immediately, but not very successfully, for while I was kissing her Montmorency put his front paws in the middle of my back and endeavoured to lick the nape of my neck. I couldn't have had a warmer welcome if I'd been away for years instead of a day and a night.

I forgot all about Spirelza—apart from a seemingly casual inquiry as to whether or not he was at home—till after supper, and then it was Freda who broached the subject of his girl friend.

"No sign of Helen Arnett yet. There's been a number of rumours flying around. Most people seem to think that she went for a bathe on Monday night, and was drowned."

"Do you subscribe to that, darling? I bet you do. I think you've been sitting here imagining the most morbid things."

"I have . . . too," she admitted. "But there must be some basis for the rumour, John. It seems that she is quite a strong and fearless swimmer, and was often seen alone a long way off shore."

"All the more reason for her not drowning then. That type of swimmer doesn't panic like a novice. I suppose the real reason for the rumour is that she was last seen, by anyone who remembers it, in her Bikini. She's probably spent so much

M

time in that abbreviated swimming suit that no one would recognize her in proper dress."

"That—or jodhpurs," Freda murmured.

We had moved into the lounge after our meal. With the curtains drawn against the mist swirling across the window panes, and the electric fire flickering a cheerful if entirely synthetic glow, the room was cosy enough. Yet Freda was not relaxed. I could tell that. You get a sort of sixth sense in time about the attitude of mind in your soul mate. My wife was worried. I couldn't guess what it was, but it worried me, for I had yet to tell her that later in the night I proposed to break into the house next door, which would give her even more cause for anxiety.

Montmorency, who was not usually allowed in the lounge, poked the door, left off the latch, with his nose quite unexpectedly so that it jerked open, and Freda jumped. The hound, wriggling his behind apologetically in a most unbecoming manner, slunk into the room, then plumped himself down beside my legs and put his ugly head on my knees.

"Traitor!" Freda called him.

Montmorency's defence to this accusation was to shut his eyes and feign immediate sleep.

"John," Freda said suddenly, in a sort of questioning tone, which told me instantly that what was worrying her was about to be revealed, "you know I was jittery till you arrived?"

"You were, darling. You still are."

She smiled. "Not so much as I was. You'll never guess who's made me jittery."

"Who?"

She nodded towards the dog at my side.

"Montmorency."

"What!" I pulled his spiky ears. "What the blazes have you been up to?" I demanded sternly.

His answer to this was to lick his chops and give a faint but reproachful belch.

"I went up to the village earlier," Freda went on. "This sea mist has been blowing all the afternoon here. On my way back I heard the most awful racket coming through the fog as

I approached the house. Montmorency was howling his head off, and Mrs. Mulraney was trying to stop him. You can imagine what it sounded like. Her language was appalling. But the strange part was that Montmorency was not in the house or in our garden at all. He was next door, squatting practically on the back-door step of Kohinoor letting off the most blood-curdling yowls.

"Mrs. Mulraney would not go in after him. She was shouting at him through the hedge. I had to go in and practically drag him away. I've never known him in such a state. Once I had him in our garden he was absolutely right in a moment, just as though nothing had happened."

"Well . . . I don't know, darling," I said. "I don't think it's anything to worry over. You know what a clown he is at times. He probably wandered in there in the fog by mistake and thought he had lost himself."

"He's not such a fool dog as he looks," Freda said darkly. "He knew you were coming this evening a good many minutes before I heard your car outside."

"That's a dog's hearing, darling. So much more acute than a human's."

"Yes. But how did he know it was you, and in a hired car? He padded out into the hall and stood there staring at the front door with his head cocked on one side. He hadn't done it before when other cars passed the house."

I let that one go because I had no answer for it. Freda didn't pursue it. But she was still worried. I thought it wiser not to tell her of my impending plan for the moment. Instead I told her the story of Sergius Spirelza from its very beginning, leaving out nothing.

Freda is a good listener, and she said nothing till I had finished. Then:

"It's all very horrible, John. But it most certainly should be reported. The man is just a beast. Why wait till the morning? Aren't you playing into his hands? He and the girl must be miles away by now setting up a new headquarters, using fresh aliases. Pretty soon he'll be sending out the same old demand notes to his victims, knowing they dare not refuse him even though they suspect him of murder. Why are people such fools as to pay blackmailers? If they would only go to the police on the first suspicion . . ."

"Easier said than done, my dear. Depends what you have to hide and from whom. All very well for the Press to call the victim Mr. A., but such things are very difficult to keep from intimate friends and relations; the very people from whom the victim wants the knowledge kept. That's why blackmailers continue to thrive. As regards Spirelza, I think there is a faint chance, in spite of the fact that he and the girl appear to have had a rendezvous elsewhere, of the house next door still holding the evidence of his trade. He doesn't appear to have moved, or to have given up the lease. He's not had time. He would have been catching up on his sleep today. His boat, for instance, is still there."

"Yes," Freda concurred. "That's still there. What are you hinting at, darling? Another burglarious entry?"

"That was the idea. Sort of catch him on one foot. Deprive him of the evidence on his victims, then slick the police on his trail."

"The police are not going to be exactly pleased at a twenty-four-hour delay in reporting Ward's death."

"I'm not looking forward to it, darling, but . . ." I shrugged my shoulders. "Is there a tin of treacle in the house?"

"Treacle? What on earth . . .?"

"Burglarious entry, my dear. The french windows, I think. You smear the treacle on a piece of brown paper, slap it on one of the small diamond panes near the lock and knock out the glass. Practically silent. No betraying tinkle of falling glass."

She laughed in spite of herself.

"We'll look in the kitchen," she said.

When I had gathered together a miscellany of articles and tools, which I thought might help me in my illegal entry and search, I was ready to go. It was then eleven o'clock. I suggested to Freda that she should go to bed but she wouldn't have it, and returned to the lounge. I thought the dog would want to follow me, but oddly enough he cringed away from the swirl of mist that came in through the opened kitchen door, and slunk away under the table.

I closed the door behind me cutting off the light. Instantly

I was in complete and utter darkness, though I could feel the
clammy touch of the fog on my face, and smell the salt of it.
Nothing stirred. I could hear the faint shirr of the sea against
the sand, and far off, like the wail of a soul in torment, the
double blare of the foghorn's warning.

CHAPTER XIV

IT DIDN'T take me long to effect an entry into Kohinoor—
roughly ten minutes, and five of those were spent prowling
around the place trying to make up my mind whether I should
use a window or one of the tall glass doors that opened directly
onto the lawn from the lounge. I had a torch but it was not
much use in the mist, which, so close to the sea, was as thick
as milk.

I chose a window eventually, arguing that I ought to be
able to get in by breaking only one small diamond pane,
whereas if I used a door I should have to break others in
addition to one near the lock in order to get at the bolts.

It was really quite simple once I had removed the pane.
The thought occurred to me again as I reached down to release
the catch that Spirelza was relying upon his complete
anonymity for security. After all if I had really been Pendleton,
who of the people he had duped would have known of this
house at Selsey?

Once inside I closed the window behind me, swept the
pencil light of my torch around the room getting a kaleido-
scopic glimpse of armchairs covered in a bright floral-patterned
chintz, of green silk cushions, of a cream-coloured carpet, and
of numerous small tables littered with bric-à-brac and glass
ash trays. The room was nothing like Spirelza, and the fact
that he had chosen a house furnished in such a feminine style
was a pointer to the transitory quality of his requirements.

I switched out the torch and stood still for several seconds
in a darkness I could almost feel. The house was as silent as a
tomb. I could not hear even the tick of a clock, though I fancied
that faintly, somewhere in the place, I could hear an irregular
drip of water. Probably the mist condensing on the roof and

dripping from the tiles. I switched on the torch, and moved swiftly round the lounge looking for likely places of concealment. It was possible that Ethel Primrose the novelist owner had a wall safe somewhere which Spirelza had been able to use. If so it was going to set me a problem. To an expert it would probably present nothing more formidable than a sardine tin but to me, pockets bulging with ordinary household tools, it might prove as impregnable as a bank. But there was no wall safe behind the pictures in the lounge, nor any bureau or drawer to contain the papers and documents I was looking for.

Passing into the hall I reflected on the habits of men living alone in a sizeable house, and decided that Spirelza had used only the room he slept in, and the kitchen. Before I spent more time searching the other rooms, prying into likely pieces of furniture, looking behind pictures, and examining the floorboards for loose planks, I ought to search his bedroom.

I went up the stairs. They creaked in protest under my weight, and I remembered how they had done just that when Spirelza had climbed them carrying his furtively collected sea-water. What had the man done with a bathful of the stuff? But the bathroom door, when I put my gloved hand out to open it—I could spare a minute to satisfy my curiosity— refused to budge. It was locked. Obviously it had been locked from the outside, and that made me even more curious. One doesn't normally lock the bathroom door when leaving the house. I fancied I could smell the salt seaweedy smell of the water inside as I had done on my previous visit. Then I told myself: "For God's sake! What the devil does the sea-water matter?" and went on, torchlight probing to find his bedroom.

He had chosen what Ethel probably designated her guest room. There was a large autographed portrait of the lady that flashed in my torchlight as I entered the room. She was not by any standard beautiful though the Bond Street photographer had done his best to soften the shock. She looked like a glamorized horse. It confirmed my opinion of Spirelza. If he could wake in the morning and see that hanging on the guest-room wall then he was a man of no feeling whatsoever.

My pencil light pinpointed the dressing-table. On it was a

large leather travelling case for toilet articles lying open, with one or two of its silver containers standing around on the glass-topped table. This it was that led me to believe he had lived in the room. But I experienced a touch of panic as soon as I examined the wardrobe for it was as empty as a cave. No clothes. No shoes. Nothing in the drawers but newspaper smelling faintly of mothballs. The bed had been made roughly but without sheets on it. Hell! Was I too late? Had the man gone for good?

Swiftly I toured the remaining bedrooms, torchlight swinging frantically across empty beds with the blankets folded in squares on the foot of bare mattresses. I doubt if the man had ever set foot in here. He had lived in the guest room all right. There was less settled dust on its furniture, and he had left his toilet articles on the dressing-table.

I sent my light sweeping around the carpeted floor as soon as I returned to it. I bent and looked under the bed, and there they were—two square and bulky suitcases of solid expensive hide. They were heavy as I dragged them out. He had packed all ready to go, but I had beaten him to it.

I settled the torch on the bed so that its beam gave me light and set to work on the hasp of the larger, using a big screw-driver I had brought with me as a lever. There was no finesse about my work, no feeling of guilt, no attempt at concealment of my intent to open. I was just a spoiler in a hurry, and the hasps came out of the locks, each with a squeal of protest loud in the empty house.

The first case contained nothing to interest me. It was nearly all clothing. A newspaper parcel of what felt like light shoes had been hastily crammed on top of suits. I burrowed into the case, flinging its contents around the floor. Nothing of any use.

The second case was obdurate. I wrestled with the hasps while the sweat poured off me, dripped from my forehead onto my hands working like disembodied phantoms in the thin ray of light. I had it opened at last, and at the bottom found a leather brief-case, locked but promisingly fat.

I had the catch bent off it in a trice, and my hands shook as I examined the contents. Spirelza was a methodical man all right. Seven unsealed linen envelopes! Each with a name typed on its cover. Ellery, Pendleton, Gribble, Swinton, Miss Piper, Mrs. Malone, and the last someone named Frampton of whom I had never heard.

I examined Pendleton's. I was, I thought, entitled to look at his, and I certainly had no desire to learn the secrets contained in the others. They would be returned to their real owners in due course.

Pendleton's contained a bundle of letters, and a small child's exercise book with his name again inscribed on its cover. I looked at this closely. The pages had been neatly ruled into columns headed: Date of Demand. Amount. Date Received. Amount. Where Received. Remarks. This last column was completely blank. Pendleton had been a steady payer. No bother at all. But he had paid far more than he had pretended to me. I began to understand his frayed suit and the darned holes round the collar of his shirt.

I stuffed the envelopes into my pockets, kicked the empty brief-case under the bed, and stood up out of the light to ease my aching knees. The house was still eerily quiet. There was only the muffled drip of the mist outside, and the faint wash of the sea on the nearby beach. I waited till I heard the double note of the foghorn's blast before I stirred.

Having found what I wanted I felt relaxed and vaguely triumphant. I was going to be fairy godmother to a number of unhappy people. Never mind what the police might think of Ward and his demise. Whether or not they caught him and hanged him, Spirelza, cut off from his large tax-free income, was finished.

On my way out of the room I kicked the newspaper parcel of shoes that had been on the top of the contents of Spirelza's suitcase. The parcel disintegrated in the circle of light from my torch. In it was a pair of woman's shoes, little more than sandals, and flimsy at that, mere strips of red leather to make a cage for the foot, and a flat shapeless base.

Curious as to why Spirelza should have these in his luggage I picked one up. It was quite small. Size 5. Tiny globules of wet sand were clinging to its low heel. Whose shoes were they? Helen Ward's?

The thought of the woman reported missing set my mind, now happily free of its main objective, questing and turning in the same old way. These were undoubtedly the sort of shoes she would have been wearing with her red Bikini outfit. What the devil had they been doing locked away in Spirelza's suitcase—crammed in at the last moment?

I found the newspaper they had been wrapped in. It was Monday night's *Evening Standard*. Then Spirelza had been here on that particular night when the girl had last been seen. Mrs. Mulraney's story of the late bus from Chichester had been, without a doubt, correct.

Quite suddenly, and without any preparatory thought, I knew the answer. Maybe it was because right at the beginning, in what seemed almost the dim and distant past, the same horrible suspicion had touched my mind for a brief moment. Now it was back, and it turned my stomach over. That bath! That bath full of sea-water. I knew now why he had wanted it; why he had taken such diabolical pains to avoid being seen collecting it.

The natural recoil from such a thought came to me in the form of doubt. Was I right? There was one way only to prove it. Before I left the house I would have to open the bathroom door.

With the decision fresh upon me I moved along the landing, intent on a swift smashing of its panels with my foot. But it was not that sort of door. Its panels were not flimsy enough to burst under a blow from my shoe, or indeed under any sort of blow unless it was one delivered by a seven-pound hammer, which I did not possess and was unlikely to find in the house. I tried the door gently against its lock, and it moved a good deal offering scope for the point of a lever. My screw-driver was not big enough or strong enough to stand the required pressure.

I thought for a bit, then went round the various bedroom doors collecting the keys in the hopes that one of them might work successfully in the bathroom lock. None of them would, and I flung them down in exasperation. I must get that door open. One look inside was all I needed, and then I would be calling for the local police.

I went downstairs, my torchlight searchlighting in front of me, along the hall and into the kitchen. Nothing of any use to me there. In the scullery I came across the boiler with its accompanying raking irons. They offered me hope for a moment, till I realized that their material was too soft. They would bend like butter when forced.

The tool shed in the garden? I could not remember that there was a shed in the garden of Kohinoor. In fact I was sure, after a moment's thought, that there was not. Yet I recalled having seen Spirelza hurrying down the garden during the previous Thursday's wild weather, anxious about the mooring of his boat, and he had been carrying a spade and a pickaxe. They might have been borrowed, and if such tools were unlikely to be found in the house of a lady novelist, Spirelza was not the type to borrow either.

I thought of our own house and the heterogeneous collection of articles to be found in the cupboards under the stairs. I returned to the hall. Sure enough when I had opened the door of the one big cupboard I found what I wanted stacked neatly just inside the door where Spirelza must have parked them after using them on the beach. I hefted the pickaxe—its handle felt deliciously smooth, the head smugly heavy—and took it upstairs.

I dared not risk turning on the house lights, and I had some trouble fixing my torch to throw its beam on the lock, but I propped it somehow, at last, between the wall and the floor so that it cast its light upwards. Then I got to work. It didn't take long. The jamb of the door was not of the same quality wood as the door itself. It splintered quickly, crackling like twigs in a fire under the fierce bites of the pick. With a gap in the wood I had direct access to the tongue of the lock. I put the point of the pick under it and levered upwards. The metal scrunched noisily and bent under the fierce pressure, but sprang back as soon as I released it. I forced it savagely again and again till finally, when I put a hand to the latch and turned it, the door swung away from me wide open.

I could not see immediately what was inside. Quite apart from the light beaming up into my face from the floor, the bath itself was behind the door set parallel to my line of entry.

I could make out the dim shape of a wash basin set under the window opposite the door, but I could smell the sea-water quite strongly above the faint odour of perfume that belonged to the place. The bath then still contained sea-water—and what else?

I had to nerve myself to pick up my torch, and step into the room. Once there even I still kept the thin ray of light at my feet whilst my heart pounded and I gritted my teeth for the effort required to look properly into the bath. I *knew* what I should see. It was as firmly in my mind as the fact that night follows day, and yet some faint hope that I would be proved all wrong sent my mouth dry with suspense, and my forehead prickling with sweat.

I jerked the light over at last, and though I was expecting it I could not help the expression of horror that came from my lips. It was a big bath, and the body, even for a woman's, was a small one. Except for her knees, which were flexed and stuck up obscenely white out of the water, she was almost totally submerged. She was on her back, and the dead face through its green veil of water stared up at me in horror; its ghastly expression heightened by the short black hair lifted from the skull by the buoyant water.

She was wearing the scarlet Bikini. The pathetic scarcely concealing strips of satin cloth looked almost black against the once tanned and now greyish-green flesh. If this had happened on Monday night then she had been in the bath for nearly forty-eight hours. When, not without effort, I peered more closely, I could see that the flesh was already beginning to puff, creasing slightly over the compressing edge of the Bikini. I saw too, shimmering slightly through the distorting water, what might be a large heart-shaped mole on her midriff. It was Helen Ward all right.

I backed out of the bathroom, closed the door on its latch, and leaning against the wall of the landing lit myself a much-needed cigarette with fingers that shook.

"Christ!" I said aloud, fighting for my nerve.

Only that evening the old priest had called Spirelza a devil, and he'd been a younger devil when Father Hobley had known him. The man was a fiend incarnate. I realized with an even greater, more searching shock that he had killed that woman, drowned her in that damned salt-water bath, *before* he had met us on Tuesday evening and gulled us into helping him deal with Ward!

I think it was this last realization which so nearly made me lose my nerve. I shook uncontrollably for a moment and the cigarette tasted like poison on my tongue. I got a grip on myself, forced myself to think rationally, sneered at myself for a craven.

After a minute or two I was thinking calmly, reconstructing the whole thing in my mind as far as I was able. So Spirelza had planned and brought off a double murder. He'd killed Ward and his niece. Why? . . . I didn't know, but I hadn't a doubt that the police would find the reason as soon as they started on it. He had killed the woman first, which lent strength to my earlier contention that Spirelza had never intended to bring Ward as far as this house at Selsey. If Kate had not made the offer of her flat—which in the role he was playing he must have thought unwise to refuse—he would have contrived to have killed Ward during the journey, probably at a place en route remarkably close to Fletton Park. How had he killed Ward? It had been done as quickly and neatly, and with considerably less fuss than the despatch of a chicken. I supposed we would learn in time if ever they were able to recover the body.

His plan for the disposal of the woman was obvious—now. She had been too good a swimmer for him to throw her overboard during one of their trips in his boat. To have knocked her on the head would have been too risky for, when the body eventually drifted ashore, an autopsy would have revealed the fact that she had been murdered. It would have been easy to fill the bath with tap-water and drown her in that, but since he had obviously planned that she was to appear to have been drowned at sea, the body when recovered must not have fresh water in its lungs. So he had conceived the idea of filling the bath with sea-water—secretly in the early hours when no one should see—and that problem was solved.

I could not recall seeing any marks of violence on the body —certainly I was not going to take another look to make sure—so that he must have persuaded her to take a drink of some sort into which he had slipped a drug—probably a mild soporific that would make her drowsy but leave no obvious traces. Then, quite calmly and entirely without emotion, for I felt sure that the house had been rented in a borrowed name, the girl encouraged, the boat purchased, the stage set for that one inhuman act, he had carried the unconscious girl to the bathroom and held her under the water till she was dead. Leave her there, for she is supposed to have gone swimming late on Monday night, and her body, which he will take to sea in his boat in due course, will when recovered tell no lies about its time in the water. As simple as that. Foolproof—almost. He had allowed for everything except me. He could not have known that an idle nosey parker, a so-called Private Detective seldom if ever in practice, would come to stay in the house next door, and make a pig of himself on the first night there, so that he couldn't sleep and as a consequence see him make his furtive journey with the buckets of sea-water. The whole framework of his elaborate plans fell apart on that one simple observation.

"You thought he was a wrong 'un, Chadwick," I chided myself. "You *knew* he was a wrong 'un. Why the devil didn't you have the sense to guess the purpose of that foul bath before he used it?"

I couldn't answer the question. The one consolation was that as sure as God made little apples Spirelza would return to the house. He *had* to come back to the house. Apart from his belongings left in the bedroom he had to get that body down the garden, over the wall, into his boat, and out to sea. He would do it at night, and he would do it soon, for he needed his belongings before he fled to another house in another name to carry on his life of blackmail and murder. But when he came back they would trap him, and if they had any sense they would let him get as far as the garden with the body over his shoulder before they pounced.

I finished my cigarette and stubbed out the end, slipped it into my pocket. All the time I had been thinking, standing with my back to the landing wall, I had paid no attention to the house, utterly silent save for the drip of the fog and the quiet pounding of my own blood. Now, as I stirred to go, I realized that an alien noise had added its quota to softly heard background of outside sound. It was the even beat of a motor engine running quietly. As I identified it so it stopped.

I listened intently, every nerve stretched, expecting the rap of footsteps to approach the house. I heard nothing. Nothing at all.

I knew that Spirelza must return soon to finish his loathsome work, and make his final getaway, but somehow I had not expected him that very night. I was certain my luck would hold. Yet I had heard a car. I could have sworn by all that was holy I had heard a car.

I waited, but there was no other sound save the trickle of moisture, the deep bass of the far-away foghorn, the sudden creak of the stair as I stopped to listen again. With a hand on the banister rail to guide me I had switched off the torch. Though my hearing might be playing tricks, some other sense was at work warning me, sending a chill down my back, lifting the hair on my neck.

Then it came. A sudden scrabble of sound. A key turning in the front door, which opened and shut gently enough, but to me, poised on the stairs, it sounded like the crash of a thousand gates. I heard a heavy tread in the hall. God in Heaven! The man was humming a tune to himself, he was that assured.

A moment's silence, then a sudden click. Simultaneously the lamp set on the banister post at the foot of the stairs blazed to life.

CHAPTER XV

HE FAILED to see me immediately, and that was natural enough. He took off the black homburg he was wearing, and the thin dark top coat, and slung them on the hall stand. Though his movements were jaunty, the smooth confident actions of a man for whom everything was going well, his face was beginning to show the strain. There were lines etched round his hard mouth, and his eyes were sunken with fatigue.

I think it was the cigarette I'd been smoking that betrayed me. He probably caught the smell of it, for he stiffened suddenly as though he'd been shot, and his mind drawn naturally to what he had left in the bathroom he swung round for the stairs, and saw me.

He started back, shied like a frightened horse. Off his guard his face showed for a second a mask of real terror, then he recovered himself and in a moment he was a figure of cold menace, a killer caught in the act. His black eyes snapped with hate, and his right hand leapt inside his jacket. I wasn't prepared for that. I should have been, and I cursed myself for a bloody fool, but there was nothing I could do about it. Not expecting it my reaction was just too late. His hand came out from under his jacket holding a long-barrelled pistol. It looked like a Luger to me.

"Come down!" he rasped.

I went down slowly, a step at a time, my hands at my sides, kept on going.

"That will do," he said. "So it's you, Pendleton. I always thought there was something phoney about you."

"Completely," I said. "I'm not Pendleton."

"It's of small moment," he returned. He was holding the gun with a dismaying rocklike ease. "Pendleton or the Shah of Persia you will shortly be reduced to a lump of lifeless clay of which I shall have to dispose. A nuisance. The sea can take you. I've a bag of cement left over from the mooring I constructed. You're heavy, but I've shifted heavier."

"Ward, for instance."

"Yes. Ward."

"How did you kill him?" I asked. The longer I could keep him talking the better chance I had, if I had a chance at all. Most killers are vain, particularly those who plan and plot, and he was no exception. He had even thought one up for me.

"Very simply," he said. "Actually he killed himself, though of course he never intended it. Ward was a diabetic. He carried around with him in a flat tin case his apparatus for dosing himself with insulin, which he had to do at fairly frequent intervals. I knew that. I knew a good deal about Ward—

our relationship was not exactly what I led you and the others to believe. He knew just as much about me—far too much!

"I long ago provided myself with a hypodermic outfit precisely similar to Ward's even to the case, which I intended to substitute for his at the first opportunity—mine being charged with a virulent and paralysing poison. Unfortunately the opportunity for making a substitution, at least an opportunity when it would not be painfully obvious that it had been made by me, never came. I had to think up another way of disposing of him, bearing in mind the whole time the awkward size of the man." Spirelza paused, and his eyes narrowed. "Really, I don't know why I'm bothering to tell you all this, except that I can think while I talk. I have to think of a way of smothering the sound of a shot. What a pity I threw away the hypodermic that killed Ward. I could have used it on you."

"I thought you said that Ward killed himself."

I found it extremely difficult to keep my voice pitched to a casual note; the sort of note that might lead him into taking up the conversation again. My mouth was as dry as hot sand. Try as I would I could not keep my mind off the Luger he was holding so expertly. I had got as far as the bottom stair, and the round hole of the muzzle was poking at my lower abdomen. I could almost imagine the searing agony of a hot bullet tearing into my guts. Or would that come afterwards? Probably feel like a blow from a sledgehammer at first. The pain would come later, unless of course he shifted his aim to some more vital spot. But he was speaking again.

"It was ironic," he said, "that the opportunity I had so longed for in my first plan should present itself so nicely in the middle of my execution of the second plan. Not that it mattered. I was going to kill him with the hypodermic in any event, though of course the process would have meant a great deal of noise. He would have undoubtedly squealed like a stuck pig as soon as he felt the needle, which would have instantly aroused the suspicions of that odious doctor. Never mind. I looked into the room where he was on my way up from the yard after turning the car. He was squatting on the bed looking very sick—so sick that he could hardly work up any invective at all when he realized that I was behind his kidnapping. He accused me of stealing his insulin. He had, it appeared, put it in the inside pocket of his jacket before leaving his mother's cottage.

"I did not think immediately of my own case, which was just as well since by now his was so much more worn in appearance. As a matter of fact he had dropped it in the car, or rather it had fallen out of his pocket, probably during the bother we had manhandling him into the back. I went down again and found it there. All I had to do was to change the hypos on my way up to the flat again. He was ready and waiting for it, with his sleeve pulled up. By that time he was in such a state he failed to notice that the hypo was already half charged. I watched the whole thing. He was so practised in it that he was remarkably quick in spite of his state. As soon as the poison began to take effect I snatched up the hypo and left. I expected some comment on my late appearance in the lounge but none came. It was rather disconcerting to find that he had managed to reach the door of the room. I was told that the poison was instantaneous—probably the effect of diluting it with insulin. Are you ready, Pendleton?"

"Ready for what?" I croaked. "And I'm not Pendleton. Any more than you're George Swinton."

"So you know that, do you?"

"I know it. You're Sergius Borodic Spirelza—a Roumanian, or something." I put as much contempt into my voice as I could muster. "You ought to go back there. You'd be an asset to the Reds."

It was a mistake to goad him, though I suppose that anything was worth trying at that moment. His brush of hair fairly bristled with hate, and his black eyes took on a peculiar glaze. He raised the pistol, and cocked it with a swift movement of his left hand. The sweat froze on my body. Then he lowered the gun.

"I suppose you're alone?" he asked. "You've not left a companion lurking upstairs? Have you?"

"Why don't you take a look?" I sneered.

He shook his head.

N

"You're a lone bird, Pendleton. I can tell that. How did you get in?"

"Through the lounge window."

"You left it open?"

"I think I did."

"Close it," he snapped. "Go along. I shall be right behind you."

"You're crazy!" I said. "Mad as a jumping bean! Why, you're——"

"I'm not mad. Sound travels through an opened window. This pistol is inordinately loud when fired. I have a silencer for it somewhere, but it is a clumsy thing to carry. Go along. I can pick up a cushion in the lounge. If I shoot you through it that will help to muffle the shot!"

"By God!" I said. "But of course you're mad. You can't even shoot a man without adding frills to it. Killing for you must be a complicated business before you're satisfied. You have to play around with a diabetic's hypo, or collect buckets of sea-water in the dead of night. Drowning a woman in a bath is more your cup of tea, Spirelza. You haven't the nerve to shoot!"

"I shall shoot," he said pleasantly, "but I will not be goaded into carelessness. You've made it abundantly plain that it is more than ever necessary to shoot—now that you've looked in the bathroom. Or are you being clever yourself, Pendleton? I think you must be some sort of policeman—except that they usually travel in pairs, like crows—and that by talking you hope to delay me sufficiently for your colleague to arrive. Is that it? No matter. I'll risk the sound being heard."

I thought that I had reached the end then. But as he spoke his last word there came through the hall from the direction of the lounge, the door of which I must have left open as well as its window, a quite perceptible thud as though something or someone had dropped heavily on the carpeted floor. Spirelza heard it. He was in the act of raising his pistol. He hesitated but he never took his eyes off me.

The thud was followed immediately by a peculiar snuffling noise. I recognized it immediately. It was the noise made by

our hound dog, Montmorency, when he had scented, or imagined
he had done so, some peculiarly fascinating smell. I knew just
what he was doing. He was padding across from the window,
through which he had jumped, towards the door with his nose
about half an inch from the carpet, blowing up dust and
breathing it in again, sounding like a miniature engine.

Spirelza didn't know what it was. It had him worried. I
saw the sweat start from his forehead, and though he never
took his eyes from the spot on my chest to which he intended
sending his bullet, I saw bewilderment and a sort of stark
terror creeping into them.

The snuffling stopped.

I thought: "He's reached the open door of the lounge.
He's cocked his head on one side. Now what will he do?
Ought I to call him?"

Suddenly the dog sent up the most hair-raising howl I've
ever heard come out of him. It wailed and screeched like
something from hell. Quite obviously, as had happened earlier
that afternoon, he'd recognized death in the house and his
instinct was frightening him.

The noise broke Spirelza's control of his eyes. He just
had to turn them towards the source of that dreadful sound.
It startled me but I knew it for what it was, and it gave me
a split-second advantage. I lunged with both hands for the
gun, forcing it down. It went off like the crack of doom in the
confined space, and I felt the fierce heat of its flash against my
leg, but the bullet passed me.

Cursing like two maniacs we began to wrestle for possession
of the gun.

I would like to record that my gallant dog came leaping
and snarling to my rescue. In point of fact I'm fairly certain
that the gunshot frightened him even more than the smell
of death, and that he went back across the lounge and out
through its opened window like a homing arrow. But I was
too busy just then to worry about the dog. My lunge for the
gun had been almost instinctive so that I had both hands
clamped on his right arm—one on his wrist, which felt as thick
and as hard as a rolling-pin, and the other just below it over
his hand which was gripping the gun. Unfortunately I still

had my feet on the bottom stair. The extra height had enabled me to bear down hard and force the barrel of the pistol towards the floor, but as we swayed—he landing a series of short-arm punches to my head with his left—I found that he was slowly withdrawing from the stairs with the result that I was stretching out farther and farther from the bottom step. His punches were quite ineffective because he was trying to hit across his own body. I got my toes over the edge of the bottom stair, gave a sudden hard shove, and the two of us staggered the length of the hall to fetch up with a crash against the front door. The pistol was an automatic, and the shock of our arrival fired it again. The stench of the cordite so close under my head and the blast of the explosion sickened me for a moment. He chose that moment to drop the gun. I think he realized that fighting as we were for a grip on the thing, it was liable to fire at intervals, with the result that the chances of it being heard were correspondingly increased. I thought then that he had no stomach for a fight, and wanted to get away.

As the gun dropped I got a foot on it and spun it away down the hall. It hit something, and pooped off again. It must have been as sensitive as a trip wire.

My attention to the gun cost me dearly. He kneed me in the groin before I could see it coming, and I reeled away from him retching with pain. He could have gone then had he wanted. For a matter of thirty seconds I was as weak and as helpless as a babe. Perhaps he thought I was tougher than I was, or maybe he saw a chance to silence me for good after all. He came at me ferociously. All I could see was his squarish head, cropped at the sides, his black evil eyes with murder in them, and the snarl of his mouth, thick lips drawn back from his yellow teeth. Then this would be blotted out as his fists rode up in quick succession to my head.

Why he chose this method of attack when he could have throttled me then with no bother at all is a matter for conjecture. I suppose I was moving away from him the whole time instinctively giving ground and riding his blows, but they were not timed well enough to finish me off. My whole concern was for the searing pain in my groin, which though it eased quickly left me feeling sick and weak.

I found myself with my back to the stairs. I dropped on them suddenly, and with my hands behind me to give me leverage, kicked out savagely with my foot. I hit him some-where—on the jaw possibly—and he went over backwards as though he'd been hit by a cannon ball. The effort had cost me something. I could do nothing but lie back on the stairs, sucking in breath while I watched him. He was out all right.

"God!" I thought desperately. "Why doesn't somebody come? We've made enough racket to fetch out the lifeboat. What's Freda doing? Surely she's heard. She must have let the dog out deliberately. I don't think I'm going to have enough strength to hold this swine."

He began to stir. His arm stretched out and clawed at the wall. I got up from the stairs and found I could stand. I stood off from him whilst he groaned and helped himself to his feet by scrabbling at the wall. When he looked over his shoulder and saw me waiting for him his eyes went blank with despair. It gave me strength.

He made a sudden dive for the door, but I swung him round clumsily. I hit him a beauty with my right—nothing clumsy about that. I stepped in and gave it to him from short range with all my weight swung into it. He caught it full in the mouth. Unfortunately there was just room for him as he fell to hit the bottom of the hallstand. It boomed away from the wall, toppled across his slumped body and fell on me.

I got away from it immediately, but as soon as I did that the top of it fell against the wall behind me. The hallstand was now jammed across the whole width of the hall with, I thought, Spirelza under its lower half.

But a blow on the mouth, however well delivered, is not a finishing one. Spirelza had extricated himself from the embrace of the fallen hallstand at the same time as I. He was reeling along the opposite wall towards the stairs. There was blood streaming from his mouth, and his collar and shirt were spattered crimson.

He saw the gun about the same time as I did. It was lying in the middle of the floor just beyond the bottom of the staircase. I thought I had kicked it far away, but it had fired when it had hit some obstacle and had probably recoiled back along the slippery floor towards us.

But the gun had not been his immediate objective. The switch to the balustrade lamp was by his shoulder. As he lunged for the gun with his right hand outstretched, so he flicked successfully with his left at the light switch. By the time darkness engulfed us I was diving for the pistol myself, my eyes glued on the burred wood of its grip. I never touched it. Desperation, the greatest of all goads, had made him faster. But the knowledge that he had the gun goaded me in turn. I rolled quickly over to the wall, flat along the floor against the wainscoting.

The pistol blazed at once—its flash brilliant, its noise and stench almost overpowering. He fired three times, wildly in rapid succession as quickly as the automatic action allowed. He was no cautious planner now—just a crazy killer in a corner. I don't know where the bullets hit. He missed me, and by a substantial margin.

If my head was ringing like a belfry from the gun's racket, then so was his. If I was blinded by the flash then he with the gun in front of his eyes was more so.

I wriggled once, shot out both arms, encountered one of his ankles, tugged hard and brought him down. In a second we were mixing it on the floor in complete darkness. He still had the pistol and I heard it click emptily. The magazine could not have been full.

"Count your shots!" I jeered. "First lesson in pistol firing! You've had it now, Spirelza!"

It was a mistake. The sound of my voice gave him rough guidance towards my head. He slashed at me with the barrel. It missed my left ear by a hair's-breadth, and landed on my shoulder close to the neck, jarring the bone. It hurt like hell.

I had the sense to jerk away, and when he repeated the process the gun clattered on the floor. He gave a grunt of despair. Anything like a prolonged scrap was no good to him. He was giving me about fifteen years, and if the thought sickened him it cheered me immensely.

I got away from his frantic clawing and punching, found

a wall, and got to my feet. I wanted light. There must be other switches besides the one I had seen him use, for there were other lamps besides the one on the banister post. I moved along the wall, my hands making wild sweeps over the paper feeling for a switch. I could hear Spirelza moving around, his breath coming in wheezy gusts. There was a sudden noisy crush as he blundered into the spreadeagled hallstand. I couldn't find a switch. It was impossible to orientate myself in relation to the rest of the house in the pitchy blackness of the hall. Then I remembered my torch. I'd had it in my hand whilst I'd stood on the stairs waiting for him to open the front door. I must have slipped it into my pocket without thinking. It was there, and in some miraculous fashion had survived the rough-housing. I flicked it on, found I'd passed three switches set in the wall, put those on and the place was blazing with light.

He was clambering over the fallen hallstand making for the front door. As he reached for the latch my hand found his collar and dragged him back. Sudden fury blazed in his eyes and he came at me again. This time his hands sought my throat and gripped expertly, his thumb sinking savagely on the windpipe. I had a taste of despair myself then. Because he was running I'd thought he was whipped and had acted carelessly. Exultation flared through the blood masking his face. For good measure he put a knee in my stomach and forced me against the wall.

To have panicked would have been fatal. Old police and Army training came to my aid. I found his little fingers with my own hands, caught them and twisted savagely. It is the only way to break a stranglehold. He blubbered at the mouth with pain as he broke away. Then I was hitting him, cold-bloodedly and savagely, till he dropped whimpering to the floor. This time he was whipped.

I forced him to his feet and urged him along to the kitchen. In one of the dresser drawers I found some cord, but in the brief time I turned away from him he summoned energy from somewhere and slipped back into the hall. He was after the pistol again, which like a fool I had neglected to pick up. He was fumbling with its mechanism. His hands were slippery with his own blood, and in his anxiety for speed he was making queer sobbing noises. He was not really human and scarcely looked it. When he realized that he could not reload, or free the jam, or whatever it was he had thought he could do, he came at me savagely, trying to beat in my head with the butt. He was shouting obscenities now, completely out of control. I dodged his wildest blows, got close into him, and kneed him expertly. I stepped away as he folded up, measuring my distance. Then I let him have it on the jaw. I put so much effort into it I grunted as much as he did when he took it.

He went down instantly, writhed about for a moment or two, then lay still, his face to the wall. I took a look at an eye to make sure that he really had passed out, then corded his hands and legs together at my leisure.

Once this was done reaction set in on me, and I flopped down on the stairs feeling like jelly. I wanted a cigarette, but I was in such a state I couldn't open my case. After a long time I felt better and managed to light one.

"Now what?" I thought. "Better fetch the cops."

I could not understand why nobody had come to the house seeking the cause of the rumpus. It was late of course, and with a sea mist blowing there was not much to do in the place near midnight except go to bed. Surely Freda had heard the shots? I realized that in the confines of the house they had sounded abnormally loud, but the lounge in our own house was on the other side of the building to Kohinoor, and the wind with its mist was off the sea. She might not have heard a thing. Why had she let the dog out? Well, of course, he might have signalled his own desire to go out as he sometimes did when we forgot his bodily functions, and the fact that he had shown no wish to go out when I had slipped out of the kitchen door earlier was just typical of the cussed way things worked with him.

It seemed damned ridiculous to be sitting on the stairs reflecting on the habits of the dog, when there was a corpse in the bathroom and a murderer tied up on the floor. Presumably Kohinoor possessed a telephone.

I found it at last tucked away in an alcove under the stairs beside the cupboard where I had found the pick, but it wouldn't work. I supposed the use of the telephone was not in the terms of the lease, and crashed it back on its cradle.

My preoccupation with it had disguised the fact that at last people were stirring outside the house. I heard the mutter of voices, and then the front door rattled under a vigorous plying of its knocker.

"Right in the nick of time," I thought bitterly. "I might be a corpse full of bullet holes for all the good they are now."

I wrestled with the fallen hallstand before I answered the door, and managed to get the thing standing upright.

They heard me outside, and a peremptory voice told me to "Open up in there!"

I pulled the door back to confront a little group of people crowded into the porch. Four men. Two of them were police-men in uniform, local chaps in flat hats. One of them was an inspector. A moment later I realized that they were all policemen, for I recognized one of the civilians as Detective-Sergeant Williams, and I hadn't a doubt that his companion in mufti was also from the Yard; possibly a detective-constable. He looked a bit young and raw. Williams didn't waste any time.

"Where's Spirelza?" he snapped.

I jerked a thumb over my shoulder. "Tied up in the hall. You can have him," I said. "What made you so early?"

He paused in the act of stepping over the threshold. He pushed up the brim of his soft hat. His brown berry eyes had no humour in them.

"You can cut out the wisecracks," he said. "I'm not too pleased with you, Chadwick. Not by a long chalk. Where is he?"

I showed him. His coterie of followers trooped in after him, eyeing me with disfavour. The Inspector had a bushy mous-tache, with pointed and waxed ends. When I had closed the door behind them, he stopped and put his finger on a slashing tear in the wallpaper, which the opened door had been screening. Some of the plaster had been kicked out of the wall and was plainly visible in the long furrow.

The Inspector's frosty blue eyes bulged menacingly. He

was about to say something when Sergeant Williams called me. He had found Spirelza and rolled him over.

I walked down the hall towards them. Spirelza was conscious though he had his eyes shut. He was jerking his head, and his tongue kept moving across his split lip.

"Did you have to be so tough?" Williams demanded.

"Look, Willy," I said, quietly and exasperatedly, "ten minutes ago this bloke was doing his best to kill me. He shot at me. He bashed me with the gun when it failed. He tried to throttle me. If I had not known the tricks he would have succeeded. I had to be tough. If you want more evidence of his pleasant nature take a look in the bathroom. Go on!"

I turned on all four of them staring at me stolidly as though I was a self-confessed wife killer. "Go on!" I shouted. "Just look in the bathroom at the top of the stairs. The door's open. I bust it open. What the hell are you waiting for?"

The Inspector bristled.

"I'd advise you to keep a civil tongue in your head!" he barked. "I'll damn soon——"

"Just a minute, Inspector, if you don't mind," Williams put in soothingly. "I've known Mr. Chadwick a long time. I'm sure he doesn't mean to be offensive. This is Inspector Garton of the Sussex Police, Chaddy. Constable Dooland. Detective-Constable Yates, my own assistant." He turned to the Inspector. "There's been some shooting, Inspector. This was on the floor." He hefted the Luger up and down on the palm of his hand.

"That's his," I said, nodding at the prostrate Spirelza. "He dropped it when I finally finished him off. I was too far gone myself to worry about it immediately."

Williams nodded.

"Now what is all this about the bath?" he asked.

"There's a corpse in it. A woman who I believe has been reported missing from the Marine Hotel. She was staying there under the name of Helen Arnett. Her real name was Helen Ward."

I paused. Williams's eyes gleamed at the mention of Ward. The Inspector turned on his constable.

"That right, Dooland?"

"Quite correct, sir. The manager reported it yesterday morning. Weren't much to go on, sir. Last seen late Monday night. . . ."

"We'd better go up," the Inspector said.

I sat on the stairs whilst they trooped up. They were not gone for long. Then the Inspector came bustling down them.

"Is there a telephone?" he barked.

"Not working," I said.

The others came down, and they held a quick conference. The upshot of it was that the two uniformed men left, taking Spirelza with them. They didn't know what to charge him with on the spot. Finally, when they had got him on his feet, cut off the cords, cleaned him up a bit, and given him his hat and coat the Inspector said, formally, "I must ask you to accompany me to the nearest police station where you will be questioned concerning the death of Edward Ward on the night of the twenty sixth, and of Helen Arnett, believed to be his niece, on the night of the twenty-fifth of this month."

Spirelza made no reply.

I nearly said, "Boy! That's funny!" but caught Willy's bright eye on me and held my tongue.

When they had gone Detective-Sergeant Williams handed round his cigarette case, and when he had given us each a light said:

"All right, Chaddy. You'd better start talking. Make it long and lucid. Take it all down, Joe."

Constable Yates, who had come down the stairs looking uncomfortably green, and was now his normal healthy colour once more, took out his notebook in a resigned way.

"I write shorthand," he said to me. "Fire away."

I grumbled a bit at the lateness of the hour, pointed out that I was practically out on my feet and suggested that we move next door where at least we could have a drink. But Williams wouldn't have it. I argued. Finally he compromised by moving into Ethel's lounge. The chairs were comfortable there, and they had to wake me up twice before I finished.

"How did you know she was in the bath?" Williams asked.

"I found her shoes. They had been wrapped in Monday's *Evening Standard* and crammed into a suitcase full of clothes

—obviously at the last moment. I told you that right at the beginning I'd been curious about him collecting sea-water. . . ."

"Where are the shoes now?"

"Upstairs in the guest room where he slept. Door beyond the bathroom."

"I'll take a look."

He came back with the shoes in one hand and the newspaper in the other.

"Fine old mess up there," he remarked conversationally. "You left that out of your statement. Find what you were looking for?"

I nodded.

"Have a heart, Willy," I pleaded. "The man was a blackmailer. His victims have suffered enough, and paid enough, without you putting them on the rack. You've got the man on a double score. If you can't hang him for Ward then you can for the girl. How did you get on to him, by the way?"

"Sidetracking me, eh?" the sergeant said, fingering his thin black moustache. He glanced at his subordinate. "Joe, go up and list the contents of those two suitcases." Yates, looking a little surprised at the order, lumbered out of the room.

"I'll do what I can, Chaddy," the sergeant said quickly, as soon as his constable had gone. "But they'll have to go in the witness box. Spirelza's got to hang this time and no mistake. I know all his victims' names. Learnt them this evening. . . ."

"But how?" I demanded. "I don't mind telling you that I was going round to see Mackintosh in the morning. . . ."

He raised an ironical eyebrow, and when I grew heated said: "All right, all right. I believe you. Doctor Gribble said as much."

"I wish to God you'd tell me what's been going on!" I protested. "How the hell did you come into it?"

"I was a bit late, but I haven't done so badly," he said smugly. "One of our divisions was keeping an eye on a patient in their local hospital—a certain Captain Ellery who'd been found bashed on the head in the garden of Ward's house—but you know that, of course?"

"You know damned well I do. I and the doc. found him. Ellery talked, I suppose? I thought he'd have the sense to have a memory lapse. He had excuse enough."

"Maybe. Trouble is they use Pentathol a good deal in hospitals these days—as an anaesthetic."

"What's that got to do with it?"

Sergeant Williams shook his sleek head in mock concern. "Such ignorance! And you a private dick! Pentathol is one of the so-called Truth Drugs. It depends on the patient a good deal but the after-effects of its being used as an anaesthetic could make him careless in answering questions. I mean by that—it's not easy to explain—but if it was in his interest to clam up and say nothing he would be inclined to forget that simple fact."

"Go on," I said. "There was a bobby at his bedside waiting for him to wake up. I can guess that much. He talked—all about Ward and his death in Mrs. Malone's flat."

"Quite so. Divisional H.Q. were a bit tardy in getting through to us. They had your statements, you see—made by eminently respectable people. They were a trifle suspicious of you, Chaddy, when they realized that you were a private dick —but Ellery never mentioned you at all, though he did mention a man named Pendleton. They were inclined to think that Ellery, so soon after his bang on the head, was talking a lot of rubbish. But when they failed to contact Ward they came through to us asking for information from Records, and that sort of thing. That's where I came in. Edward Ward rang a bell with me. He and his niece Helen Ward had provided Spirelza with his alibi at the time of the murder of Elsie Gold!"

"Well, I'll be . . . So that was it!"

"Yep! That was it! Remembering your call upon me last week and our chat about Spirelza I got cracking. I had a word with your Captain Ellery in hospital. I didn't have much difficulty in identifying the man he called Swinton as my old friend Spirelza. I didn't need much persuading into the idea that Ward's death had not been natural.

"Ellery, by the way, never went inside Ward's house. Spirelza slugged him on the way to the front door."

"So that he doesn't know whether or not Spirelza went into the house?"

Sergeant Williams took out his cigarette case again, and helped himself absent-mindedly without bothering about me.

"No. As a matter of fact Ellery was not precisely clear when exactly he caught his packet. I was only allowed five minutes with the man, and he was in a bad way. I had to more or less put the words in his mouth. I got the impression he was slugged on his way to the front door. It doesn't matter a scrap. I feel sure that Spirelza went into the house, and opened the safe." He paused for a moment to light his cigarette.

"Don't waste any sympathy on Ward, Chaddy. If the alibi he gave Spirelza for the night of Elsie Gold's death was false, and I feel sure it was, then Spirelza had to pay for it, and pay plenty. It wouldn't suprise me to learn that he had to write out a confession to murder and lodge it with Ward in return for the alibi."

"By God!" I said. "No wonder he was after them. He used the girl to build up his blackmail business, and once it was thriving . . . but go on, Willy. Then what?"

"I had a word with the Chief. He suggested that I find you. I eventually got around to the Can Can Club shortly after you had gone. The doctor was just leaving. When he and Mrs. Malone realized that Ellery had been talking they obliged with the truth. . . ."

"Obliged?" I echoed. "They stood about as much chance against you as the Babes in the Wood! The doc. tell you about this afternoon?"

"Yep." The sergeant dragged out his watch from an old-fashioned fob pocket and dangled it in front of me. "See the time?" he demanded. "Ten minutes to midnight. I left them about seven-thirty. Gribble said you'd be here and were expecting Spirelza. In four and a half hours I've contacted the Surrey Police to see what can be done about recovering Ward's body, I've found Inspector Garton in Chichester to bring him here, I've learnt with his assistance which particular house was rented to a Mr. George Swinton and found it—in a fog—and you had to make a crack about my being early.

Jeeze! If Garton wants to pinch you for breaking and entering I shan't stop him!"

"All right," I said, changing the subject. "What about coming next door for a drink?"

"Later, perhaps. Buzz off, if you want. I've a hell of a lot to do. Don't go to bed, though. The Inspector will want a word with you as soon as he gets back."

I left Kohinoor by its front door and entered our own house by the back one. Downstairs the lights were burning. In the lounge I found Freda asleep, curled up on the settee, with the dog stretched along the floor below her. He opened one eye and raised one ear when I went in, then struggled reluctantly to a sitting position. He yawned. I spoke to him softly, and Freda stirred, and woke up.

"John," she muttered drowsily, then seeing me properly she jumped to her feet. "What on earth has happened? Your face! . . . For goodness' sake! I'll get you a drink."

"Magic words," I grinned, and fell onto the settee. When I'd had the drink and another to keep it company I told her what had happened but left out the more lurid parts.

"And you didn't hear anything?" I asked her.

"Not a thing."

"But you let the dog out?"

"Oh, he got fidgety. You know how he is at times. He was back in next to no time—shivering. He's an awful baby—really."

I thought of Spirelza raising the Luger, and of the dog's sudden life-saving howl. I stroked one of his silky ears.

"Oh, I don't know," I protested drowsily. "I don't know."

I must have dropped off to sleep then, for the next thing I knew the house was in pandemonium. Montmorency was barking his head off, and Freda was shouting at him. Both were in the hall. Then cutting through the noise with all the directness of unquestioned authority Inspector Garton's voice inquiring for me.

I struggled to my feet. Freda had left the decanter on the small table by the settee, and I snatched a quick reviving drink. It was as well I did so, for the noise in the hall took a dramatic turn. The dog's bark had dropped to a bloodcurdling growl, and the Inspector's voice was becoming shrill. Freda rushed in.

"For heaven's sake, John! It's Montmorency. He's bitten the Inspector!"

I put down the glass and made for the hall.

"Here we go again," I said.

THE END